V. Mahanenko

CONDEMNED

Lord Valevsky: Last of the Line

A Progression Fantasy Series
Book 3

Magic Dome Books

Condemned Book 3: A Progression Fantasy Series
(Lord Valevsky: Last of the Line)
Copyright © V. Mahanenko 2023
Cover Art © Lunar 2023
Cover Design V. Manyukhin
English translation copyright © Taylor Elise Margvelashvili 2023
Published by Magic Dome Books, 2023
All Rights Reserved
ISBN: 978-80-7693-199-2

This book is entirely a work of fiction.
Any correlation with real people or events
is coincidental.

All Books
by Vasily Mahanenko:

The Way of the Shaman LitRPG Series

Dark Paladin LitRPG Series

Galactogon LitRPG Series

Invasion LitRPG Series

World of the Changed LitRPG Series

The Alchemist LitRPG Series

The Bear Clan LitRPG Series

Starting Point LitRPG Series

The Bard from Barliona LitRPG series
(with Eugenia Dmitrieva)

Condemned
(Lord Valevsky: Last of The Line)
a Progression Fantasy series

Table of Contents:

Chapter 1

"YOU MEAN WE'RE NEVER returning to the academy?" I clarified once again, assessing my new lodgings with interest. The Silver Goose wasn't the most fashionable hotel in Turb, but compared to where I'd been forced to live for the past month, it was the peak of cleanliness and perfection. The two-room suite we'd settled into was on the fifth and final floor, with a phenomenal view of the Fortress, academy, and even the Imperial Palace. The greater part of the capital was at my feet, and I, unaccustomed to such magnificence, was rendered completely breathless. Who would have thought that the capital of the Zarak Empire could be so beautiful?

"You're no longer a doomed soldier, Max. Your status is still not entirely determined—I must discuss it with the High Priest—but you are no longer obligated to waste your time on useless humdrum at the academy," replied Mother Alia, who had donned the purple robes of a bishop. The girl was only eighteen years old, my age, but she behaved as if she were a wise old man who had lived a long and eventful life. Of course, this behavior could be attributed to post-traumatic shock—just three hours ago, the girl nearly perished in the cleansing fire of the church, but even before that, Alia had seemed not of this world.

"As for useless humdrum, I strongly disagree. Some of the Evil Engineer's training sessions are worth something! Plus I have the right to ten rapier classes. Since I'm no longer a doomed soldier, I should have my own personal weapon. Dance, history, law—there's a lot more the academy has to offer me! And I have obligations to the chancellor. He believes the rift underneath the academy has reached a critical depth and must be closed. He invited me to participate in this event. I agreed. All my stones were pumped up to level six and they promised to give me a facet, and new stones to boot, once I figure out which ones I need. Plus, we've got to deal with my weapon situation— my katars have already demonstrated their limitations. On level eight, I met beasts that could block steel. All in all, the academy is a useful place and I shouldn't avoid it."

"All your prior promises and obligations are no longer valid. From now on, you have only me. If someone requires your assistance, they must go through me," Alia responded calmly. I couldn't bring myself to call the girl "Mother Alia." What kind of mother was she?

"So we're not going to help the academy with the rift?"

"One facet, buffing your stones to level six, and the promise of some unknown stones in the future?" She looked at me like I was a stupid little boy. "That's the price for clearing a five—maybe six-level. Alright, the rift under the academy is a unique case, since it's constantly being cleansed, so you could agree to go to level ten for a price like that. But they're talking about level fourteen, and maybe even level fifteen. No one has ever closed rifts that deep, so the academy won't be able to get away with awarding you trinkets. I think we should visit the chancellor as soon as possible and discuss the conditions for your participation and further education. I agree that you need an education and polished manners. Closing the rifts is just one part of what you and I will be doing."

"You want to send me off to hunt converts?"

"They're much more dangerous than beasts. The creatures living beneath the earth are ordinary animals, even if they are dark. The beasts found among humans are the true monsters, able to influence your consciousness and the purity of your thoughts. I tried to prove to the High Priest before that your place was among the aristocrats and not in the rifts, but no one listened to me. Father Urg believed that doomed soldiers have no place in high society. But now everything has changed. Yes, Max, you and I are going to hunt down converts. This is the top priority. The rifts are a nice bonus and way to earn some money. Nothing more. Now let's go! I see no reason to postpone our meeting with the chancellor."

"In the middle of the night?" I gazed pointedly at the setting sun.

"Do you have other plans?"

"To be honest, yes. I've never been to the capital—the incident with the convert doesn't count. Look how beautiful it is. Ultimately, I just want to walk around the city, go shopping, sit in the park, listen to music. Remember—I'm still a person, not just a tool for closing rifts or sniffing out converts."

Alia stared at me as if seeing me for the first time.

"Max, let's outline some boundaries here. My duty entails overseeing your development and progress. So that you grow stronger and learn to destroy the dark ones, in all their manifestations. However, I do not intend to oversee you sitting on a park bench and enjoying the beauty of the city at night. No shops, no music and no other bells and whistles distracting from the main goal. You are a weapon in the hands of the Light. I am the hand that wields this weapon. That's it! You won't get anything more. Just because you stopped being a doomed soldier doesn't mean you're suddenly free. I understand perfectly well that you are stronger, faster and more dangerous than me. Try to run away and I can't stop you. But I know you won't. From now until the end of our days, we are bound together, Max, whether you like it or not. So let's learn to live in peace and harmony. I will provide you with everything you need, but in return I require your absolute trust."

"You'll provide me with everything? Okay, I have a need you can fulfill right away: I need the three doomers I closed the rift with. What needs to be done to transfer them under your leadership?"

"I do not know," Alia responded honestly. "They did not discuss this point with me. I agree that you need help. I agree that some of the skills these doomers have are quite useful, especially since we will constantly be negotiating contracts with the Fortress. I will think about how I can arrange this, but I cannot promise that I will succeed. They are doomed soldiers who are slaves of the Fortress. You...I do not know who you are, but you are definitely not a doomed soldier. You don't even have an internal Fortress ranking anymore. It does not apply to you."

"So I guess the forty-one thousand ranking points I earned are just down the shitter?" I was outraged. "What about the fact that, for instance, a protection amulet that blocks lethal damage costs three thousand points? Are you trying to say that thirteen amulets have been stolen from me? Thirteen extra lives that could end up being vital to our cause?"

Alia frowned and said thoughtfully:

"I didn't really consider that, if I'm being honest. You're absolutely right—the Fortress doesn't have the right to deny you your rank. After all, you received these points when you were a doomed soldier. As well as ten percent of the booty that you are owed for cleansing the fault. Max, I will resolve these issues as soon as possible. If you recall, four hours ago I stood tied to the stake, awaiting my meeting with the Light. These things weren't really on my mind. Alright, let's go. We have to get to the academy before dinner."

The perks of my new status were immediately apparent as soon as we made it to the front office. No one looked askance at me, no one had whispered discussions of where this doomed soldier had come from, and—I appreciated this the most—no one made me do anything. Alia took care of everything: renting a room, driving to the academy, even ordering food for the morning. The girl was like a roosting hen blowing dust off her chick. I can't say that I was upset, or even unnerved—for the first eighteen years of my life, servants had fulfilled, if not all, then at least most of my desires. The fact that Alia had voluntarily assumed this role was completely her choice, and I wasn't going to argue. It suited me perfectly.

The academy greeted us with the usual evening hustle and bustle. It was dinner time, and most of the students were hurrying to the dining room. I involuntarily snuck a glance at my peers who had just finished training. I wanted to see if at least one of them had a pastry like the ones filling my former roommates' bags. But I didn't notice anything of the sort. A huge crowd of people passed by us, but none of them carried rolls.

"Something's bothering you." Alia had

obviously learned to read my emotions. "And it's bothering you a lot. I feel the tension but don't understand the cause. Will you elaborate?"

I wanted to snap at her and keep silent, but something inside me resisted. It wouldn't be ideal to start my relationship with my personal servant by cursing at them over such a trifle. Especially without any reason.

"When I was a doomer, I lived in that house," I said, pointing to the doomer dormitory. "Two men lived with me. Ordinary peasants who got their hands on some magic stones and put together a gang of robbers. They were caught, sent here for training, and in a matter of weeks they managed to establish a small business reselling sweet pastries. This morning when I ran back to the house, there were twenty-one bags of sweets that my roommates promised to distribute by the end of the day, but I'm looking at the students and don't see them holding anything of the sort. It's quite possible they've already eaten them or plan to eat them this evening, or the pastries are still in the bags...it's nothing, of course, but for some reason it bothers me."

"Two peasant doomed soldiers?" Alia frowned. "As far as I know, the Fortress didn't send anyone to the academy while you were here. Where did they get the stones from? How did they manage to activate them?"

"What do you mean, they didn't send anyone? There are two scruffy looking doomers, one tall and one fat. They were wearing the academy's steel blockers. Apparently there's something they didn't tell you. I don't know the answers to your other questions. We didn't talk much."

"The Fortress didn't send other doomers to the academy, Max," Alia stood her ground. "Let's pay your roommates a visit. The chancellor can wait."

Shrugging, I led Alia to my former dormitory. The students shot strange glances at us—it wasn't every day you saw such a young cleric wearing purple robes strolling through the academy. Opening the door, I let Alia inside. But there was no one in the house. No roommates, no bags. Only the saccharine smell of baked goods, which seemed to have soaked into all the bedsheets, proved that I was not delusional. Alia looked at me, demanding details, so I had to show her the beds and bedside tables of the two men. My personal attendant shamelessly reached inside, pulling out personal belongings and underwear. The girl was not satisfied. She walked around the house, looking everywhere she could. Finally, standing next to me, Alia said:

"Alright, we've determined that they exist. Now the question is, where did they run off to? It's dinner time now, as I understand?"

"Maybe they're at the training grounds? Training their mental block?"

"How are they doing? Were they able to pass through the first cave?"

"First? From what I remember, they finished the entire initial level and were preparing for the second. Again, we didn't talk much. I was never around."

"Two peasants who adapted to the first level of the training grounds in a week," Alia repeated thoughtfully. "Remind me how Karina Fardi coped with this?"

"Poorly," I agreed. "She had to relearn everything under the careful guidance of Father Nor."

"Meanwhile, two robbers who are no match for your partner passed this test with ease. Why didn't you find it strange?"

"Because I had enough unpleasant things going on in my own life, without keeping an eye on others. Finally convinced the doomers were here?"

"I'm convinced that two men are living here. Clean men. Have you met many thieves in your life? Or simple peasants who care so much about their clothing? Look: everything is laundered and folded neatly. I happened to live in the countryside for a while. There, no one cares so much about their clothing, especially underwear. I want to talk to this pair. Take me to the training grounds."

"Shouldn't we invite Father Nor? The academy is his diocese. He'll tell you everything about these two."

The look the girl gave me could have frozen me solid. However, she nodded.

"A rational idea. Let's go to Father Nor."

"Alia, can I ask you a question? A personal one."

She stopped and spun around abruptly to

look me in the eyes. Some time passed, after which she said: "I don't know what you want to ask, but something tells me I should speak a little about myself. I was given to the church at the age of three. Right after the dark ones killed my mother, brothers and sister. I was the only survivor. That was fifteen years ago. All this time, my father was preparing me to replace him. Became the personal attendant of the Evil Engineer. That's why I know so much about you. My father has always been a model for me—for a long time, he was the leader of the Dark Inquisition. He was a gray cleric. I went out of my way to prove that I was worthy of him. That I deserve my position because of my own capabilities, and not because of the blood I share with the infallible Father Nor. I became the best in all fields and was set to replace my father in ten years. No one thought that another dark one acknowledged by the Fortress would appear in the empire, but reality turned out to be much more multifaceted. The High Priest offered me this position, and I agreed, knowing full well that you would see me as a girl of the same age, but not a personal attendant. This brought me to the stake. What else...Alia is the name given to me by the church. I don't remember the one I was given at birth, I was never interested in my past. The church has been my family since I was three years old, and the rest does not matter. Perhaps that's everything. What did you want to ask?"

"Nothing, now." I was taken aback by such openness. "Let's go. Father Nor's usually in his office at this time."

It turned out I was right—the light burning in the cleric's window and the servant of the Light standing at the door, protecting Father Nor's peace from pesky students, proved that Father Nor was at his desk. His guard did not stop us, but first knocked on the door.

"What occasion brings Mother Alia to my office?"

Father Nor remained the same as ever. Dry, insensitive and accustomed to seeking out darkness in everyone. He paid no attention to me at all. This suited me perfectly well. The less I communicated with this man, the stronger my nerves would be.

"The two doomed soldiers who lived under the same roof as Max. Where are they?"

"They should be there," Father Nor replied calmly, but something that he alone noticed told him that we'd already been to the house. "Then they're in the rift. After successfully completing the initial level, they are permitted to visit the rift, up to level two. Why have you taken such an interest in ordinary doomed soldiers?"

"Over the past month, the Fortress has not sent anyone to the academy except Max," Alia said slowly, emphasizing every word. "Where did these two come from?"

I had to hand it to Father Nor. He didn't argue, ask again, wring his hands or try to figure out who was to blame. He silently stood up and walked over to a cabinet where all sorts of folders were stored. Removing one of them, he returned to his desk and started leafing through it.

"The two doomed soldiers were admitted almost four weeks ago. Admissions documents. Waybills. Signed and sealed. You are mistaken, Mother Alia. These two were sent here by the Fortress."

"Two hours ago I had a conversation with the High Priest, in which he mentioned that the number of doomed soldiers is dwindling. That only Max has been sent to the academy in the last month. I don't think Father Urg has been kept out of the loop. Father Nor, I need to see these two with my own eyes. Do you think they are in the rift? Escort us there."

Again, he remained calm. Turning over the documents, he found a waybill with my name on it. For some time, Father Nor studied the documents, looking at one, then comparing with the other, and finally gave his conclusion:

"The documents were written by different people, although they bear the same signature. Perhaps different clerks, but one signer. There is nothing special about this, it is common practice. I checked these two personally—there is no darkness in them. If you are right, the question arises: who in their right mind would voluntarily agree to become a doomed soldier? Who is trying to deceive the academy?"

"If I knew that, I wouldn't be so worried. There were twenty-one bags in the doomer dwellings this morning. Twenty-one, Father Nor. You know where this number appears."

"That is impossible," said Father Nor, showing his first hint of emotion for the entire conversation. He frowned.

"But it is a fact. Max, what size were the bags? Ordinary backpacks?"

"No, they were huge, you might even call them potato sacks. Definitely over a meter high. And I'm certain there were exactly twenty-one of them. I counted them when I changed into my academy uniform this morning. Where does this number appear?"

"There are no bags in the residence now," Alia said, ignoring my question. "Not even a hint—I checked everywhere they could have hidden them. I have a very bad feeling, Father Nor. When did the doomed soldiers gain access to the rift?"

"This morning." Father Nor was still scowling. "Two hours before we left for the Fortress. Follow me. I hope you are wrong, Mother Alia. Call the Evil Engineer, it's urgent! I'll be waiting for him at the first level of the rift."

This last part was addressed to the cleric standing guard. He ran off at full speed, but we were already approaching the administrative building at a quick pace. The entrance to the first level of the fault, if you weren't traveling through the mine, was located here. Not far from the torture chamber.

The first alarm bells went off in my mind as soon as we reached the basement. The huge steel doors leading into the rift were open. The guards that were supposed to be monitoring the area were nowhere in sight.

"Blood." Alia pointed to several red stains on the doors. "They forgot to wipe them off. Didn't notice. Max, go ahead. I approve the use of force. Those who came here have no business with the Light."

The anxiety gripping Alia had transferred to me. I recalled my roommates once more—ordinary, shaggy peasants. Just like most of the inhabitants of our former barony. They had their peculiarities, of course, but their behavior had been quite standard. In line with the way any ordinary peasants who had seized power would act. But the commercial spirit they seem to have acquired was troubling. This was extremely unusual for robbers.

The first cave on level one was empty. No resources, no dark beasts, no students getting ready for dinner and bedtime at this late hour. Simply silence. But perhaps not—a muttering sound began to reach my ears, emanating from the second cave. Checking that I had five mana and recovery elixirs on my belt, my mana bar was full, and my golden dome was activated, just in case, I slowly crept forward. Father Nor and Alia kept their distance, but kept pace. That's why they didn't hear the muttering immediately, but as soon as they did...

"Max, stop them!" Father Nor cried, suddenly remembering my existence. "This is the dark one's song! They're doing a ritual!"

There was no point trying to sneak anymore—his shout must have echoed all the way down to the Riftmaster's cave. I rushed forward as fast as I could go. I passed through the corridor and ran into the third cave, where I noticed a strange group of people, but then was dealt such a brutal blow that I was knocked five meters to one side. I rolled inside my golden dome of protection, which absorbed the damage as my mana sank by ten percent, and I saw the reason I'd been sent flying—a huge protective dome spanning nearly half the cave was surrounding the strange group. Jumping to my feet, I ran up to the dome and struck it hard. My body ricocheted, but the katars penetrated, unhindered. Protection against magic! Damn! Why didn't I have a crossbow?!

As I jabbed through the dome with all my might, I was finally able to make out what was going on inside. Twenty-one bodies lay on the floor, forming a monstrous circle. The bellies of the poor fellows were ripped open, their insides pulled out and dragged to the center, where they united into a terrible lump of flesh. Nearby was one of the two suicide bombers. The fat one. He had been stripped naked and, like all victims, appeared to be dead. His entrails spilled out of his open stomach and onto the floor, but he wasn't dead yet—he was still breathing and his head thrown back to the ceiling. The tall doomer was reciting the dark spell and slowly walking in a circle, slitting the poor student's throat. Only then did I realize that those whom he had not yet reached were also still alive!

I began beating frantically against the dome, hoping to destroy the shield and interrupt the monstrous ritual. Father Nor and Alia appeared beside me, but they could not help in any way—they didn't have their crossbows. Finally, the doomed soldier completed the circle and as he straightened up, suddenly noticed us.

"What a fortuitous meeting. Father Nor, in the flesh. Came to personally witness his own failure. What, you couldn't detect the darkness within us? That's because there is none! Darkness can only be sensed in those who have souls. We gave ours up to our Lord to become something more than ordinary humans. People like you can't detect people like us. The Lord will be pleased that you, the doomed soldier who has foiled his plans twice, are also here. Now you will die along with everyone else at the academy!"

"Why'd you call? Mother of Skron!!" the Evil Engineer ran up to us. Like me, he immediately tried to break through the shield, but flew off to one side. The dome held.

"It's no use!" The doomed soldier laughed hysterically. "You can't stop me, it's already done! Twenty-one sacrifices made! Only one remaining! Go, brother! Skron is ready to receive you!"

The fat doomer standing there with his guts out suddenly sprang to life. He raised his hands, and I saw a knife in them. The Evil Engineer crashed into the protective dome again, and again ricocheted off. Cursing, the dark one began to break off the tip of the spear that he'd retrieved from the rift, but didn't have time—the fat one finished the movement, drawing the blade down his throat. Unable to remain standing, he fell to the ground like a corpse.

"The location has been set! The strength has been given! Let the passageway open!"

With these words, the tall doomer took off his jacket, exposing his torso. The Evil Engineer finally broke the tip off of his spear and launched it with great force without needing to swing, but was too late. The beast inside the dome slashed through its own stomach with one swift movement, and its throat with a second. For a moment, the floor under the corpses flickered with red light, after which the dome disappeared. The tip of the spear crashed into the already dead doomed soldier.

You have learned the symbol "Worm."
2 upgrades available.

The rift shook so hard that stone chips fell from the ceiling. I turned toward the Evil Engineer, wanting for some explanation, but nearly pissed myself in fear. The dark one was whiter than chalk! In the blue light of the rift crystals, he looked especially eery.

"Twenty-one victims and two keykeepers," Alia said, and sighed convulsively.

"Can someone explain what happened here? What did these two freaks do?"

I received my answer from Father Nor. And he sounded calm, as if nothing extraordinary had just happened. Outwardly, the cleric kept his cool. No more shouting.

"It is a Wave. In a few minutes, all the beasts below us, as well as those that were called here through the gate, will rush into the city, sweeping away everything in their path. Dark One, you know what to do. Alia, send your dark human along with mine—he may need help. You and I also have business to attend to—we need to warn the chancellor and arrange for the students to be evacuated. According to Kimal Sarento, he has cleared the rift up to and including level nine. We have about five minutes before the dark beasts rise from the lower floors. And among them there will be fifteen guards... Dark One, why are you still here? Move!"

Chapter 2

"FOLLOW ME!" ORDERED the Evil Engineer and without waiting for a response, ran off into the depths of the rift. I looked at Alia. The girl was on the brink of shock. A Wave forming underneath the academy clearly hadn't been part of her plans. Nevertheless, she nodded, allowing me to follow after the dark one. Hoping he would know what to do, I summoned all my strength to chase after him. But he was already gone! The speed the Evil Engineer had cultivated was far beyond human capabilities. I passed through the first level and made my way to the third by memory, but I couldn't catch up to him. Level three was still unfamiliar—I didn't have the slightest idea where the passage to level four was, but the trail of dead beasts my mentor left behind helped. The beasts the chancellor had failed to finish off rushed toward the surface, driven by the will of the ritual, so it was easy to trace the direction the mentor had taken. Soon I managed to overtake him—the dark one was standing near the passage to level four and wielding a huge hammer. And he wasn't whacking monsters on the head as they rose from the depths—in fact, there were no beasts in sight. He was pounding on the wall.

"What are you up to?" I asked as I approached. At that moment, the head of a krona popped up through the passage and I had to raise my mirror and stop the monster. As well as the few dozen other kronas that followed behind.

"We knew that sooner or later, something would happen with the rift, so we prepared," he said without pausing for a second. "This will block the passage and slow down the Wave. Not for long, but enough to evacuate most of the students. Step aside—it's going to collapse."

"The Wave...and the beasts really can't resist it? They're all rushing up?"

"Yes. The dark ones are powerless against the will of Skron. The Wave will drive the creatures onward, even against their own will."

"The Riftmaster too? Or will it stay put?"

"The Riftmaster is not a living being. It's a spawning ground for beasts. In theory, it's not going anywhere. But damn it, how do I know? No one has ever launched a Wave in the rift before! Especially in such a deep one."

"I'm going down! I'll block off the passage. I'll try to kill as many beasts as I can along the way without going too overboard."

"Now is not the time to be a hero," the Evil Engineer reacted sharply. "We need to survive. Let the chancellor deal with the Wave. Our task is to give him time to orient himself and ensure the academy is secure. That's it!"

"I'm not planning on being a hero. I'll go down to level seven or eight and wait until the beasts from the very bottom pass me. Including the guards. When the lower floors are empty, there will be no monstrous influence, which will allow me to safely reach the Riftmaster. If we finish this creature off, the Wave will die out."

"Are you deaf? That's the academy's problem, not ours. Our task is to survive!"

"Do you know what *Devour* is?"

The look my mentor gave me spoke volumes.

"When I closed the eight-level, I received three fragments from the Master. Three out of a hundred. Do you still think that I should be cautious, stick with you and leave? Or is it better to take the risk? I got three shards from the eight-level rift. How many do you think I'll get from fourteen or fifteen?"

"You die and I'll kill you," the Evil Engineer replied after a beat. "When you get back I'll tell you what *Devour* is and what it eats. Come back through the mine. Through what remains of it. If the creatures can not break through the blockage, they'll start breaking through the steel plates. Alright, get out of here! Guards are pretty nimble bastards. Where do you think you're going?"

The last sentence was directed at a krona

squeezing through the gap in the corpses of its fallen brethren. The dark beast had no idea what was going on around it. It longed for only one thing: to get to the exit of the rift as quickly as possible. I activated my blades, sending the creature to its eternal rest, after which I cleared a passage for myself with a few kicks and dived into level four. As I landed I had to run a few meters away as a terrible clamor was heard behind me. Clouds of dust rose, and when they cleared, the passage up was gone. A huge stone block had not only broken the path, but also sealed the hole tightly shut.

"Alright, Max, you wanted this. So no complaining, only action. The main thing is to survive."

The thought was not unwarranted—the rumble emanating from the cave in front of me did not make me particularly happy. The dark ones were rushing forward at full strength. Both on the floor and ceiling—the rapses were almost outpacing the kronas. All I could do was move toward the wall. Within seconds, the cave was filled to the brim. Somehow, the creatures knew that there was a passage to the upper floors here and, not finding what they were seeking, let out such a howl that I nearly went deaf. My katars showed their effectiveness against ordinary beasts. Without any way of protecting themselves, they died by the dozen. However, their place was immediately taken by others—new creatures constantly poured out of the passageway, shamelessly clambering over the heads of their comrades. The realization dawned on me that if I didn't hurry, I would simply be crushed under the writhing mass. Especially when the heavyweights showed up. The three-meter guards would flatten the kronas like pancakes. And me along with them, given that I was completely unprepared to handle dark beasts from such depths. So I had to act like and become one of the dark ones. I jumped onto the krona and ran through the living sea to the exit, kicking away the ones blocking my path. It seemed I made it just in time—the neighboring cave was already so jam-packed with beasts that they clogged the passage that I had just squeezed through a few moments earlier. And this, as I understood it, was just the beginning. The main avalanche just hadn't had time to reach us yet...

The race for survival began. Fighting against the flow of monsters barreling at me proved so difficult that I nearly fell to the floor several times. If not for my shield, which deflected the particularly zealous and blind beasts, I certainly would have been bowled over and trampled. Never ceasing to wield my katars, I moved into the stream, leaving a mountain of corpses behind me. Finding the passage to level five turned out to be quite easy—an avalanche of beasts were pouring from the hole. But discovering it was one thing, and passing through was another. The flow of beasts was so dense that for a long time, I couldn't squeeze through. And it started to get darker—now there was the occasional exclusive flickering among the masses. Apparently, the chancellor had not finished off all the red beasts on level five. Or had they traveled all the way from the ninth? Judging by how awful I felt, the latter seemed more likely. So the monsters from the even lower levels must not be far behind. I needed to pick up the pace.

While before I had cursed everyone and their mother for the fact that the level six passage was in the same cave as the passage up to level four, now I was glad for it. I passed through level five without having to linger too long. True, I only managed to pass through with great difficulty—first I had to kill several dozen kronas blocking the way, then throw the bodies aside and squeeze under the paws of the rushing beasts. Once I got to level six, I didn't try to go further—the cave containing the passage down was completely blocked. I was pressed against the ceiling, but I couldn't stop now. Turning my back to the kronas crawling over one another, I began to crawl with my hands and feet, pushing off from the stone wall. This proved much more effective—the monsters could not move me, so I inched toward the passage, slowly but surely. The one drawback to all this was that I couldn't kill any of them. Once I made it through the passage, I fell to the floor—there were significantly fewer beasts in the next cave. My body began to convulse—among the mob I noticed several exclusive beasts and, judging by how terrible I felt, these beasts had risen from the deepest depths of the rift. The red-auras paid no attention to me, and paid the price for it. I couldn't move any further due to the aura they generated, so I had to solve the problem on the spot. Nearly losing consciousness, I let the crowd of kronas carry me to the first "boss" and, before it recognized the intruder, I activated my weapons. The exclusive turned out to be a krona heavily studded with spikes, growths, and additional plates that very much resembled armor. It also had a protective field, but it started only a few centimeters from the body and could not effectively deflect steel. The katar blades passed into the body of the first red beast without obstacle, making me a very happy guy for a few minutes. The influence of the dark creature had disappeared, relieving me of the monstrous pain.

1 of 12 *Amplify* shards obtained. Total: 5 of 12

The pain immediately returned. There were two more red creatures in the cave, but the second of respite had done me good. I could once again adequately perceive the world around me. And I absolutely did not like what I saw. The number of dark beasts exceeded all reasonable limits. Creatures scrambling on top of one another, unable to squeeze through the passageway. Those who were at the very bottom wheezed and stopped moving—they were simply crushed, but this didn't seem to faze any of them. Such a small loss was a drop in the bucket compared to how many dark beasts were rising from the lower floors. There couldn't have been so many beasts down there! It was just impossible. This meant that most of the monsters had entered the rift through the gate the Wave opened. I just needed to find it and somehow block it off.

A fantastic plan. Especially considering the fact that the influence of the two red monsters nearby was twisting me into a pretzel. Before I did anything, I'd have to deal with them. If that was the case...

1 of 12 *Amplify* shards obtained. Total: 7 of 12

Saying I felt better is an understatement! As soon as I finished off the last red beast in the cave and got my *Amplify* shards, it was as if the red-hot pokers had been removed from my body and I'd had a dose of healing magic.

Wait! Healing magic? Why hadn't I thought of that earlier?

Turning around, I began to scrabble back into the cave with the passage to the fifth and passed straight through to level four. I wasn't immediately successful—the dark ones resisted, shoving and trying to get ahead of me. Again I had to anchor myself and push off from the ceiling, only this time in the opposite direction. After struggling to get to the center of the cave, I clung to the rocks as best I could and activated Healing Aura. Boosted to level six, the magic stone's radius increased to twenty-five meters, so I also managed to hook the upper cave, and the amount of damage inflicted to the dark ones struck me with its sheer multitude. If that didn't stop their rapid ascent, then there wasn't much that could...

The inhuman howl heard from hundreds of throats burned alive by the Light was deafening. It seemed like my ears were bleeding, but the healing aura immediately repaired all the damage. My mana began to drop rapidly, but I did not turn off the aura until the creatures below me stopped moving. And, most importantly, screaming.

Stretching my hand to my belt with difficulty, I withdrew one of the mana vials and, pulling out the cork with my teeth, poured the contents down my throat. The dark beasts wouldn't budge—I managed to create a huge traffic jam. I squeezed into the next room and snorted in discontent—there were kronas up to my eyeballs. Once again I had to crawl along the ceiling, moving toward the passage. The next cave was a similar story—monsters climbing from the lower floors, compacting the space as much as possible. Only after I passed through four caves did I have the opportunity to jump to the floor and run. Or more precisely, I was knocked around in the dense stream, but I moved much faster than I could along the ceiling.

I stopped at the descent to level seven—the mob of dark beasts was again so dense that I couldn't break through. On top of that, I began to feel more and more pressure as the denizens of the depths approached from below. This was the last straw—I decided to back out and hide in some side passage. It was not difficult to find one—the beasts that inhabited this area were already at the surface, and the lower branches had lost their appeal. I entered the empty cave and even rejoiced at the freedom as the pressure became so overwhelming that space itself turned upside down. For a moment, I think I even lost consciousness. The dark aura permeating throughout the level exceeded the limits of what I could withstand. The pain came in waves. This was apparently because another dark beast from the lower floors passed by the cave where I hid. The belated thought flew through my head that these beasts might not be from the bottom level, but only, say the tenth. Soon, the true monsters would appear and I'd be crushed into the stone floor. Concentrating, I crawled away from the stream of creatures. To the next cave. Here things became much easier, but I was not going to stop— I had to pass two more empty rooms before the influence of the dark ones dropped to an acceptable level. It still rolled through me in waves, but now I could at least stand on my feet.

Suddenly, the rift shook violently. Another hysterical howl rang out and quickly subsided, but something had changed—the dark aura no longer rolled over me in waves. It started to weigh down on me so heavily that I was sprawled on the floor, unable to even move my hand. I ignored the danger and activated healing. In theory, it wouldn't reach the stream of creatures. It got easier, albeit not by much. My mobility never returned to me, but it became clear I wouldn't die instantly. The pressure lasted for a long time. It gradually grew stronger as the beasts from the lower floors passed by. I really wanted to believe that this was the last of them, because otherwise I would simply be crushed when the guards arrived.

I jinxed myself. At some point I felt like I couldn't even breathe, that's how heavy it was. The rift filled with a teeth-rattling screech. It seemed that something huge and steel was trying to worm its way through the narrow passageway, grinding the stone to dust in the process. I realized that the traffic jam I had created would not stop the monsters that were moving along the corridor. They would simply gnaw through the entire cave and move on. The question was, would the boulder brought down by the Evil Engineer be able to stop them? From what I was hearing, the answer was no.

That moment when time froze, I'll probably remember for the rest of my life. I was critically starved for oxygen. My body almost stopped working. I was blind, deaf and practically choking on my own vomit, unable to spit it out. My thoughts swirled into a full delirium as suddenly everything stopped at once. The contents of my stomach rushed up, and as soon as my mouth cleared, I inhaled convulsively. The monsters that almost killed me had left level five.

I wanted to lie down and think about the

future, about my place in this world, but I forced myself to get up. Even if the block managed to delay them for a few minutes, the guards would still break through eventually. I was sure the Evil Engineer would be able to block the passages to the third and second, which would win the defenders a few more minutes. Then they would all die. I didn't think that even the chancellor could hold back such powerful beasts. I needed to hurry. If my calculations were correct...

I didn't manage to finish the thought—I fell into another endless stream of monsters. This was rather strange, as I thought the monsters had come to an end, however there they were, continuing to move purposefully toward their singular goal. And the flow wasn't dying down. Kronas, rapses, lurges, shtryks, even a few flying ousels—the caves were bursting with beasts. Strangest of all was that despite the fact that the creatures were rising from the lower floors, their auras weren't too terrible. They appeared to be ordinary monsters like those found on the first and second levels. Terrible for any other person, yes, but not for me. All this mass of dark flesh only prevented me from moving on, but could not harm me in any way. Now that I'd tested the effect of *Healing Aura*, I was more than sure of it.

However, this was not the only oddity I noticed. First and foremost was the passages between caves. Previously, they had been small corridors that two people could barely walk through shoulder to shoulder. Now they had turned into gaping holes, as if something massive and incredibly strong had managed to shove its way through, breaking through the stone. Which, by the way, was lying in piles next to the passage, hidden by a dense stream of dark creatures. Were there creatures that huge on the lower floors? It was clearly not the guards—even the three-meter giants could easily fit through the gaping hole.

Wait...could it have been a metamorph passing through? What did I know about these beasts? Absolutely nothing, save for the name. Its aura was truly monstrous, its strength was immeasurable, and its mass, as I understood it, was also considerable. Was my campaign futile? Maybe by the time I got back up, the capital would be gone? What was the point of all this? Maybe I should lie down and rest? How long have I gone without rest? An eternity, really. I was constantly running around, doing something or other, following other people's orders like a dog. Now I had a personal servant. Soon the guards would appear. I needed to wait for them and throw myself at their feet so that they trampled me. Because all I was good at was prostrating myself before Skron, in all his majesty.

The beasts conjuring these images in my head got a little too close. I had never seen anything like it—the flying head of a krona with long snake tails, each of which ended in a lobed fish fin. Above the open shark mouth was a row of three eyes that were all staring at me. It barely exceeded a krona in size, but the red aura betrayed that I was being attacked by a dangerous opponent who knew how to ignore my mirror. It pulled whatever it wanted from my mind. Anything that could slow me down and break me.

Naive little flying monster.

The katar strike was so fast that the creature didn't even have time to react. It clearly believed that I was under its power and was going to devour me. It even opened its tooth-filled mouth, ready to chomp down on my shoulder. The blade passed through all three eyes with ease and exited the other side of the torso. I twitched my fingers to return the katars to their place and my head was immediately cleared of foreign thoughts. The creature collapsed on the stone, expired, and a moment later was hanging from the mouths of the dark kronas rising from below. The monsters never missed the opportunity for a meal. My head cleared and I struggled to control my trembling. If it weren't for Father Nor's warning that there were creatures capable of influencing the mind in the depths of the rifts, if it weren't for the constant training with the Evil Engineer, if it weren't for my mirror, which still managed to reflect part of the enemy's attack, my adventures would have come to an end right then. I had no defense against penetration into my mind, except for the realization that the thoughts there did not belong to me. That they contradicted everything I used to believe. To put it simply—it was sheer luck. There was no other justification for the fact that I managed to resist the creature boring into my brain.

1 of 12 *Amplify* shards obtained. Total: 8 of 12.

The message notifying me that the dead monster was an exclusive raised my spirits and with a few bounds I found myself at level seven. Maneuvering among the indelible onslaught of monsters and distributing blows left and right with my katars in an attempt to cull the herd (although the dark beasts were handling this well enough on their own), I managed to get down to level nine, where the ugliness once again overtook my soul. The beast I'd just killed gave me a hint as to what exactly was rising from the depths of the rift. Fourteen or fifteen guards that could turn me into a bleeding piece of meat with their aura alone. Spinning around, I ran as if all the monsters in the world were chasing me—which wasn't too far from the truth. I knew full well that as soon as these three-meter giants set foot on this floor, I would most likely be dead. The only thing that could help me was the fact that there were only a few caves between the descent to level ten and the ascent to level eight. The guards would have to cover the distance fast enough so that I wouldn't be driven mad. Reaching a dead end at the maximum distance I could move away from the passages, I sat down near the wall and activated *Healing Aura*. Just in time! The aura swept over me with such force that all the previous times seemed like child's play. When I woke up, I groaned in pain—my shield had been exhausted and my body was one continuous wound. The guards' aura had managed to pierce through all seven caves and almost finished me off. There was such a large pool of blood under me that I seriously feared for my health. My hands were trembling, and it took me multiple attempts to gulp down the recovery and mana elixirs in order to switch on *Healing Aura.* I wanted to drink. No, not like that—I just wanted to DRINK! It felt like I'd give anything for a sip of water right now. Any secret, any item, any promise. Anything for a gulp of life-giving liquid.

But no one was rushing over to me with a bottle. Swallowing to prevent my saliva from escaping my mouth, I pulled myself together with difficulty and, leaning against the wall, managed to get to my feet. The idea of licking up the puddle of blood occurred to me, but I didn't know how much the dark aura had affected it. Maybe if I did this, I'd turn into a monster that hunts people at night and drinks their blood. No, this wasn't an option, no matter how thirsty I was. One thing I could say for sure—I still wasn't ready for level fourteen, let alone fifteen of the rift. And if the guards had such a strong effect on me, it was unlikely that I'd ever make it there. Alia was right—the reward Kimal Sarento offered me for closing the rift didn't even come close to the danger I faced. If not for the Wave that made all the creatures rush up, I would never have gotten below level ten.

Gathering my will into a fist, I peeled myself off the wall and took a few hesitant steps. My legs held, but weakly. I really hoped it had been the guards, the last and final creatures in this rift. Because I couldn't take that kind of damage again. Alright, enough feeling sorry for myself! One foot in front of the other—there are still six levels ahead. Logic dictated that I shouldn't bet on fourteen. The rift had reached its maximum depth and the metamorph would soon be born. After the guards passed me, I was one hundred percent sure that the giant that broke through the passages was not a metamorph. Just a huge monster, a product of the insane dark lord Skron. The only question is, would I have time to get to the Master before it gives birth to an even deadlier beast?

Chapter 3

LEVEL TEN... as far as I knew, no one alive today had ever descended to such depths. It was considered impassable. Not by the Evil Engineer, nor Kimal Sarento, much less any of the doomed soldiers. I calmly walked forward, leaving a trail of dead kronas behind me. The flow of creatures racing to escape the rift as quickly as possible did not diminish for a second. It was frightening to imagine what was happening on the surface now. For some reason, I had no doubt that the vaunted defenses that Father Nor and the Evil Engineer were counting on had proved useless in the face of the monstrous creature capable of punching out its own passages between caves. Judging by its speed, the monster was about to break free from the rift, permitting the mobs of smaller beasts to pass by along with—and this concerned me the most—the guards from level fifteen. Even if Kimal

Sarento had some sort of answer to the giant beast, there might not be anything that could protect against the monstrous aura that broke my defenses. If this was the case, I had to hurry. I had too many plans involving the academy to let the dark ones destroy it.

Upon entering the next cave, I stopped dead in my tracks. There was a passage to level eleven here, but that wasn't what made me turn into a statue. A huge window gleamed against the wall, away from the collapsed passageway. Several carved stones formed an archway and inside was a water-like substance. It moved in waves, shimmering, if not with all the colors of the rainbow, then most of them, but most surprising of all was that the river of beasts of all shapes and colors constantly pouring into the rift originated at this source. I stepped aside to move out of the stream. The passage to level eleven was free—there were no beasts emerging from the hole, which gave me hope that I'd be able to make the rest of the journey without further issue, but I couldn't just ignore this archway. Even if I managed to reach the Riftmaster and stop the dark beasts that originally inhabited the rift, there were thousands of kronas, lurges and other horrors that would turn the capital into a wasteland. I liked the city too much to lose it now.

That meant my first task was dealing with this archway. Or, as my memory dutifully informed me, the "gate" through which the Wave emerged. But this raised a question I didn't yet have an answer to: how to destroy them? They obviously hadn't covered this in class.

I approached the arch from one side and peered around the back. There was no shimmering veil. Just an empty space between stones, from which dark monsters magically materialized. Activating my katar, I ran the tip of the blade along the body of the arch. It sparkled as if someone was trying to break through my golden dome with steel. There wasn't even a scratch on the stone, but this wasn't what made me leap back and assume my battle pose. What did was the huge, shimmering red banner that suddenly appeared above the arch with the words "99999 out of 100000." No one attacked—the dark beasts continued their swift ascent to the surface, and a bloodthirsty grin crept across my face. I had a plan.

Singling out the chunkiest krona in the mix, I made short work of it and grabbed it by its legs and dragged it over to one side to prevent the other beasts from devouring it, then began to swing it around me in a circle. As soon as the body gained enough momentum, I, still spinning, took a few steps toward the arch and brought my improvised club down on it. There was an unpleasant crunch as the krona folded in half, and my shoulders were nearly torn from the sockets as its body vanished into the gate with a sickening slurping sound. The number on the banner instantly fell by fifty. But why? Because I hit the arch or because the monster was sucked back in? I needed to test! I had to find myself another beast immediately!

The stream was still going strong, so I quickly grabbed another victim. This time I didn't spin, instead throwing the body straight through the shimmering veil. The result was the same: minus fifty units. Excellent! Now for my next trick—let's see how the structure behaved under the influence of *Healing Aura.*

The hysterical howl that rang through the cave nearly deafened me—the rift beasts were vehemently opposed to light magic. But the gate was even less fond of it. Every second that I held the aura, the number on the banner dropped by fifty. Every second! I grabbed the screeching krona that was still trying to rend its own flesh from bone to still the flame of light inside it for just a moment, I threw its live body back through the gate. This did not produce any particular result. If the numbers had changed, then it was only very slightly. I was unable to track them. No problem, I had one more weapon left! *Dark Spike* (which I periodically forgot about due to its overly destructive and uncontrollable nature) finally came in handy. I stretched out my hand and, without disengaging *Healing Aura,* slammed a dark icicle into the base of the arch.

Oh, yeah!

The number on the banner instantly fell by a thousand! On top of that, the explosion threw several kronas back into the shimmering shroud, further damaging the source of the Wave. Not wanting to waste my mana on *Healing Aura,* I switched it off, activated both katars and windmilled them around me, destroying the dark creatures and sending some of them back through the gate with a kick. Once every five seconds, I jumped to the side and activated *Dark Spike*. After some time, a satisfied smirk broke across my face. The stream of creatures leaving the rift had dried up completely, and the number on the banner had dropped below fifty thousand! I had succeeded in accomplishing something that Gustav, my old mentor, had considered essentially impossible! I had single-handedly stopped a Wave!

This went on for some time—I spent another two whole vials of mana. I'd have to thank Alia—she was the one who insisted I have ten recovery and mana elixirs on me at all times. In any situation, even during our meeting with the chancellor. A fun meeting that had been...

Weird things started happening once it reached ten thousand, when magical and elite creatures began galloping out of the gates. And some of them were quite dangerous, equipped with shields, spikes, and additional abilities. My shield began to spark as it deflected lightning, fire, and some horrendous green goop that the lurges were spitting. The giant praying mantises posed the most trouble. Their weak spots were located so high up that I had to jump up to reach them and expose myself to the other beasts. *Dark Spike* was still damaging the gate's integrity by a thousand points each hit, but had stopped doing any significant damage to the beasts. My mirror no longer worked. The dark beasts emerging from the rift could sense their opponent perfectly well. Once again, I had to activate *Healing Aura* to put us on more equal footing. Fighting several dozen magical beasts at once was a challenge. My mana was seeping away like water through sand, but drop by drop I fought my way through—five more hits from *Dark Spike*, and it would be over. It makes no sense for me to kill all of them now. Just hold out a little longer and...

And it was all I could do not to scream in horror when instead of a krona, purge, rapse, the rare schtryk, or even one of those terrible flying tadpoles that wanted to burn into my brain, a huge horned head emerged from the rift, barely clearing the arch as it caught on its horns. The beast's muzzle was very similar to a goat's—elongated, with a funny beard, nostrils, two red eyes and meter-long horns capable of piercing through any startled doomed soldier. But I had no time to laugh at its little goatee. I was crushed by its monstrous aura. It wasn't as strong as the guards' had been, but powerful enough that I could hardly stay on my feet as I fought off the remnants of the dark beasts. The huge goat couldn't fit completely through the gate—it would simply destroy it—but it could attack. Taking a giant inhale, the creature took aim in my direction and released a jet of fire. Apparently, I'd also need to thank the Evil Engineer. Previously, I had always asked why I, the owner of a one-of-a-kind mirror, needed to do all these physical exercises, jumping through hoops and other seemingly unnecessary stresses?

After all, none of that was required for what I did. I could kill dark beasts with impunity. But this was why! So that I could avoid being burnt to a crisp by this powerful jet of flames! I managed to jump back, although part of my golden dome still caught the flames. One hit and it vanished, completely depriving me of mana. The damage that the monster dealt was colossal!

For the two seconds it took for me to pull out one of my three remaining mana vials, I felt the full force of the creature's power. *Healing Aura* switched off—without mana, it couldn't work. *Golden Dome of Protection* also evaporated, so there was nothing to protect me from the goat's influence. And the only thing I could say about those two seconds is that I never want to experience them again in my life. Even the guards that nearly finished me off had been more merciful than this.

However, everything eventually comes to an end. As did these two terrible seconds—my shield and healing aura once again flickered into place. I was glad for one thing: the flames had damaged not only me, but also the elite beasts I hadn't dealt with yet. They were wallowing on the stone floor, still able to twitch, but no longer able to rise to their feet. The huge goat had also been affected by my healing aura, if only imperceptibly, so I extended my hand and activated the *Dark Spike*. Down a thousand units! Just four more blows and the gate would be done for. Twenty seconds. I just needed twenty seconds! A tiny fraction of the time

I'd already been hanging around the gate, but an infinity to spend in the face of the threat looming over me. The goat's muzzle began to draw in air again, and the mouth changed in a strange way, turning into a wide nozzle. I felt rather than understood that the next strike would be a whole fan, and not just a jet of flames, which there was no way I'd be able to avoid. It was too late to flee the cave—the gate was located too far from the entrance. Jumping down to level eleven was also not an option—the fire would reach me faster than I could hide. So I took advantage of the only reasonable option swimming around in my wretched brain.

I ran toward the monster. When it finished sucking in air, I managed to jump up and, clinging to its horns, flip around and land flat on the creature's head, right between the horns and the gate. Stretching out, I rested my feet on one part of the arch and my hands on the other, so that the huge monster would not inadvertently draw me into the shimmering veil. The monster flinched and released its flame. The fire filled almost the entire cave, turning the bodies of the dark ones into ash. It got so hot that my mana level began to drop rapidly, but my shield held strong. And then it was my turn—another five seconds had passed. Extending my hand, I aimed at the part of the rift directly under the creature's head and activated *Dark Spike.* It shook so hard that it threw the beast's head back, but my body and the huge horns that I was blocking prevented it from flying back.

Now we were getting started! The bearded monster roared with all its might and started to shift, but I was saved by the fact that the magnitude of these movements was rather small. The beast's own body prevented it from moving further through the gate and the fact that I was wedged against its horns prevented it from moving its head. Bones popped, muscles screamed from the tension, my arms and legs wanted to buckle and allow the beast to retreat back into the portal, but I held strong. I'm not sure how I did it, but I held! So that five seconds later, without even trying to move or aim, I could activate *Dark Spike*. I didn't have the opportunity to raise my head and look at the number hanging above the arch—I was struggling to keep myself from snapping in half. The beast pressed hard against me, but not with as much force as a creature of that size should exert. As if it had nothing to rest its paws on (it surely did have paws, right?), so it could only wiggle its jammed head. Another tongue of flame spewed out, this time aimed upwards. The jet hit the ceiling and ricocheted, flying not in our direction, but straight into level eleven. It had missed, but I had no doubt that the next shot would definitely hit its target. The creature has already shown that it could draw the right conclusions and adapt to the situation. My vision began to go black—the pressure really was enormous. My body still hadn't recovered from the previous break, so I didn't have much muscular strength left. I was basically holding the creature back with my bones and willpower. And these bones were no longer just popping—they were crunching and breaking. However, before consciousness left me completely, I saw a welcoming flashing of the cherished icon. Already only barely aware of my movements, I activated *Dark Spike.* There was an explosion, and...I collapsed to the floor, rolling over the rocks. Judging by the pain, it had still broken me in half. Now the owner of meter-long horns would once again take a deep breath and there'd be nothing left of me, not even ashes. It was coming, now. Or maybe now. Come on, you horned freak, burn me! I'm ready!

But it seemed no one was in a hurry to turn me into a cloud of smoke, so I gathered the rest of my strength and opened my eyes. My head was turned toward where the gate should have been, but it wasn't there! All that remained of the Wave were the warped stones that once comprised the archway. No shimmering veil, no huge monster. It ran off, the bastard! It broke me and ran away to be torn apart by Skron! I reached for my belt and growled in pain. It felt like every cell in my body was in pain. Like after a training session with the Evil Engineer! Nevertheless, I managed to reach the vial and even bring it to my mouth. Of course, if my spine was broken, this wouldn't help, but at least it would reduce the pain.

Imagine my surprise when, after just one bottle, I managed not only to roll over on my back, but even sit up! The first thing I saw, which caused a wave of relief to pass through me, was that my legs were still in place and hadn't been snapped backwards. From the outside, my body looked whole and unharmed, despite all the sensations I had experienced. The second thing that caught my eye and made me forget how to breathe properly for some time was the huge horned head of the creature lying a few meters away from me. My *Dark Spike* had closed the gate, slicing off the unknown monster's head. My hand flew once again to my belt—I needed some more strength. Only after my fourth recovery elixir was I able to rise to my feet and approach the monster's head. Its dimensions were terrifying. Even without taking into account the meter-long horns, the head reached my shoulders. This beast turned out to be two or three times taller than a guard! It was unlikely that such a huge head could be supported by a body any smaller than that.

I touched my own head and cringed, ready to receive a whole load of dark notifications, but nothing happened. Finding an icon on the status bar describing my current acquisitions, I studied the list and frowned—there was nothing new there. For destroying such a terrible beast, Skron or the Light (I didn't know which of them distributed the awards) didn't give me anything!

For a while, I stood there staring blankly at the destroyed arch. It was kind of upsetting, to be honest! I had destroyed a whole army of the dark beasts, shut down the Wave, killed the monster, and what did I get for all this? Broken bones, torn muscles and nearly all my elixirs gone, that's what I got! Where were the bonuses? Where were the awards? Where were my Skron-damned shards of *Devour* or *Amplify?* Where were they, I ask you?!

The space was silent, offering no answer. I glanced back at the entrance to level eleven, then back at the giant head, and decided that I wouldn't be left without my trophy! I wouldn't let the dark beasts devour the single piece of evidence proving the extremely dangerous and difficult experience I had endured. Grabbing the horn in my hand, I took a few steps toward the passage. Strangely, I had no issues dragging the head along. It weighed two or three times less than it should have. By changing my grip to grab the second horn, I was even able to lift the head off the floor. Yes, it was difficult, but nothing too bad—forty kilos at most. If that was the case, I would take the trophy with me. It wasn't that far to the bottom of the rift.

Thus began my descent, code named "Mad Max." I wasn't about to leave my prize behind, so I stubbornly dragged it along behind me. I almost got lost on level eleven. There was no stream of dark beasts hinting at where to go. There were no dark creatures here at all—they had all run to the surface. Level twelve. Thirteen. Fourteen. The rift seemed dead. It was like level one, turned into nothing but inert stone by the students. Not a single beast, not even the scrappiest runt. When I got to the final descent, I stopped to appreciate the scale of the cave. The Warden that had once inhabited this space was truly colossal. Approximately the same size as the goat I'd destroyed. It was the largest cave I had ever seen in the rifts. Fifty meters tall, no less. Moreover, there wasn't a single pit, ledge or pebble anywhere on the walls, ceiling, or even the floor. Everything was smooth, as if the Warden had been particular about its living space. Or it had fed itself on rocks. Or simply pounded all outcroppings into dust. If I was right, then the Warden was the terrible creature that had so effortlessly smashed its way between caves. Considering the fact that the creature must be an exclusive with a whole heap of abilities and and a monstrous aura that could easily crush anyone flat, the academy must have been razed to the ground. As well as a good chunk of the city. Kimal Sarento alone won't be enough to counter such a creature. I wondered—had the Evil Engineer had managed to escape? Had Father Nor ceased to be his personal attendant?

As always, my questions remained unanswered. Grabbing the horn, I began the last descent. Level fifteen. The deepest level in the rift. One no one has ever reached. Although this immediately raised questions for me—how did the clerics and doomed soldiers know that the rifts maxed out at level fifteen? They knew for certain, didn't they? They did. So someone had already reached such depths and lived to tell the tale. I needed Alia, I had a lot of questions for her. I was sure my personal servant of the Light knew more than most clerics. I just needed to shake it out of her. It looked like I'd have to share some of my own knowledge. Incidentally—why hadn't I looked all this up before?

As I continued along my path, I found the *Symbols* icon on my status bar and opened the list of available upgrades. Now I was able to apply two symbols at once—either the same or different, as the situation demanded. *Yat,* as I already knew, was an amplifying symbol. I just had to figure out what the symbol that generated the Wave gave me.

Worm. *Curse symbol. Applied to the body. Grants the owner the curse "Vampiric Aura," allowing you to absorb all positive emotions from light creatures within a radius of three meters. For each light creature within your curse area, you gain +1% to all stats for 1 hour. If the creature is under your curse for more than 1 hour, it will die in terrible agony. For each creature that dies, your stats are permanently increased by 0.1%. Symbol duration: 1 day. Requires chabre powder to use.*

To say I was stunned is an understatement. The darkest of all dark auras that could possibly exist. With the help of *Vampiric Aura,* I could become the most powerful being in the world! All I had to do was kill a thousand people to max all my stats out to 100%? They'll die in terrible agony, you say—who cares? I could turn into the perfect warrior, capable of defeating any creature of the dark. Or light, if the Fortress decided to get rid of me. And if there were ten thousand victims? A hundred thousand? A million? There was Light. There was Skron. And there would be Max. The third god of this world! A world built on bones and sacrifice. A world filled with my cursed *Vampiric Aura...*

I shook the obsession from my head. Now I knew how the Fardis would die. And only them—I would not become a new Skron. The symbol I had just received was so monstrous that I earnestly searched for a way to get rid of it. To avoid the temptation of using it. But there was no way to refuse the gift. *Worm* was not a permanent fixture in my stats. Alia would definitely not be happy.

And I wasn't too happy about what I saw in the final cave. The Riftmaster on level fifteen turned out to be the same as the ones I'd encountered on levels one and eight. A cubic creature with a huge heart-like organ in the center. So in that regard, everything was pretty standard. What I didn't like was the creature standing next to the cube that, judging by the density, was in the final stages of spawning. It was small in stature—about two meters. Legless. Headless. Winged. And from what I could see through the still transparent body, it had four hearts. Its appearance wasn't what caused me concern, but rather the fact that my gut fell to my heels when I saw it. I rushed forward and struck at the Master with all my might to stop this beast from incarnating as quickly as possible. The body twitched one final final time and I was bombarded with notifications:

3 out of 5 location map fragments obtained. Total: 5 of 5.

1 of 12 *Amplify* shards obtained. Total: 9 of 12.

10 out of 100 *Devour* shards obtained. Total: 13 of 100.

The notifications were intriguing, of course, but I paid them no mind. The creature causing me this visceral horror had not vanished! Despite the fact that the Master was dead, the monster continued manifesting itself, although the process slowed significantly. I tried to swipe the monster aside, but my hand passed through it as if through something incorporeal. Panic set in—from the looks of it, the creature would fully incarnate in a matter of minutes. If I failed to do something, a metamorph would appear in the capital. That this unremarkable seeming creature was a metamorph, I had no doubt in my mind. The animalistic terror that gripped me every time I glanced in its direction left no room for interpretation. Backed into a corner, I looked around frantically, then stared at the goat head I had brought with me. Not just at the head, but at the meter-long horns. Turning my gaze toward the substantiating metamorph, I ran over to my trophy and dragged it toward the ghostly figure. The horns pierced the disembodied creature with the same ease as my hands, but this was exactly what I needed. I adjusted it to ensure that the horns passed through two of the hearts. I stuck my katars through the other two, laying on the head and positioning myself so that the blades would remain in place, even if I lost consciousness. I turned on *Healing Aura* and waited. Exactly thirty seconds later, the creature blinked for the last time and solidified. At that moment, my consciousness faded. No explosions, no pain, no inhuman torment. I just switched off, unable to withstand the presence of a god-like entity. It couldn't be anything else. So this was what death felt like...

Chapter 4

OPENING MY EYES, I stared at the immobile body of the metamorph lying a few meters away. For some reason, I was in an upright position. Lowering my head, I saw the reason—I was pressed against the wall by the goat head. Its horns were stuck into the wall to the left and right of me, piercing the stone almost to the very bedrock foundation. A couple of centimeters to the right or left and no shield in this world could have saved me from certain death. I reflexively flexed my fingers to activate the katars and gazed at the vestiges of my weapons with a detached look. Only a few miserable shards of the blades remained. With great effort, I managed to move the head enough to slip out. Knowing that there was no way I could leave my trophy behind, I just barely was able to pull the goat head out of the wall. The monster's horns had broken off, just like my blades. Neither the steel nor the dark beast's ossified flesh could withstand the protection of the metamorph.

Only then did I realize what had been nagging at me this whole time—a new icon had appeared on my status bar. It was blinking to get my attention, and when I focused on it, an explanation appeared: *Catalysts.* The word meant nothing to me, so I kept my eyes on the pictogram. A new window opened before my eyes. In the upper section there were three cells with very strange contents—small multi-colored piles of sand. Near each was the number "4" and, as soon as I focused on the piles, the details popped up.

Rainbow Catalyst: *enhances a quality by improving the resistance characteristic of a ring or amulet. Cancels out other types of qualities.*

True Catalyst: *enhances a quality by improving the characteristic of a ring or amulet. Cancels out other types of qualities.*

Poison Catalyst: *enhances a quality by improving the attack characteristic of a ring or amulet. Cancels out other types of qualities.*

Very informative, neither too much nor too little. The bottom part of my vision was occupied by another field, significantly larger than the first, but completely empty. Below the field was the word "*Enhance,*" but no matter how I stared at it, nothing happened. Basically the only thing that became clear was that nothing was clear.

Whatever these catalysts were, they were of no use to me—I had neither amulets nor rings.

But the ordeal reminded me that I had to deal with the awards I'd received. That incomprehensible little icon couldn't have been all I won from my battle with the metamorph, right? There had to be something else. Something I could use right here and now. Opening up my stats, I stared at the new notifications:

Amplify shards: 10 of 12
Devour shards: 63 of 100

For some time I glanced back and forth between my personal stat bar and the metamorph. While everything was more or less standard with _Amplify_—I received one shard because the beast had been an exclusive—the situation with _Devour_ was much more interesting. Fifteen shards. An incredible quantity. From what I knew, the shards fell from Riftmasters in high-level rifts, starting with level five. I'd gained three shards for the level eight master and ten for the level fifteen. That all added up. But then here came the metamorph, gifting me fifty shards in one fell swoop. Whatever _Devour_ was, it was now a huge step closer to being reassembled.

There were no other new additions, so I stepped over to the beast. Even motionless, it evoked a primal, uncontrollable terror in me. I pulled myself together with difficulty and began to study the beast. Fragments of my blades and the horns could be seen protruding from its body. Well sure, it's hard to stay alive when you incarnate with extra appendages through all four of your hearts. Learning down, I touched the body, and it felt as if a bolt of lightning ran through me. Even dead, it was trying to defend itself. Jumping back—to Skron with it anyway—I stared, astonished, at how the dangerous creature had crumpled into nearly shapeless wads of flesh, having completely lost all integrity. Suddenly I realized that there was something in its clenched fist. Slowly, as if afraid of an explosion, I pried open the fist and found myself face to face with the most beautiful ring I'd ever seen in my life. It had clearly been crafted in a masculine style—a massive face with a huge diamond in the middle and a smattering of smaller surrounding stones. It was made of some unfamiliar blue metal, and despite its massiveness, weighed almost nothing. And most striking of all—it made me gulp—was that the ring exuded a noticeable red aura, just like a living dark beast.

Ever since childhood, I'd been taught that if you don't know what something is, you shouldn't use it. Noticed some unfamiliar berries on a nearby bush? Don't even think about sticking them in your mouth. Found some unknown species of mushroom? Great job, now go toss them out. Spotted an unknown plant? Fantastic! Don't get anywhere near them! And the same thing applied here—I wasn't going to put on an unknown ring that had just fallen into my hands. Because I had no idea what might happen to a person who wore an exclusive dark ring. Maybe I'd instantly go so dark that I'd no longer be able to return to my humanity. No matter how carefully I inspected the metamorph's gift, I gained no further explanation of what I had gotten my hands on. I knew that amulets were mined from elite dark beasts. Perhaps some exclusives also dropped rings and the church knew what they were and how to use them. I urgently needed to find Alia. I hoped she had survived. Before I talked to her, I wouldn't even consider sticking this little red wonder on my finger. Into the pocket it went to await better times.

There was nothing else of interest in the Master's cave, so I collected the remnants of the katars and horns, grabbed the goat head and slowly trudged to the exit. I had fifteen floors of "happiness and joy" ahead of me.

The first beasts started popping up around level six. I didn't leave a single one left alive, turning them into formless hunks of meat, but they didn't drop anything at all. From what I could surmise, these were the dark beasts that had come through the gates, and as soon as they closed, they had transformed into statues. Nevertheless, I slogged on, continuing my terrible mission of sterilization. Finally my efforts were rewarded:

Magic stone *Ice Spike* obtained.
Blank for magical amulet obtained.

On level four, I came across a half-crushed

elite creature. The crazed Warden, who had turned most of the more sluggish dark beasts into mincemeat, had trampled this dark beast, but didn't finish it off. There was no trace left of the stone block the Evil Engineer had toppled into the passage—the creature had simply knocked it aside. Level three also didn't yield anything good, but as soon as I had ascended to level two, I realized that I'd be here for a long time. All fifteen guards were here. These bastards still hadn't made it to the exit.

The question immediately arose—did I have the right to harvest these monsters? The answer came immediately—of course I did! No one else in the whole world had as much right to these bodies as I did! But, before touching the nearest three-meter giant, I sat down on the stones and began to study my stats. Thanks again to Alia—she suggested that we should not rely on chance. As practice had shown, I was sorely lacking in mana. The 80 units I had at my disposal was a pittance when it came to maintaining *Healing Aura* or blocking damage with *Golden Dome of Protection*. The goat, whose head I still stubbornly dragged behind me, was a witness to this. Nearly burned me, the filthy bastard.

It took me a long time to figure out how to place a checkmark before the desired state. The very existence of this checkbox was a discovery for me—in desperation, I had pulled my gaze away from the table of stats to the blank space next to it. A little squiggle had appeared, underlining the entire line. I had to spend some time messing around with it, and as it turned out, this was exactly what I needed. Placing a green checkmark next to the "Mana" line, I approached the first guard and, closing my eyes in trepidation, reached out and touched it.

Enhancement obtained. Selection predetermined.
Mana +1. Total enhancements: 2

It worked! Aside from the buffs, the guards didn't reward me with anything else, but I didn't need it. I had the unique opportunity to become an order of magnitude stronger. After the previous break, my physical stats had fallen even below the initial values. Exhaustion didn't do anyone any good. Periodically changing the checkbox between my parameters, I bypassed all the remaining fourteen giants, transforming myself into, if not a monster, then at least a warrior to be reckoned with.

Mana +4. Total enhancements: 7
Elemental Resistance +4. Total enhancements: 5
Speed +2. Total enhancements: 3
Constitution +2. Total enhancements: 3
Strength +1. Total enhancements: 2
Agility +1. Total enhancements: 2

Was I worried about the fact that someone

wouldn't receive their yem? Not at all!It was my rift, and, given the chump change that the chancellor was planning on paying me, I had every reason to get all the kicks I could. After finishing with the guards, I walked around the whole cave, touching each of the dark ones as I walked by. At some point, I had to take off my jacket and tie it up to make a backpack for the magic stones and blank amulets I was getting. I tossed the nux and chrone to the side, not wanting to mess with the normal resources. Priority was given to chabre and trama—the latter was unfamiliar to me, but there was so little of it, and I was clever enough to understand its value. By the time I managed to crawl through the entire second and first level, there was a huge sack filled with various valuables dragging behind me on one side and a huge horned head on the other. I had just found more than a hundred magic stones! And at least ten of them were gold. But the personal victory I held in most esteem was a rather interesting little line in the personal stats:

***Amplify* shards: 43 of 12.**

I had managed to obtain at least three *Amplify*s, but I didn't absorb them immediately. For one, I didn't know how—I'd have to tinker around with that. Secondly, who knew how the chancellor would react to my winnings? Maybe he'd demand I give him all the hard-earned loot I'd pulled from the rift? It was much easier to defend your rights when no one could confiscate your possessions.

The basement, as such, no longer existed. The powerful steel doors had been blasted off at the hinges. The charred corpses of dark beasts lay everywhere—magic had run rampant. There was no ceiling. The administrative building of the academy had been destroyed. I followed the Warden's path through the huge hole leading outside. Climbing over the pile of rubble, I placed my bag of loot by the wall and looked around. My heart sunk to my toes. The sun had already risen above the horizon, allowing me to see the full extent of what the academy had become. Only the tower remained intact, where the chancellor's private room and the dining room were located. Everything else, including the doomed soldier den, the academic building, the dorms, and even the training ground, was razed, completely demolished. Dead dark beasts as far as the eye could see, hundreds, if not thousands of creatures had found their death within the walls of the academy. But not only them—in some places, I saw human remains. An arm, a leg, a rare torso. Scraps of fabric showed that they were slow students who hadn't had time to evacuate the academy before the dark army had broken through.

The park surrounding the academy was no more. One got the impression that a dark beast had spent most of its time carefully destroying every single tree. Judging by the tracks, the monster had circled around the academy, gradually increasing its radius. Not a single tree was left standing! I walked a little further along. The houses closest to the academy were also in ruins. Immediately after leaving the park, the monster had rushed toward the city, where it now remained. The huge carcass was stuck into the next house down. The beast hadn't managed to topple the structure completely before the Master had met its demise. Its carcass was already smoking—sunlight had a negative effect on dark beasts. Nonetheless, someone would have had to put in serious efforts to destroy a body like this. It looked like an earthworm that had grown to an incredible size. I couldn't see the face, but the tail was enough to horrify. I really wouldn't want to cross paths with this grub. It would crush you without even asking your name first. I was about to touch the monster to receive the spoils I was due, but someone stopped me.

"Don't do that," came the calm voice of Father Nora. I turned around and got a good look at him. His mantle was torn, his face covered in blood, one arm hung like a lifeless whip at his side. Nevertheless, he was alive and in relatively good health.

"Where is Alia?" I immediately clarified the issue that had been haunting me. She had too many questions to answer, she had no right to die.

"In the Fortress, preparing the defense," came his reply, which eased the weight on my soul a little. My personal servant was alive, which meant that not everything was as bad as it had seemed at first glance. It was unlikely that Alia would have left the academy until it was completely evacuated.

"The Evil Engineer?"

"Somewhere under the rubble. That thing that crawled out of the rift proved too strong, even for him. Did you manage?"

"The rift is closed, the Wave has been stopped," I nodded. "Where could the dark one be?"

"Anywhere. Maybe even in the belly of the beast. Don't touch it and turn it into inert flesh. There aren't any monsters like this in the registry. We must study it thoroughly."

"What about the chancellor?"

"What was left of him was sent to the Fortress. If the Light is merciful, he will survive," Father Nor sat wearily on the ground. "Many honorable people died here today to ensure the life of the city. The city was not ready for a Wave like this. Nobody was ready."

"And what were you doing here? You're clearly not a mage. Or is there something I don't know about you?"

"I was looking for the dark one. I'll consider him alive until I see his body. How many levels deep was the rift?"

"Fifteen. When I got to the Master, it was finishing forming the metamorph. If I had hesitated even a few minutes longer...It's even scary to imagine what that creature could have done. I think this enormous grub is just a cute little caterpillar compared to the metamorph. By the way, this is the Warden. It dwelled on level fourteen."

"Do not burden me with unnecessary information, that's what you have a personal servant for. Mother Alia is waiting for you in the Fortress. She should know that you survived, the rift is closed and nothing else threatens the city."

"I will certainly go to the Fortress as soon as I help find my mentor. I have too many questions for him, so his heroic death is canceled for today. Do you have any idea where he was fighting?"

"Last time I saw him was near the training grounds, when the Warden wriggled off that way. There's practically nothing left, so you'll need to look elsewhere."

"You mean he ran after the worm? That's something, at least. By the way, Father Nor. If you suddenly find the strength, get to the entrance to the rift. More precisely, to the building. I found an interesting specimen and dragged it out. I really want to know what it is. Do you know all the beasts? Excluding this worm, of course. Basically, can you help me identify it? Next to the head is a jacket filled with my loot. Don't touch it. It's mine! Alia will figure out later what to leave to us and what to give to the Fortress or the academy. Agreed? Alright, I'm going to look for the Evil Engineer."

My speech had puzzled Father Nor—I'd never seen an expression like that on his face before. But this didn't bother me. I set off to look for my mentor. After the last time I'd found the dark one with stumps for arms and legs, for some reason I was certain this time that the Evil Engineer had survived. He might have been crushed, perhaps once again left limbless, but he had survived, that was a fact. The only thing I had to do was find him somehow in that jumble of stones and wood that the academy had become.

And I succeeded! True, I wouldn't have without help from the Evil Engineer himself, but I found him! After an hour of fruitless running around the rubble, I had already begun to despair, and then a stone moved over near the ruins of the doomer dorms. Good thing I wasn't far and heard it roll. Behind the first stone came another one, and by the third I was there, tossing the particularly large blocks aside. After the enhancements, I had become an order of magnitude stronger than before without having to suffer such incredible pain. First, a hand appeared, then a body, and by moving just one more stone, I freed the head of the Evil Engineer. His face was one big bruise, but the dark, pupil-less eyes were intact and open.

"Alive..." the Evil Engineer croaked, and then a committed perhaps the most horrific act of his entire life. He smiled! That repulsive grimace cracking across his eternally gloomy face, I will not forget until the end of my days! I immediately switched on my healing aura, gave him my last recovery elixir and, throwing back the remaining stones, pulled him to freedom. Judging by the position of his arms and legs, they were broken. The art of healing was unknown to me, so I did not pretend to be a great mage, capable of coping with such injuries with a wave of the hand. Instead I found a suitable piece of wood, dragged the Evil Engineer onto it and dragged my finding to Father Nor, who was hanging around near the head I had extracted from the gate.

"Sign for the delivery," I said, slumping down next to the cleric. I was nearly completely drained, even despite my updated stats. I wanted to sleep, eat and—more than anything—to have something to drink.

"Hard times are coming," Father Nor said obscurely.

"So what's already happened wasn't hard times?" I looked around the ruins of the academy. "How much harder can it get?"

"The dark ones will take revenge. The murder of one of Skron's incarnations is not easily forgiven. This happened a few hundred years ago—humans almost lost the Wall. The dark ones were driven back with monstrous sacrifices. Now history will repeat itself. A Wave is coming that could easily overwhelm our empire. The only good news is that another dangerous dark beast has left our world. But how many human lives will we have to pay for this..."

"You mean it would have been better if I let it burn me up in the rift?" I was amazed at the soulless man's words, and broke off, looking into his eyes. He didn't need to respond—I could read his reply easily enough in eyes. Yes, I should have let myself perish!

"You know, you and your little ruminations can go to hell!" I exploded. "If I hadn't destroyed that bastard, I wouldn't have been able to close the gate, and the Wave would have continued to spawn dark beasts. If he had burned me up, I wouldn't have been able to get to the Master and stop those dark ones that got out of the rift. I wouldn't have been able to destroy the nearly-formed metamorph. The capital, with its vaunted Fortress, the emperor's palace, the academy on the hill, the army and the countless number of aristocrats would have simply disappeared if I had not been able to finish this creature off. Are all the people I've listed worthy of death just because the dark ones will avenge the death of this goat? I have nothing more to say to you, Father Nor. Let's go through Alia for all further communication. I hope my personal servant of the Light has a different opinion about the value of human life. And those who exist now are much more important than those who may die in the future. And maybe they won't die, because it's not guaranteed that the dark ones will take revenge. On whom and for what? Who knows that it was I who destroyed the creature? Nobody. I'll drag the head out into the sun and within a couple of hours, all that will remain of it is a small wet patch on the pavement. Take care of your dark one. He needs treatment."

I stood up, barely able to contain my anger. Rationally, I knew that my anger was in vain—it was foolish to expect anything else from Father Nor. But now that everything was over, I could be treated like a human again, if just for a few seconds!

"Max, wait!" I heard him call suddenly. Father Nor rose to his feet and came close to me. The churchman's heavy gaze was oppressive, but I had too much anger boiling inside to pay any attention to him. "There's no darkness in you."

"You don't know for sure," I quipped. "The pair that caused the Wave didn't have darkness in them either."

"They didn't have souls. You do. I can feel it," Father Nor said, ignoring my tone. And then something happened—something that I would never have anticipated. The cleric put his good hand on my shoulder and said: "I rarely say this to anyone, but this may be a unique moment where I have no right to remain silent. Thank you. From the bottom of my heart, thank you! Never before have I been glad that someone else was able to dissuade me. You have proven your value. In the beginning, I was against you even going to the academy. I counted you among the converts. I am sincerely sorry that the Fortress treated you the way it did at first. It was wrong. Now that you've saved an entire city—not just a city, an entire empire, I only have one thing to say to you. Thank you. Please hurry to the Fortress. Those preparing for the final battle there must be warned that it is over. I will take care of the dark one and promise that as soon as he can, he will answer any of your questions. Even more, he himself will tell you everything he knows about the dark ones. You can leave your winnings with me. I swear, no one will lay a finger on them. I, Father Nor, as the official representative of the Fortress at the magical academy of the Zarak Empire, acknowledge that everything you brought out of the rift is yours to keep. Whatever it may be. Let it be so!"

Chapter 5

WHAT A LUXURY IT WAS to lie in a huge, warm bath (more like a small swimming pool), a beautiful girl on one arm, drinking delicious wine without a care in the world! Not thinking of the fact that somewhere deep in the dungeons of the Fortress, a real battle was being waged for the rights to resources obtained from the rift. Not thinking of the capital's five districts in ruins or the several hundred—perhaps thousands of civilians who thought it prestigious to live next to the magical academy and who will never again open their eyes. Not thinking of the difficult conversation ahead with Alia and the Evil Engineer. Not thinking of anything at all!

But these luxuries were unavailable to me—despite my soft and pleasant surroundings, my thoughts kept turning to the events of the past few days. After I came to the Fortress and reported that the Wave had been quashed, and that the rift under the academy no longer existed, such a flurry of activity began that it sucked in anyone and everyone in its path. Even representatives of other academies came to help clear the rubble and find the victims. Guards, aristocrats, townspeople, students, churchmen, doomed soldiers...several thousand people gathered in one place with the sole purpose of undoing the consequences of the dark breach and saving at least someone.

I didn't get the chance to take part in this "working vacation"—the Fortress representatives were putting me through the ringer. From what I understood, the special response team had already made it through the rift and realized that there was practically nothing to extract, so then the servants of the Light had settled on me, demanding a full report. This was where Alia came in handy. At that moment, I was even ready to call her Mother Alia—it was delightful to see how she bent the other more experienced and older clerics to her will. Soon Father Nor appeared, dragging behind him my jacket filled with all sorts of goodies. The servants of the Light were about to stretch out their hands to take it, but two others immediately stood up to protect my property— Father Nor and Mother Alia. How much was abuse, how many shouts and threats! In the end, after some time, I was sent to a hotel, a girl was sent over from the most expensive brothel in the capital, and for five hours, I had been indulging in sweet, non-stop bliss.

Suddenly, the door almost flew off its hinges. Alia burst into my bathroom. Angry Alia.

"Get out of here!" The girl snarled, barely able to contain her anger. The busty beauty squeaked something and, flashing her magnificent bare bottom, ran out of the room.

"Assholes!" Alia said furiously as she stopped pacing the room.

"Hello to you too," I said. "Let me guess—they took all of my winnings?"

"I'd like to see them try—I'd rip their arms off. What you took from the rift is yours and yours alone. Neither the Fortress, nor the academy, nor the empire have rights to your spoils. Later we'll think about what we should keep and what to sell. I saw a couple of interesting stones in the mix. They will definitely suit you."

The girl sat down in a chair and stared at me. It became uncomfortable—Alia had Father Nor's look. Heavy, penetrating to the very core. Funny thing was, it didn't bother either me or her that I was naked in the bath. Who cared about such trifling things when there was so much more at stake?

"Then what happened? They blamed me for the destruction of the capital? Do I need to pay for the restoration of the academy? The dark ones just issued an ultimatum demanding that the Fortress give me up?"

"If only. You were recognized as a hero, the savior of the city. The emperor wants to see you in a month in order to personally grant you your reward."

"Um…and that's why you're so annoyed?"

"According to the rules of the Zarak Empire, doomed soldiers are not permitted to meet with the emperor!"

"Well I'm supposedly not a doomed soldier," I frowned. "Or is there something I don't know?"

"The thing is, your status is still undetermined. And the High Priest still cannot agree with the Council of the Heads of Regions on your unique position. Yes, you are not a doomed soldier, but you are not an ordinary inhabitant of the empire either. You still don't exist. And therein lies the main snag. The representative of the emperor who bore this 'good news' said that for saving the capital, you will be granted life and will have your name returned. You will once again become Baron Maximilian Valevsky, and we cannot change this in any way. The invitation was handed over to me personally in the presence of the Council of the Heads of Regions. Refusing to meet with the emperor would put the Fortress under fire."

"So if I go before the Emperor in a month, I will get my name back and the Fortress will no longer have influence over my actions?" I asked. "What's the catch?"

"That now, you only have one person to be accountable to. As soon as you become a baron, there will be a huge number of such people. The Duke of the region you reside in, judges and prosecutors of all stripes, mayors, the emperor with all his heaps of advisers and heirs, all kinds of counts and viscounts who are higher than you in status. You will fall to the very bottom of the empire's food chain, where you will be used by anyone with even a modicum of power. Including the Duke of Odoevsky. Damn—you can't even go into the church! For a whole year, a person who received a title personally from the hands of the emperor is unable to refuse the gift, under pain of death!"

"Listening to you, you'd think it was time to prostrate myself before the Fortress and beg them to keep me," I quipped. "Only you forget, dear personal servant, that by returning to the land of the living, I not only gain a mob of new bosses, whom I already have more than enough of, I will also have the right to defend my honor and dignity returned to me. And by any means available to me, and I'll tell you, I'm quite capable. Besides, nothing obliges me to sign vassalage with any of the dukes—I may well exist for some time as a landless baron. Where will I get the money to survive? Simple: I will be free to choose my own rifts. All I need is to assemble a team of people who can butcher dark beasts. Gold, materials, artifacts, boosts—all this will flow toward me in a bountiful river. I will purchase an estate for myself within the city limits of the capital, thus leaving the influence of the duke, and I will live well and gain wealth. For some reason, you didn't mention that part."

"Rifts are located on other people's lands. The

Fortress has to pay thirty percent of the estimated value of the rift to the landowners each time."

"Not a big loss. I only have to close two or three five-levels before barons, viscounts and counts of all kinds will invite me to their lands, simply for me to pass through their rifts. Because thirty percent after doomed soldiers have gone through and thirty percent after me are different amounts. Or am I wrong?"

"You're not wrong about that," Alia said gloomily. "But as for the other point, you are. Rifts belong to the Fortress. This is the law. No one will let you inside without an agreement and their fair share."

"And for this, I have a specially trained person who knows how to resolve issues related to the obstacles of the clergy. Weren't you loudly declaring that you would stay with me until the end of my days? What keeps you in the Fortress, Mother Alia? Especially now, when you are equals with the bishops? Personally, I'm glad that I can get out from under Fortress control. Think about it—the High Priest publicly acknowledges that I am not a suicide bomber. But the Council of the Heads of Regions is impeding the process of determining my status. Why? Because it suits their purposes, of course. Father Urg can talk all he wants, but as long as he has nine bishops, the Fortress will be of no use. And the High Priest himself also betrays his own inconsistency. He loudly proclaimed that from now on, I belong to neither the Fortress, nor the empire. But as soon as the emperor declared that he wanted to see me, you turn into a raging shrew. Why?"

"Because we're not just the church, but the church of the Zarak Empire," Alia muttered. "At the pinnacle of which sits the emperor."

"Then please explain why in Skron's name you kicked out my pretty lady? I paid for two more hours, by the way, and I plan to use them to the fullest! Wow, you still managed to find a problem—your ward has been returned to the living. You should rejoice that you no longer have to protect me from any sort of riff-raff who wants to assert their dominance over me. So I definitely still need to continue training my sword skills. Without that, I'm nowhere now. And I need to buy myself a sword. Are you listening to me at all? Hey, what are you doing?!"

My exclamation of surprise was completely warranted—Alia had suddenly stripped off her robe and the garments hidden underneath, appearing entirely naked in front of me. For the first time, I saw the girl without her formless frock, so I was able to solemnly appreciate her perfect form. A flat stomach, a small upturned chest that just begged to be in the palm of your hand, a thin waist, long slender legs and not a single hair on her body. Without a hint of embarrassment, Alia climbed into the bath with me and, dunking her head all the way under water and then leaning back against the side of the tub, rolled her eyes back in delight.

"I haven't taken a real bath in ages. You can't

even imagine how envious I was when you went to the bathhouse with your group after that one-level rift," Alia said without opening her eyes. "Do you have Shurgan wine there? Pour me some?"

"Take it," I repositioned myself to lay floating next to Alia.

"I need to pull my group from the Fortress. Will you do that?"

"They're doomed soldiers. The only way to get them out is to exchange them for an *Amplify*."

"That's what I'm talking about," I said, causing Alia to open her eyes abruptly. The look she shot me crumpled me, completely dashing any hope of any romantic motifs I might have imagined.

"There weren't any *Amplify*s among your winnings. Max?"

"Max what? I know full well that I have to tell you everything I went through in the rift, but when you come here, looking so pretty and hopping in my bath, my thoughts turn in another direction. And don't look at me like that! I'm a young man in my prime, and instead of allowing me to relax a little, you kicked my lady friend out. What else was I supposed to think when a naked beauty climbs into my bath and asks for wine? Certainly not about what happened in the rift. Or are relations between dark ones and their personal servants of the Light forbidden? I propose we decide this issue right now, so that I don't have any illusions about it."

"That issue remains unregulated," Alia

responded after a long pause. She glanced down at her glass of wine, took a sip, and set it aside. "Before our case, personal servants and the dark ones were always of the same sex. I'm sorry, I didn't consider how you might react to seeing me naked. Where I studied, there was no division between boys and girls. There were only children of the Fortress. Therefore, we have developed a different attitude toward nudity. Not like normal people. If it bothers you, it won't happen again in the future."

"You know, that would actually be good," I said after pondering it. "I won't hide that I like what I saw. You have an amazing figure, and if you don't take your heavy look into account, then without a doubt, you're a beautiful woman. It's hard to see you naked and know that I can't have it. Better to just never see you like this."

There was an awkward pause. Alia looked at me, I moved to the opposite edge of the pool and looked at her. Finally, she said:

"Serving the Light does not imply renunciation of carnal pleasures. The only restriction is no relationship with doomed soldiers. Or, if we take our case, with those whose status has not yet been determined. During my time spent in the Fortress, I did not have the opportunity to start any sort of relationship. After all, for everyone, I was not just sister Alia, but the daughter of Father Nor, head of the dark inquisition. No one wanted to touch me, lest they angered my father. You can't imagine how annoying it was. Maybe I really did get too worked up about your upcoming meeting with the emperor. If it takes place and you again become officially a living being, I will have nothing against us getting to know each other better. If you still want it. Until then, you'll have to be patient. Because I'm not going to give up taking baths. I hope we have resolved this issue. In that case, please explain to me why there are no *Amplify*s among the spoils that Father Nor so fiercely defended?"

"Well...perhaps we have reached a unique moment where I'm ready to be as open as possible. Set up a canopy, my dear personal servant of the Light. What I'm about to tell you, even the walls of this hotel have no right to hear..."

How lovely that the water in our pool was heated! It took me around an hour to tell Alia about my adventures in the rift and beyond. Whatever one may say, the girl proved that she was worthy of my candor. It's amazing what one trip to the stake can do. I told her everything I learned so far. About symbols and how to get them. About the creatures that could get inside your head. The fact that steel does not always help in the rifts. About how I managed to shut down the Wave and where I obtained the head of Skron's incarnation. And about the metamorph, catalysts and my own enhancements, of course. The final note in my story was the ring, which I handed over to Alia without any hesitation.

"Now you know everything about the dark

ones that I do," I finished my story and drained my glass of Shurgan wine in one gulp. Alia, after pondering for a while, followed suit and said:

"For ages, *Devour* was thought to be the stuff of ancient legend. The first mention of the stone dates back to the hundredth year after the appearance of Skron. It was received by a man who drove the darkness back from the center of the mainland, divided the lands into three empires and organized the construction of the Wall. The first human emperor. The second and final mention of the stone was five hundred years ago, when the descendents of the first emperor uncovered his tomb to take the valuables for themselves. For a long time, the stone was considered a fairy tale, a fiction of ancient storytellers, until the eight-level rift was closed twelve years ago. The Evil Engineer took the most active part in that battle—he was one of the thirty-two doomed soldiers who came back from the rift. The father of the current emperor highly appreciated the feat and sacrifice of the doomed soldiers, granting them all life. Actually, it was then that we learned that high-level rifts can be used to get fragments of *Devour*. They knew that you had received some for closing your eight-level rift, but did not force the events. Why the hurry, when there's a separate servant in the Fortress who keeps complete statistics on the rifts you close and their levels? The Fortress monitors your every step, but only interferes when necessary."

"And you ask me why I so desperately want

my freedom?" I burst out suddenly. "For that very reason!"

"Anyway, now onto what exactly *Devour* does. If we are to believe the ancient archives, it's a stone allowing the holder to absorb all the resources within a certain radius. For example, say you found yourself some chrone, which they use to make potions to increase the levels of stones. *Devour* absorbs all the energy of the stones and, as soon as it's enough to increase the energy level, notifies the wielder with an option to make the improvement. And so it is with all resources. Chrone, chabre, nux, tram, yem…Everything that can be obtained in the rift or from the dark beasts on the surface. We must talk about what those who use *Devour* might transform into. You remember the curse symbol…it's practically the same thing, but without human sacrifice."

"You know, that raises the question—how many people are snatched up by dark beasts? Does the Fortress have yearly statistics?"

"*Worm* was a surprise for me—the church had no information on this symbol. The Evil Engineer has four symbols, but they're all geared toward enhancing strength."

"I believe my mentor already has five symbols. He gained the fifth with me, when the pictogram summoning the Wave was completed. You didn't answer—how many people are lost every year?"

"Dark beasts devour or drag back ten thousand people into the rifts every year," Alia replied reluctantly.

"The church is certain these people are being devoured?"

"I'm tracking, no need to press the point," she cut me off. "And I don't like where you're going with this. We've already discovered the unpleasant news that dark ones can integrate stones and place them at will, without relying on chance. If it turns out that they have also significantly increased their numbers through people…It certainly must be investigated, the only question is how? The highest hierarchs of Skron have so far evaded our capture."

"You mean to say that the Evil Engineer didn't tell you anything about the stones?"

"The dark one doesn't have any stones other than *Analyze.* They check him on a monthly basis."

I bit my tongue so as to not blurt out too much. Oh, man! Turns out my mentor was a cunning bastard! He kept silent about the fact that he wields several exclusive stones. Or did he? What if Father Nor hid this information from the church? I wouldn't put anything past him. I'd need to check.

"I have a not entirely appropriate question, so you don't have to answer, but I'm compelled to ask—are you going to relay everything I just said to the Fortress? Meticulously record it in some report, attach it to my case file and leaf through it on long, sleepless nights, searching for inconsistencies?"

"Do you think Father Nor has something to

hide from the Fortress?" The girl narrowed her eyes, which made me almost swear. Why was I assigned such a clever cleric? Nevertheless, Alia answered after a long pause, "That is not an easy question. We know that the dark one's spies are operating in the Fortress. There is even a suspicion that these are high-ranking spies with high levels of access. So yes, I will record everything you told me in a separate report, but no, it will not go to the Fortress. Only two people will know where and how this report is stored: the High Priest and I. I received information on the dark ones from Father Urg—he gave me a summary of Father Nor's reports. I haven't seen the reports myself. The High Priest himself will decide what to convey to the public from our conversation, and what should remain hidden until better times."

"And what's better to forget entirely," I added. "For some reason, I feel like the Evil Engineer has had the *Worm* symbol for quite a while. But for some reason, he didn't report this information to you."

"I will clarify this point," she said. "Father Urg would have reason to behave this way—never before have there been two dark ones recognized by the church within the empire at the same time. Not to mention with a mirror. All the experiments the Fortress conducted ended in a crushing failure. Even masters capable of entering combat meditation could not open the mirrors within themselves. At the moment, you are unique."

"Uniqueness implies a huge responsibility that I don't need. Better to tell me what you're going to do with the ring."

"It's rare, but sometimes dark beasts drop jewelry instead of amulets. They're usually unsightly magic items with two qualities. Rarely, one in a thousand, an elite ring with four qualities appears. Nobody has seen a red ring. Their existence, of course, was predicted, but for the thousand-year history of the confrontation with Skron, there is no mention of exclusive jewelry in the archives. The ring's qualities are currently inactive. They will remain so precisely until the moment the object is placed on someone's finger. It is believed that at this moment, the ring adjusts to its wearer, and from the whole variety of parameters, of which there are almost a hundred, those that are ideally suited to the characteristics of human development will be selected. I may be wrong, but for such an unactivated ring, the emperor could easily appoint you a duke."

"If only I needed that. May I?"

Alia didn't hesitate for a second. As soon as I reached out my hand, the ring immediately appeared in my palm.

"You said you had five of the five map fragments," Alia said before I managed to slip the ring on. "What does a full map give you?"

"To be honest, I forgot about it, somehow," I admitted. "Everything started spinning as soon as I finished off the Master that the map completely slipped my mind. Hold on a minute, I'll find out."

It took a few seconds to figure out how to assemble the map fragments. As soon as I focused on the stream of notifications with everything I had acquired, a message popped up asking if I wanted to combine the pieces into one whole. I wasn't canceling now, so I accepted, and after a moment, I was looking at a huge map of the central region of our empire. Everything was here: cities, villages, rivers and even the roads between settlements. There weren't any footnotes and explanations, but all I had to do was look at the capital, which was hard not to recognize, and think to myself that this was the city of Turb, and suddenly the first label appeared directly on the map. I was also able to change the scale—as soon as I focused my eyes on a certain area, it immediately zoomed in. Not by much, but if I really wanted to, I could make out the individual homes in the villages. The cities and roads, however, were not the important part of this map. Rifts were scattered in red spots throughout the central region, and the numbers next to them indicated their levels. The rift in the capital was also present, only it was not red, like everyone else, but gray. I fixed my gaze on it and received an explanation:

Rift closed. Levels will vanish in six days.

"Looks like we've got a little problem," I said slowly, evaluating the new map. "There's a ten-level rift in the central region. And, if I'm reading the map correctly, the Riftmaster here will soon have a new floor at its disposal…Alia, why does no one know about the nearly eleven-level rift located in the city in the north of the central region?"

"A city in the north of the region? Hearth? Are you certain?" She frowned.

"Judging by the map, absolutely," I told Alia what area the map pertained to and its features. "Why are you so surprised?"

"Because Hearth is the patrimony of the Bishop of Zwat. A place he practically never leaves, despite the fact that there's a capital in his region." Alia jumped to her feet and began to pace around the pool, not at all embarrassed by me shamelessly gazing at her naked figure. Finally, the girl stared at me with her heavy gaze and said: "Max, I urgently need to get to the High Priest. Looks like you have a new job."

Chapter 6

"I AIN'T GOING IN ANY eleven-level rift! My limit is eight. And look what it did to me. Eleven will kill me! I have a counter offer: let me go through all the regions and create a map of the rifts in the Zarak Empire. So that there are no more surprises like what happened with the rift under the academy. So that the Fortress has time to react to the situation. Why haul ass now to close the rift in Hearth?"

Alia exchanged glances with the High Priest. My proposed idea was tempting, especially with the Fortress' fanatical desire to control everyone and everything. However, the High Priest suddenly balked:

"The active rifts aren't as concerning as the fact that one of the highest-ranking members of the church is a traitor. No one is asking you to close this rift—you must only prove that it exists, as well as pass through the first five or six levels and completely cleanse them of dark beasts. But even these are trifles compared to your main task. There are two ways this situation may unfold. First, you find an untouched rift, clean it up to level six, return to the surface and start an exciting journey through the empire to create a rift map. I sincerely hope for this option."

"But there is a second possibility," Alia said. The rift may be in its active phase of development. There are so-called dark miners—those who can close rifts between two to four levels deep. Considering that in this particular case we have a ten-level, I believe that five or six levels may be in active development. Resources, magic stones, amulets, the innards of dark beasts...And now let's imagine that not only dark miners, but also converts went to the rift. Dark ones with the same abilities as you. For example, the ability to hold a mirror. Then we're talking not about five or six levels, but about all nine or ten. Think what the dark ones have to gain from such depths? How many exclusive creatures are there that can bestow, for example, a whole *Amplify*? Or something even more valuable? The dark ones are getting stronger every day as we postpone our campaign through this rift."

"Stop trying to put psychological pressure on me, I can do that too. First off, the rift has existed for many years up to this point, it can continue to exist a little longer. Second—the only people who know about the existence of this rift are the three of us. It makes no sense that the dark ones would somehow push the plan forward or somehow react to the fact that the Fortress discovered this secret. And, I want to point out that this only occurs if Bishop Zwat has really been covering up this hole in the ground. Maybe no one has any idea that it exists? Is that possible? It's possible. Third, can you guarantee that at the moment, there isn't, say, a fifteen-level rift forming in the western region? Are you ready to lose that much territory? Why can't we conduct a full-scale reconnaissance mission first, and then decide how to act? Why rush headlong into this rift? What are you not telling me?"

"The High Priest is an elected position. Every four years the heads of the regions meet to re-elect the head of the church. The next election is due in three months, and Bishop Zwat is my main competitor. Yes, why hide it—he is now my main opposition. I must ascertain what will happen if he takes my place, and now I find out that he is collaborating with the dark ones? I'll have to give him all the information, including what I got from you and the Evil Engineer. Everything that the Fortress currently has on dark ones. I sincerely want to be wrong about Bishop Zwat. I sincerely want to believe that he has nothing to do with the rift and that this…'hole in the ground,' as you put it, remains untouched. But I am compelled to respond to this new information. I must verify everything."

"So send some spies. Aren't there people who

know how to sneak into even the most tightly secured places?"

"As I've already said, they will only confirm the existence of the rift, of which we already know. Perhaps they will be able to determine where the extracted resources are going. But they won't be able to get inside the rift. But for now our priority should be Bishop Zwat—if the dark ones really are helping him, they will be on the lower levels. There's no way for ordinary people to access them."

"So you want to confirm not whether the Bishop is developing a rift, but whether he is collaborating with the dark ones?"

"Developing a rift, although it is a crime, is not so serious as to be charged with treason. All of us, to a greater or lesser extent, are involved in the unauthorized extraction of resources. Even me. About twenty years ago, when I was still a bishop, I also committed the sin of bypassing the Fortress and extracting resources from the rift. Yes, my girl, I, too, am human, you don't need to make that face. So we have no choice, Max, but to go into the rift and find out what's going on on its lower levels."

"And there won't be dark beasts there. There will be people."

"That is correct. There will be people. And I sincerely pray to the Light that they are ordinary people. Even despite the fact that there's a high degree of probability that I will lose the upcoming elections."

I pondered this. It was one thing to fight dim-witted beasts, especially under my mirror. Humans, on the other hand, were a different story, especially converts. It was unlikely they'd just sit there all wide-eyed and beautiful, waiting for me to come skewer them through with my katars. Especially considering the fact that my blades were broken!

"Okay, let's say I agree to visit this rift now. What will I get in return?"

"First and foremost, you will receive a weapon," replied Father Urg. "Yours, as I understand, has fallen into disrepair. You will receive a wrist crossbow with steel bolts. You should have been given one a long time ago. Three amulets to block lethal damage. Two healing amulets—they work similarly to your aura, but do not require mana. One elite ring that increases protection. All this will remain yours after the operation. Alia has already made a preliminary assessment of the magic stones you have obtained—we will help you to identify those that you consider important. Don't forget, the academy has been destroyed and it's impossible for them to integrate the stones now, but we also have such devices. We cooperate with the academy because it is beneficial for us. You will also receive an *Amplify,* and we are ready to enhance your capabilities as much as possible. Do you need anything else?"

"Yes, two points. The first: I need three doomed soldiers from my former group."

"For what? They are useless in combat."

"In a month, the emperor will return my title to me. I need people to develop my clan. Hiring from the outside is not an option—I need either those who can be trusted, or those who are indebted to me. In fact, I would like to purchase those three doomed soldiers from the Fortress in order to make them my doomed soldiers."

The High Priest looked at Alia as if asking for clarification.

"A middle-class merchant, a legal clerk and a teacher with the rudiments of a mage," the girl explained.

"That is correct," I confirmed. "I don't know how to bargain at all, I don't deal much with the law, and many things that are considered the norm for others are a revelation to me. Geography, history, the natural sciences. I was never taught these things, and now that the academy is no more, there's really nowhere to learn. I don't want to go to a regular academy."

"A completely logical desire. What's the second point?"

"A little over a month ago, Duke Odoevsky closed our lands. I will not delve into the justice of this, I will settle that with the duke personally. My concern lies somewhere else: all the inhabitants of our estate were evicted and sent somewhere. Cooks, maids, grooms, tutors. All those who faithfully served my family. I have no idea where they were all assigned. It is unlikely that they were executed, like my relatives. I need them. All of them. Find my people, ransom them, if they fell into slavery, gather them in one place. It won't be an easy task, but what you require of me is no walk in the park either. My people in exchange for the rift."

"Let's imagine a situation in which your meeting with the emperor does not take place," Alia immediately suggested. "You do not return to the world of the living and remain in your current undefined status."

"Nothing will change. I can still buy an estate in the city. If not myself, then through one of my people. And if not through them, then through the Fortress. Those who remember what the Valevsky name once was will settle in this estate. Even if everything goes badly and I remain who I am now, I will have the opportunity to relax, and not in some random hotel, wondering whether or not the cook spat in my dish, but among my people."

"I have no qualms," the High Priest said after thinking for a moment. "You go to the rift in Hearth and study what's happening to it on location. I initiate the process of collecting your former subjects. All that's left is resolving the issue of the three doomed soldiers. We can't just release them to you—we need a reason."

"Will three *Amplify*s—one for each—suffice?" I stared into the High Priest's eyes. He frowned and nodded. Wow, they just promised with such confidence to hand over an exclusive stone, and here I was ready to spend three *Amplify*s at once. How could I help but grimace? Alia just physically hadn't had the time to tell the High Priest about either the ring or the stones.

"In that case, go get the contract and sign it." I dove into my inventory and manifested the three exclusive magic stones. After the map, this was child's play. "When can they be considered free? I need to assign them the task of finding the estate. And one more thing, Father Urg, I am entitled to a share for closing the eight-level. When will I receive it? I require gold to purchase my property.

"In addition, Max has forty-one thousand points in the doomer rankings. I would like access to the store," Alia said.

"You're killing me here!" the High Priest threw up his hands, grabbing the *Amplify*s with a quick movement. A moment later, Father Urg was already ringing a small bell, calling for a personal assistant. The cleric who had once escorted me to the golden throne entered the office and bowed.

"I have urgent orders for you. First, arrange for Max and Alia to have access to the closed section of the doomer shop with a limit of forty-one thousand four hundred units. Second, prepare a decree on the withdrawal of Max's group from the ranks of the doomed soldiers on the grounds that he provided the required number of *Amplify* stones. Third, give Max the weapons and ammunition on this list. Fourth, start the search for servants from the Valevsky family estate. Everyone who was there at the time of the execution. I think the servants of the Light there should be able to help you with that. Fifth, prepare a waybill for Max and Alia, tomorrow morning they are going to Hearth. Sixth, make sure that a full report on the Fortress' financial obligations to Max for closing the eight-level rift is prepared within the week. It is not good when the church owes someone gold. You may begin."

"Please follow me," the assistant looked up at Alia and me. "Let's start with store access. We'll pick up weapons and ammunition for you there."

Up to that point, I'd never had the occasion to set foot in the doomer store—my previous visits to the Fortress had been cut short. The store was located in the basement and was a large, elongated room lined with various racks and shelves, all of which were listed in the labeled catalog with prices. Bargaining, like One had wanted, did not work here. I looked with interest at weapons, stones, elixirs, various tools and appliances that would make life easier on a campaign. Like a flint, a tent and sleeping bags. No one would issue them on default. However, our escort strode confidently past all of this stuff toward an inconspicuous little door.

"Please follow me," he said, pulling a heavy key from his pocket. Behind the door was a narrow corridor illuminated by blue crystals mined from the rift. Without even expecting it myself, I put up my mirror. My body worked on pure reflexes. My actions did not go unnoticed—Alia smiled and put her hands on my shoulder:

"Relax. Nothing will threaten you in the Fortress."

This statement seemed very dubious to me, but for now I conceded, lowering my mirror. We ended up in a small room, just like the previous one, lined with various racks. This was where the Fortress housed their exclusive items.

"Katars, a crossbow, a number nine ring, three lethal block amulets, and two healers," the High Priest's aide began listing as he pulled the items he needed from the shelves. "The rest is on your coin. You may choose. If you have any questions, ask."

"I guess I'll take something, I don't know," I muttered, but Alia came to the rescue.

"We need a tent and sleeping bags, two sets of clothes for each, and a hunter's camping kit."

"Don't they have those in the other room?"

"They're better here, although more expensive. The material is tougher, but they weigh less and are more compact."

"Alright, we'll take them. We'll need a spear as well, to shake the rapses off the ceiling. Let me take a look around. Then I will decide what to get here, and what I can find anywhere else…"

Let's just say that the Fortress' exclusive store turned out to be a pretty interesting place. I hung around the elixir counter for a while and, having set aside thirty thousand points for better times, I moved on. Why did I need so many ranking points? For the facet-adding elixir! Yes, such rarities could be found within the Fortress. After collecting tens of thousands of little useless things, including some that Alia advised, I still couldn't resist and pointed to the potion:

"I'll take that."

The cleric merely nodded, making another note to himself. However, Alia did not approve of my choice:

"You could buy lethal-damage-blocking amulets for that price," she noted with obvious annoyance.

"I could," I agreed lightly. "Only now, I have the opportunity to add a second facet to *Dark Spike* and attach two support stones to it. I am sorely lacking in speed and damage. I've got defense, I've got healing, but I have problems with my attack. The mirror doesn't work with people, as you know."

"You're planning on attaching your *Amplify* to this stone? Not to your shield?"

"Again, my defenses are more than sufficient. I don't think any dark human I'll encounter will match the level of that goat that almost burned me. If I'd had a decent attack then, I wouldn't have to play the hero. So the choice is quite obvious and justified. You said that you looked at the extracted stones and even made a choice of what to install. Will you tell me?"

"Have you finished with the wares?" The cleric hurried us out of the closed section. "If you don't require anything else, please continue this conversation somewhere else. I need to fulfill the High Priest's orders."

"Let's go, I have a room in the Fortress, we'll talk there." Aliaa took up half of our purchases, and a few minutes later we found ourselves in a small cell. A bed, a table, a chair, a wardrobe, and a window. That was it! My personal attendant's room was bare, save for these items! There was no toilet, no shower, not even any paint on the walls, not to mention the wallpaper! Throwing the goodies we'd gotten down on the floor, I sat down on a chair and turned to the girl.

"Alright, let's see it," I grinned.

"See what?" Alia was taken aback and blushed.

"Look, let's not pretend, okay? As soon as I heard you say the phrase, 'I saw some interesting stones that might suit you,' I was certain that you not only set these stones aside, but also drafted the layout of my magic field. With all the stones, connections, levels. You are Father Nor's daughter. You could not do otherwise."

"Am I that predictable?" Alia sighed. "Yes, I drew up the plan, but I never dreamed that you'd be able to get your hands on a facet elixir. Here, look. This will make you stronger."

The girl handed me a piece of paper containing a five-by-five field of cells with a schematic representation of the stones. In addition to the stones I currently wielded, there were several new ones, but as soon as I read the description, I looked in surprise at my downcast attendant.

"Alia, what are you playing at? We're supposed to be on the same team! Why in Skron's name do I need *Analyze*?"

The scheme the girl handed me was nearly an exact copy of the one that the High Priest had once tried to foist on me. Yes, "foist," without explaining each magical stone and the effect it would have on me.

"Don't tell me one of the stones I received was *Analyze.*"

"That's it!" Alia defended herself. "It's a sign from above! The Light itself wants you to integrate *Analyze.* A stone with four facets! Max, I think the rifts are a profitable aspect of your life, but weeding out converts among the aristocrats is much more vital. Save the souls of those you can, before Skron can recruit them to his ranks. *Analyze* will help you in this task. Combined with *Amplify* and *Dark Essence,* it will allow you to find those with darkness in them. You will become one of the dark inquisition. I think you will even be able to detect those with no soul. Like the dark one who summoned the Wave."

"One? There were two of them."

"One. That was one person, Max. Or rather, no longer a person. The High Priest told me about humans without souls. It's awful, Max. According to the archives, the highest hierarchs of Skron have the ability to split their soul into fragments and implant them into living people, completely absorbing their essence. Once upon a time, these two peasants were indeed robbers, but ordinary, devoid of magic. Someone from the top, I believe Magister Elor, who is now hiding in the capital, managed to divide his soul into three parts, two of which he implanted into this couple. These were not two independent people—they were one being enacting the will of its creator. We do not know if there is a connection between the soulless and their creator. In general, we know practically nothing about them, except that they cannot be detected by standard means. Now imagine how many of these bastards there are in the empire. Do they live lives, act in the darkness' interests, perform various rituals? You have learned to close rifts perfectly well, Max, but you won't be running around underground your whole life, will you? You have the opportunity to seek out the beasts among humans. But for this, you must trust me and keep with this structure."

"Alright, let's say I agree. Tell me, will *Analyze* somehow affect *Devour*? I have no intention of giving up this stone."

"Counter question: what do you need *Devour* for? As soon as the Fortress or land owners realize that closing the rifts does not bring them profit, they will immediately revoke your access. It is easier to call in a group of doomed soldiers, without a second thought about the fact that half of them will perish, than to lose profits. The rifts belong to the Fortress, the lands where they are located belong to different clans and families. Where do you fit in this narrow scheme? Or are you going to do everything in secret? Using maps?"

"That isn't an option?"

"I won't allow it," Alia scowled. "Yes, I am involved in your development, but I am not obliged to permit you to violate every conceivable law. No, Max, using *Devour* is not an option. In any case, not in the way the description suggested. For some reason, the first emperor did not refuse you this stone. Why? For personal gain? If this were so, he would not divide the lands into three parts. Let's do it this way—once you collect *Devour*, we will return to this issue. If *Analyze* bothers you, we will remove it. Researchers have already learned how to do this. Agreed?"

"Not really. What are 'mental defenses?'"

"Are you talking about *Amplify*? That doesn't apply to you. If an ordinary person uses an exclusive dark stone, as was the case with Viscount Jurmal, the emperor's healer, his defense against the influence of the dark ones will decrease. In particularly severe cases, he can become a convert, even without initiation. Because Skron decided so. One stone is dangerous, two are deadly. No ordinary person can withstand such a load on his soul. But you are dark. And if Skron could not sweep you away in the first minutes of your initiation, if you survived the meeting with that high-ranking convert, then *Amplify* will not affect you in any way."

"And that's all? I was punished for such a small thing?"

"You were punished for arguing with the High Priest. And that was before you proved your worth to the Fortress. No point in remembering the past, Max. Let's live in the present and the future."

"No, Alia, you can never ignore the past when

constructing the future."

"I can't comment on something I didn't take part in. Yes, perhaps the High Priest got upset. Perhaps you were wrong. What is the use of discussing with me the time when I was not your personal attendant? If you want, I will arrange a meeting with Father Urg, and you can pose your questions to him personally."

I was so tempted to curse—she had backed me against the wall, then removed herself from the situation effectively. After waiting for a pause and making sure that I was not going to yell, Alia looked away and said:

"But that's still not all, Max. In light of the new stones we're introducing, I think your magic field needs to be changed."

"Of course it does. We need to figure out what support stone to pair with *Dark Spike*. What's that?"

I looked at the hastily corrected drawing.

"Your new field."

"I don't even have the emotional energy to be indignant about this. Spending the extra facet on *Analyze?* Are you serious? So when I said I sorely lack casting speed, it just bounced right off your eardrum?"

"No, I'm just thinking about the future. What's the point of a two-faceted *Dark Spike?* What is the point of this stone? To deal damage. Great, let's follow that thought. No other support stone will give you an effect like *Amplify*. If you link it to your attack, it will not only increase your speed, but also greatly increase your damage. We will add it here, linking two stones at once. I can't even imagine how strong *Analyze* will become in this case. You will be able to see almost everything about whatever being you use this ability on! As far as I remember, the chancellor promised you a facet. You can use this one for your attack, as soon as Kimal Sarento wakes up and gives you your well-deserved reward."

"A second *Amplify?*" I looked slyly at the girl. "Good idea. You could even call it a great idea! But the question immediately arises—where will I get it?"

"In the rifts," she replied without a hint of embarrassment. "After killing that incarnation, you have seven shards out of twelve. Two or three rifts and you'll get what you want. Max, we can go back and forth on this forever, but this is the only way you'll become a truly strong and dangerous opponent of any dark one."

"You're crazy," I muttered, dumbfounded as I looked over her proposed layout once again. If I buffed my attack ability with *Amplify*, it would truly become twice as powerful. As well as my defenses. There were too many pros to pass up. We needed to consider things before deciding, but I didn't have time for this—we were leaving for Hearth in the morning. I needed to make a decision here and now—was I ready to trust Alia? Once applied, reassigning *Amplify*, from what I understood, was impossible. The exclusive stones would root themselves in my magical field once and for all. Looking over at at the girl silently awaiting my decision, I said:

"You haven't led me astray so far. I hope these stones won't be the first time you do. I agree to your proposal. Let's do this thing…"

Chapter 7

"SO HOW DO I STOP SEEING all this?" I muttered angrily, closing my eyes. It didn't help—a huge stream of messages continued to flow by, ignoring my closed eyes, as if projected straight into my brain.

"Anything interesting?" asked Alia, who was sitting next to me, to which I mumbled something inarticulate and continued to deal with my new ability's settings. Fortunately, I had more than enough time for this.

The open wagon moved slowly toward the north of the region. Three, acting as coachman, was silent, as if he did not believe his luck and was afraid he'd soon wake up. But who was Three? Mentor, teacher and mage (albeit with only one stone so far) Alexy Snor. Last night, the High Priest prepared a petition for the pardon of the three particularly distinguished doomed soldiers, and this morning the emperor signed a decree that returned Demitr Turbin, Bagration Rubinsky and Alexy Snor to the world of the living. The former doomers in my group, who bore the unofficial nicknames One, Two and Three, respectively. I set the task for the first two to find a worthy estate within the Turb, to ensure it was purchased and prepared for our future settlement. The Fortress took over the financial side of the issue, with a hint that I would have to pay back all the funds spent on me, plus ten percent per annum on top. For the inconvenience and bookkeeping fees, as the blue-robed churchman explained to me. Given that I did not have my own money to buy the estate, after consulting with the team, I had to agree. Demitr promised to do everything in his power to talk the final amount down to the smallest sum possible. He wasn't about to drive his master into debt.

Yes, all three had sworn their allegiance to me. From now on, I was considered their master, they were my subjects, despite the fact that a month remained before I had my barony. But who cared about such trifles? As a result, Demitr and Bagration went house hunting and Alexy volunteered to accompany me in whatever capacity he could. Even as the coachman. The nature of the accompaniment was simple—I had to spend at least two hours a day studying, and Alexy was meant to help me with this task. In the wagon lay a whole pile of books on history, geography, social studies, jurisprudence and other boring disciplines that I'd so stubbornly ignored as a child. It was time to reap the results of my stupidity.

"Alright, again." I looked at my new teacher and activated *Analyze*. Once again, a river of messages appeared, but this time my settings were saved, significantly reducing the number of numbers and inscriptions that appeared. I don't even know if I was lucky or not that Alexy was my guinea pig—most of the data I was seeing was related to his magic stone. *Analyze* with two *Amplify*s attached worked real miracles, revealing not only the stones themselves, but also their description, parameters, and even the dull and tedious numbers that I always ignored. As I did now, mentally minimizing several windows, leaving only the name of the stone, its description, the number of facets and the level, I drank a mana elixir and activated the ability again. There! That was much better! Yes, the window that appeared still had to be tweaked and adjusted, but now at least it did not block my entire view. When I had activated *Analyze* for the first time, I'd almost panicked, everything was so insanely confusing. But it seemed like I was slowly getting the knack of it.

Where did I get the second *Amplify*? A reasonable question. The answer was actually quite mundane—the High Priest lent it to me, leaving me once more indebted to the Fortress. As soon as Aliya showed him my magic field and informed him that I needed to modernize, Father Urg offered to participate in the enhancement process as much as possible. He escorted me to the basement, where the stone integration devices were located, personally started the mechanism that prepared the stone and inserted it into my essence. Everything that Kimal Sarento did to me. As Alia later explained, this was a mandatory precautionary measure. No one in the Fortress was supposed to know that I could integrate them myself, and what levels they were at now. For everything that concerns me and my stones was a mystery with seven seals. I once again opened my upgraded magic field. If someone had told me a couple of months ago that I would soon be mage with so many powerful stones, I would never have believed it.

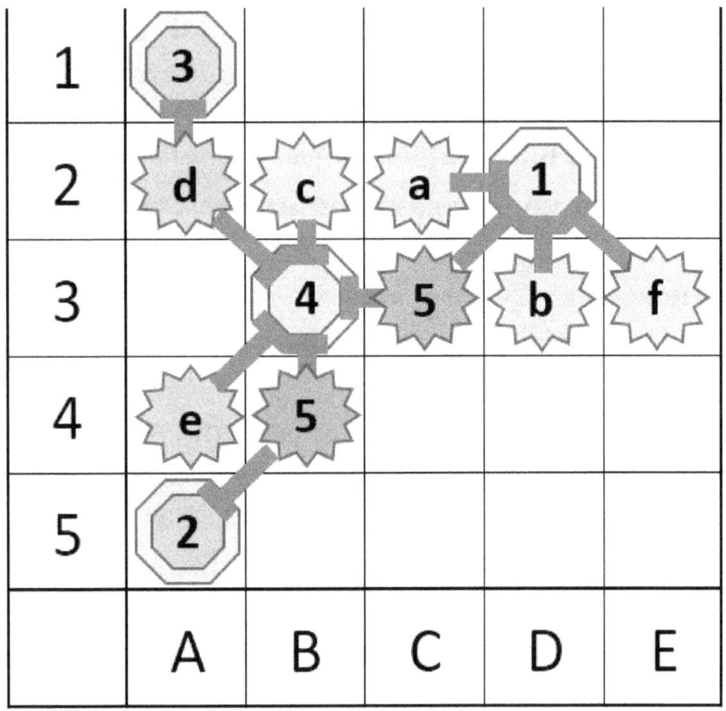

Max's Magic Field Key

1 — *Golden Dome of Protection.* Elite stone. 4 facets. Level: 6.

2 — *Dark Spike.* Magical stone. 1 facet. Level: 6.

3 — *Healing Aura.* Magical stone. 1 facet. Level: 6.

4 — *Analyze.* Elite stone. 5 facets. Level: 6.

5 — *Amplify.* Exclusive stone. Level: 1.

a — *Steel Resistance.* Elite stone. Level: 6.

b — *Damage Reflection.* Elite stone. Level: 6.

c — *Dark Essence.* Elite stone. Level: 6.

d — *Cost Reduction.* Magical stone. Level: 6.

e — *Casting Speed.* Magical stone. Level: 6.

f — *Fortify.* Elite stone. Level: 6.

The stones' power had increased significantly, and as far as Alia and I were able to agree, if I ever got a *Devour,* it would be able to fit nicely in the "C-4" field. Just under the two *Amplify*s. So that I would simply have to enter the first cave and all the resources would instantly become mine. Oh, dreams and fantasies.

"I need to find a dark beast," I finally said, having finished with Alexy. The amount of information displayed was significantly reduced, but if necessary, I could expand any of the tabs I needed. And what struck me the most and pleased me greatly was that the ability formed a separate icon on the status bar, where it stored all the data. A sort of directory, accessible only to me.

Moreover, using the ability on the same person did not duplicate the record, which only worked to my advantage.

The only disappointing aspect of this update was that, despite the cost reduction support stone, my new ability required a monstrous amount of mana. A third! Thirty-three Skron-damned percent of a full mana bar! So I wouldn't be able to constantly analyze people. A max of three, then I'd either have to drink an elixir or wait until my ring shows its true power.

Yes, my exclusive ring. How could I forget? You keep a ring like that on for the rest of your life!

Exclusive dark mage's ring. *Increases spell speed, increases shadow damage, reduces shadow influence, allows you to block mental attacks, restores 1% mana per minute, increases Mana by 1.*

When Alia saw the description, she fell into an actual stupor. There had been no dark ring in the history of the Fortress, and no one could even imagine that mana could restore itself, without the use of elixirs. The ring given to me by the Fortress paled in comparison to this one.

Elite mage's ring. *Increases the range of spells, reduces the cost of spells, increases the wearer's magical parameters by 1%.*

"Dark beast?" Alia said, tearing me from my

reverie. "What for?"

"I figured out the basic settings, now I need to test it on something serious. I'm looking on the map—we're going to pass a two-level rift. Can we go?"

"Max, we've already discussed this!" Alia grumbled indignantly. "We're not climbing down into any rifts without consent from the church."

"No one's climbing anywhere. I'll just go into the first cave, have a look at a krona and leave. I won't even kill anything."

"You? Stop at the first cave? Who are you fooling? You'll go all the way down to the Warden, and then to the guards. Max, don't provoke me. I can be mean too."

"Sir Max, we are being pursued," said Alexy, putting an end to this senseless skirmish with Alia. Turning around, I saw two riders quickly overtaking us. I had my dome up at all times, and just in case, I edged closer to Aliya, covering her with my shield.

"What made you think they were chasing after us?"

"I turned off the main road when I saw them," Alexy explained. "We have been riding along a country road for several minutes, the main road is a little off to one side. So these gentlemen turned after us. Why such a coincidence?"

It was only now that I noticed that the road we were driving on did not much resemble the broad paths of the thoroughfare.

"Is that Karina Fardi? What's she doing

here?" Alia said with a frown as the distance between us and the riders narrowed. I was amazed at the girl's keen eye—I personally could not make out anything from such a distance. After some time, it became clear that Alia was not mistaken. Karina Fardi, accompanied by some unknown man, really had caught up with us. Judging by my attendant's reaction, there was no point in asking why my former partner was giving us chase.

"Stop the cart!" Karina demanded as soon as she caught up with us.

"On what grounds?" Alia asked.

"These! I have a letter for you!"

I frowned—Karina Fardi didn't look like a courier. The girl pulled out an envelope marked with the High Priest's seal from her pocket. Alia and I looked at each other, not expecting this development. Things got even weirder when we saw what the letter contained.

"Greetings, my children! Unfortunately, circumstances have developed in such a way that the affair I sent you to deal with will have to be postponed. The Duke of Turb, imperial manager of the central region, somehow found out that the dark one was traveling through his lands, accompanied by his personal attendant. Apparently, even our walls have ears. The Fortress has been presented with a note of protest, with which we must comply. In three days the duke will visit Hearth, where you will be introduced to him as companions of Karina Fardi, daughter of the Duke of Odoevsky. This will

smooth out the wrinkles and unbind your hands. Do nothing until this meeting. Along with Karina Fardi, one of the Duke of Turb's most trusted men has been sent. Be careful what you say. Now you are the companions of the duke's daughter, and nothing more.

Father Urg, High Priest of the Church of the Light

"It's definitely his handwriting and style," Alia whispered, glancing at Karina's companion. Small in stature, slender in build, he was outwardly unintimidating, but all I had to do was drain my mana bar by third and I could barely hold back my exclamation of surprise. The person who arrived with Karina Fardi turned out to be no common subject. Twenty-three body enhancements, four magic stones, eight support stones, exorbitant attack and speed stats. As far as I could tell, there was no dark in him—in any case, the structure of the highlighted data did not differ much from the one that Alexy had.

"I thought we were meeting at Hearth, Your Radiance," Alia said and inclined her head. "My apologies for being curt—I was tired from the journey and didn't yet know who had overtaken us. I didn't expect that you would be accompanied by..."

"Viscount Kurpatsky, at your service," the companion nodded. "Confidant of the Duke of Turb."

"The Viscount travels so lightly?" Alia was

surprised.

"We had to hurry in order to catch up to you. It's not often that you encounter a situation where a duke's daughter must catch up to her servants."

"Companions, Viscount. We are Karina Fardi's companions, not her servants," Alia corrected. "Children of the Fortress are servants only to the Light."

"Here, I see, there are not only servants of the Light, but also ordinary civilians," the viscount's gaze stopped on me. "Introduce yourself."

"According to the order of the High Priest of the Church of Light, the former doomed soldier Max has the right to refuse questions from representatives of the empire at any level, up to the emperor. I, Mother Alia, am his full representative and, if necessary, his voice. If you have any questions for this man, Viscount Kurpatsky, please ask me."

"Doomed soldier?" The viscount frowned and turned to Karina. "You travel in the company of a doomed soldier?"

"My father destroyed his family line, so the Fortress decided to test my endurance," Fardi said so serenely, it was as if she was talking about the weather. "Besides, this doomed soldier owes me his life, so I have to drag him everywhere with me, hoping that someday he will be able to repay his debt."

"A doomed soldier owes you a life? A doomed soldier whose family was destroyed by the Duke of Odoevsky?" The viscount was even more astonished, and, as I understood, the surprise was sincere. "Verily, the ways of Light are inscrutable. I have never heard such a cruel joke in my life. Let me ask you a question—why did you depart from the main road?"

"We were searching for a place to stop," Alia lied. "It's only two days to go to Hearth, we were supposed to meet her ladyship in three, so we had no reason to hurry. Is this forbidden?"

"No, I just found the behavior strange. Which hotel in Hearth did you decide to stay in?"

Alia kept silent—the question turned out to be a trick. Neither Alia nor I knew the names of the hotels in the northern city of the region, and to say that the duke's daughter's companions did not bother to book a place of residence for her ladyship would be to admit their own incompetence. And there would be even more questions about who we were and what we were doing here.

"Are we on a break, madam?" Alexy's voice suddenly sounded. "If so, I'd like to tend to the horses, we've been driving them for half a day without rest. They're tired. If we push them now, we won't even get an old mare in exchange for them at the Red Goose. Who needs tired, unkempt horses?"

"Yes, go ahead," Alia nodded. "I beg your pardon, Viscount, I was contemplating the difficult fate of doomed soldiers. Did you ask me something?"

"No, nothing in particular." Viscount Kurpatsky gave us an appraising stare once more, then turned to Karina. "Your Radiance, as I understand it, your mission has been fulfilled? You delivered the letter? In that case, I propose to return to my servants and continue the journey in comfort. In three days you will meet your companions at the Red Goose. Not a bad choice, by the way. The central hotel in the city offers a gorgeous view of the lake. What floor did you book the room on?"

"Is that really an appropriate question?" Alia asked.

"I beg your pardon for my lack of tact." The viscount apologized, but it was impossible to tell from his visage. "Personally, I really like the view from floors four to six. The windows overlook the central square, where they execute criminals of all kinds. All those who considered themselves above the laws of the empire!"

"I'm sorry, Viscount, but I'll have to stay with my companions, despite all the comfort you can provide. I propose we meet in two days at Hearth, where you will show me the most interesting places in the city. Then I will tell my father about what wonderful assistants the Duke of Turb has."

"No need, really," the viscount's smile did not reach his eyes. "In that case, all the best, Your Radiance. In a few days there will be a dinner party in honor of the arrival of the Duke of Turb in Hearth. I dare to take the liberty of inviting you and your companions to this event. I trust my master will be pleased to meet you. Invitation cards in your name will be delivered to the Red

Goose.”

Turning his horse, Viscount Kurpatsky rushed back at the same speed with which he overtook us.

“What in Skron’s name is going on?” I blurted out as soon as the viscount had galloped a decent distance away.

“You’re asking me? They woke me up at dawn and forced me to trudge out to the middle of nowhere to give you a letter! I was forced to do the job of a courier! Do you even realize what a blow to my reputation this is? If father found out about this, he would give the whole Fortress what for!”

“Who woke you up? Did you see Father Urg?”

“No, his assistant brought me the letter and ordered me through him that I stay by your side no matter what. As I understood it, the High Priest had already left the palace. He had been called to the palace. Because of you, by the way! Why did you suddenly decide to travel around the region without a contract?”

“It’s not a contractual matter, but that’s not the point,” I said, waving off her interrogation. “Alright, we’ll deal with the problems as they come. Alexy, are you sure that there will be a vacancy at the Red Goose? What exactly is this place?”

“The central hotel in Hearth, sir. The upper floors are usually free. Too expensive for ordinary guests of this unremarkable city. The bishop’s residence in Hearth is the only thing that draws the interest of both travelers and a whole crowd of suppliants. Some even travel across the entire region to get here."

"Sir?" Karina clung to the words and stared at me, demanding an explanation. "When did you manage to acquire servants, doomer?"

"Your Radiance seems to have missed something. Max is no longer a doomed soldier, and all his obligations as a doomed soldier have been waived. He doesn't owe you anything, Karina Fardi. By order of the High Priest."

"Just don't tell me fairy tales," Karina grinned. "Max is in my debt whether you like it or not. The High Priest has no right to influence the internal laws of the doomed soldiers. When Max acknowledged his blood debt, he was a doomed soldier. The fact that he was granted whatever kind of special status is the Fortress' problem. I have no intention of waiving mine."

"What do you want from me?" I asked. "How can I fulfill a blood debt if you won't even go down into the rifts? Even though that's exactly what the Evil Engineer was preparing you for."

"Why don't you die?" snorted Karina. "That would be an excellent way to fulfill your debt."

"I can't," I said, feigning a sigh. "Too much to do. Until I slaughter the entire Fardi family, I am forbidden to die. When you are left alone, when I come for you, then we will talk about who owes what to whom. Until then, live."

"What a complex dynamic you two have," said Alia. "Karina, I can't say that I'm glad for your appearance, but since the High Priest ordered so, so it must be. Will you come with us or on your horse?"

"With you," Fardi answered after a pause. "My status forbids me from making long journeys on horseback. Let Max take the horse. I don't want to be in the same carriage with him."

"Max is riding with me. You are a guest. If you'd like to join us, you are welcome to. If not, no one is holding you here. You can dictate your conditions in your own estate or to people who answer to you. I hope that this has clearly defined the boundaries of our communications? Then I will ask the question again: are you riding with us, or separately?"

"With you," sniffed Karina, sliding off of her horse. "Do you remember our last ride together, freak? Look at me sideways again and I'll give a repeat performance. I'll beat you so hard your own mother wouldn't recognize you. Oh, wait, what am I talking about? You don't have a mother."

I kept silent and even turned away, trying not to make any rash decisions. One of my hands lay across the other, as if completely casually, in order to slowly and, as it seemed to me, imperceptibly cock my crossbow. A few seconds ago, I spent thirty-three percent of my mana examining the duke's daughter's stats. Whatever anyone might say, Karina really had been stronger than me before, but I didn't know her exact stats. And, from what I could tell, I might never know. Because the creature that climbed into our wagon and sat down opposite Alia was in no way related to Karina Fardi, except for her appearance and trashy personality. *Analyze* gathered all the available information on this creature and gave me the results, calling the creature a "shifter." A dark beast was appearing before us now under the guise of Karina Fardi. Rational, dangerous, possessing the memory of a girl and sky-high attack and defense stats, which is why I did not attack right away. I needed to think it over and discuss it with Alia. Apparently, the creature had decided to play the role of my former partner in order to understand the purpose of our trip to Hearth. Then a reasonable question immediately arose—where was the real Karina Fardi? Would that she were dead…

* * *

(Turb. Secret residence. That day.)

"Magister Elor, explain what that was."

"It was a failure," replied one of the highest-ranking hierarchs of darkness. "A monstrous, painful failure that makes you wonder about the true power of the Light, but nothing more than a failure."

"Not just a failure, but *yet another* in a line of failures, Magister Elor. I'm beginning to regret that I started working with you. Even the armored creature of the capital coven caused more trouble than the Wave and the metamorph, so carefully prepared by you personally. Yes, Magister, a metamorph was born in the rift."

"Nevertheless, the capital continues to live a normal life. Nobody is evacuating."

"I see you are quite saddened by this news. The metamorph has been destroyed, the fifteenth level rift has been closed, the Wave has been shut down. And all this was done by one of your kind, Magister Elor. Kimal Sarento only slowed down the creatures, it was the dark one who did the majority of the work. Here, read this. I think you will learn many interesting things."

Magister Elor accepted the small folder with disbelief, but as he read its contents, the dark one's eyes narrowed more and more. Eventually, they were just two narrow slits.

"We need him."

"Do you think? Did you read everything carefully? Dark Max serves the Fortress."

"We need him," repeated Magister Elor forcefully. "We are ready to pay."

"Without a doubt. But before we continue this discussion, I need what is rightfully owed to me. The fact that your Wave choked is your problem. You promised me the head of Kimal Sarento, that upstart who decided to become emperor. The fool still thinks that no one knows of his plans. But he survived and, according to the doctor, will soon awaken. This is not just a failure, Magister Elor. This is professional incompetence. Maybe I should find another Magister to work with?"

"We need this boy," Magister Elor stubbornly fixated on this point, as if he could not hear the other.

"Everyone needs the boy. Including me. Don't forget: he is the only living person who can close the rifts alone. I was able to get the extraction bill from the eight-level—my head is spinning from the totals. Moreover, there are materials here about which you told us nothing. And no equipment for processing it was supplied. I'm talking about the tram in particular. I see that this word is not new to you. However, we learned about it only recently. Why is this? It's a very good question, dear partner. So yes, we're in the business of getting the boy out of the Fortress. Thanks to the timely intervention of our mutual friend, the Duke of Odoevsky, the emperor declared Dark Max a hero and is going to meet him in a month. This will automatically remove the doomed soldier from the Fortress' control. I suppose it will not be difficult to find a law that will force the newly-minted baron to become a vassal to the duke of my choice. Any of the five that serve me faithfully. The rifts will be mine, and I see no reason why I should refuse such an advantageous acquisition. The dark one will bring me what you so stubbornly refuse to give."

"But I do see a reason," the Magister said and took out a small box. Opening it, he presented the contents to the other, who froze. "And they are far more powerful than all the resources that you can get in the rifts, my future emperor. In a month, when Dark Max gains his freedom, he will make a showing on the Wall. And then you will have a complete set at your disposal."

Chapter 8

I PRIDE MYSELF IN THE FACT that I was able to keep my emotions under control. If the shifter hadn't killed us as soon as Viscount Kurpatsky went about his business, then it had some plans for us. Perhaps it was waiting for an attack from our side, not knowing about the true relationship between me and Karina, as well as the abilities I had gained after the most recent rift. So I needed to pretend like nothing important was happening. That I fully accepted the fact that Karina Fardi was riding with me in the same wagon. And, while there was still time, I needed to thoroughly study this monster's stats to find its weak points.

The shapeshifter's magical field measured six by six and was packed to capacity. It contained four magical ability stones, each of which was enhanced by eight support stones. My stomach almost twisted when I realized what I was looking at—four eight-faceted stones! I'd never seen such a thing, even in fairy tales!

Faux-Karina's abilities were centered around the exclusive *Shift Essence* stone. Judging by the description that popped up, it allowed the wielder to temporarily assume the appearance of their victims, and the support stones gave the shifter the memory, voice, habits and other details that might catch the attention of someone who knew the victim. It couldn't remove the victim's entire memory, only the last four weeks, and even that came with some restrictions. I needed to do more research on my own—the description here was lacking. Thoughts, for example, cannot be taken in this manner. The *Extra Time* support gem increased the duration of *Shift Essence* to twenty-four hours when active. The ability turned out to be not as perfect as I initially thought—it only lasted a day, after which the shapeshifter returned to its original appearance. But even here there was a caveat—the timer stopped when the wielder was asleep. I squinted at Faux-Karina. She had already realized that no one was going to attack her, so she sat comfortably between the pillows and pretended to be asleep. I'd need to use *Analyze* again after a while to make sure.

It turned out that twelve hours ago, Karina Fardi had been alive—this was precisely how much time had passed since the shapeshifter had gained its new appearance. Even if the beast slept all the way to Hearth, it still wouldn't have a lot of time to enact its scheme. My conclusion: this

Karina was riding to Hearth alone in order to gain the opportunity to change her face. Unless I was mistaken and this monster's mission was to finish us off in the dark of night. Alright, we'd deal with that later. First, the hunt for weaknesses.

The defense stone. It was essentially an analog of my dome, but its range was located in close proximity to the body. A second skin, or as the name suggested, a *Magical Suit of Armor.* I examined the support stones with interest. Some of them were the same as mine. *Steel Resistance, Amplify* and *Fortify*—a stone that Alia had suggested. It reduced damage received by 20%, which would be a significant boost during any battle. *Cost Reduction* made any concerns about mana moot. The shield would absorb less mana for more damage. I had this one too. However, the rest of the stones were a discovery for me—I hadn't yet heard of any of them. *Physical Damage Reduction, Magical Damage Reduction, Elemental Damage Reduction,* and *Poison Damage Reduction,* were four separate stones that reduced the opponents' attacks (translated into numerical values) by another 50%. Quite an interesting decision—why pump up your defenses in this way when you could significantly reduce the incoming damage? By 70% up front, as it turned out. The shield itself, located under the *Amplify,* would handle the rest. This was the ideal security solution, I needed to learn from this. If I managed to survive this encounter. Now I understood that holding back had saved my life—a steel crossbow bolt never would have penetrated these defenses. Because all of the stones, save for the *Amplify*, were level fifteen!

Healing stone. I didn't find anything particularly relevant or interesting to me, as this turned out not to be an aura, like mine, but a focused pinpoint healing ability. Although, it looked like I'd have the opportunity to make Magister Smalog or Viscount Jurmal my debtors—one of the elite support stones had the uninformative name *Reflection Blocker* and allowed the healer not to spend their own life force on healing. Or rather, not to accept the consequences of the treatment. Just for information about this stone, they'd shower me in a mountain of gold.

And finally, the attack stone. The shapeshifter didn't overcomplicate things and used the most mundane of fireballs, which, as I had already found out, the vast majority of mages possessed. The distinction, as always, lay in the support stones, which added additional types of damage to the ball. Cold, lightning, darkness and even poison. As well as the well-known *Amplify*, which no ability could do without, *Reduce Cost*, which reduced mana consumption by 70%, and finally, two stones that aroused my particular interest. *Elemental Concentration* greatly increased elemental damage but prevented any physical damage. In fact, being hit with a fireball wouldn't even push you back, because inertia is a physical phenomenon. It would simply create a huge fiery/electrical/dark/poisonous/ice sphere, capable of transforming a creature from a living state to a dead one in a matter of moments. *Multiple Shots* formed not one, but three balls at once and reduced the damage dealt by 20%. My *Dark Spike* could definitely use these last two stones.

In fact, this was the opponent's main strength. As far as buffs went, he only had +5 mana, bringing his total to just 240 units, and no more. Even the shapeshifter's physical stats were significantly lower than mine. I was wrong—Faux-Karina turned out not to be dark, at least not in that sense of the word. Not a convert, not some terrible beast. He was definitely a man, and quite old, with unique stones. That didn't make him any less dangerous. On the contrary, now I had no idea how to proceed. Although...why not? I needed to not reveal that I know and try to survive until we made it to the city.

"Alexy, stop the wagon. We need to take a brief pause anyway."

"I hope you haven't forgotten what awaits us in Hearth?" Faux-Karina said grumpily, thereby betraying the fact that she had no intention of sleeping.

"Wish I could forget you," I replied. "Actually, we have to make a stop to cover your ass. Alexy, get back on the horse and hurry on to Hearth. Drive the animal hard if you need, speed is key. We need to rent three rooms at the Red Goose. One on the upper floors, and two more economical ones. They can even be in the basement, I don't care about the view. And this must be done before Viscount Kurpatsky arrives to check. Your Radiance, it's time to spend our gold. Come on, Fardi, get the cash—I'm not paying for your highborn lifestyle."

Faux-Karina wrinkled her nose in displeasure, but did not dare to refuse, pulling out a heavy purse.

"How much do you need? Will two or three gold cover it?"

"That might cover the tip," replied Alexy. "A room on the upper floors in the Red Goose starts at ten gold per day, without any of the frills. The minimum stay is three nights, Your Radiance. The lower floors are three to five gold per day, depending on the occupancy.

"Here," I handed the purse to Alexy. "There should be enough for two rooms for a week. Fardi, are we going to have to wait for you forever? Or is this too rich for Your Radiance to afford? I can give you a loan. I'll give you gold if you consider my debt paid."

"Don't get your hopes up," Faux-Karina snorted and threw her heavy purse to Alexy. "You, there. I need the best room. That's enough for a week's stay."

Despite the fact that Faux-Karina got herself a partial memory and had even adopted the demeanor of the real Fardi, there were still moments that gave it away. Whatever our relationship was, Karina would never be so rude and dismissive of the servants. It was a small thing, but conspicuous enough that I didn't need *Analyze* to see there was something wrong with the girl. Alexy caught the purse and looked at me demandingly, waiting for permission to leave. I nodded toward his horse, indicating he was free to run the errand. A few minutes later, the three of us were left alone.

"I hope you know how to drive a wagon," Faux-Karina said and yawned loudly. "We should reach Verse by evening, it's a little village between Turb and Hearth. And just see what happens if we're late. I'll beat you."

"Mother Alia, will you accompany me?" I moved over, inviting her to sit next to me in the cab seat. "I don't want to leave you alone with this...wonderful girl in every respect, may I never see her again as long as I live."

Faux-Fardi grimaced and lay down, taking up the entire back seat. Which left Alia no choice but to accept my offer. Gustav taught me how to drive the wagon, so soon we returned to the main road and moved at a jaunty pace toward Hearth, periodically overtaking travelers on foot. There turned out to be an obscene number of them, forcing me to maneuver between particularly large groups. Nobody was going to leave the road—the Fortress gave us the most ordinary wagon, one without any identification marks that could belong to any family. What was the point, then, of moving away from the comfortable and level road, when those who are in a hurry could turn into the field?

Let them ride over potholes and see how they like it!

Half an hour later we found ourselves on a relatively empty stretch of road. I turned around and used *Analyze* again. That thing's stats had not changed, with the exception of one item—the *Change Essence* ability timer had decreased by twenty minutes. Faux-Karina had been sleeping for ten minutes now.

Allowing the horses to take the lead, I turned around and pulled out my writing instruments. I opened a book and pretended to read and take notes in my notebook. Against an opponent like that, even the slightest misstep could be fatal. After finishing my note, I handed it to Alia:

"Could you check if I answered the questions correctly?"

She took the notebook warily, but as soon as she read the first line, all her skepticism vanished in an instant.

Just don't flinch and don't turn around. Analyze showed me that this is not Karina, but a very strong shifter. A person who took on the identity of Karina Fardi, including part of her memory and demeanor. I can't attack—it has very powerful defenses. And an attack. We need a steel net and hoops. Can you get all of that in Verse? I have an idea about how to handle this beast. It would be better if we could discuss this all out loud, but it's dangerous. From what I can gather, if the shapeshifter feels that it has been discovered, it will kill us. And no, I cannot defeat it, even while it's sleeping.

"Max, are you sure about these responses?" she asked in such an unperturbed tone that I mentally wanted to applaud her. I have never been able to turn off my emotions like that.

"My answers? Yes, absolutely. Do you have some sort of doubts about them?"

"If you're confident in them, then there's no point in checking. Have you finished with this book? Then I'll try to buy you a new one in Verse. Watch out—people."

Indeed we had caught up with another crowd. I finally recognized what they all had in common— practically every group had someone who was crippled in one way or another. With bandages, splints, crutches, they stubbornly pressed on in the same direction we were going. I remembered Alexy's words and only then realized that all these people were traveling to Hearth in order to touch the greatness of the local bishop and beg him for some kind of grace. To stand within the radius of a healing aura in the town square, for instance. Not a bad idea, by the way—gathering all of your subjects once a month and exposing them to mass treatment. Remembering my life as Baron Valevsky, I could say that there were often people in our territory who fell ill. There were no magic stones among the peasants, especially not healing ones.

Alia plunged into deep thought, periodically

turning around, as if casually and briefly glancing at Faux-Karina. When the sun almost touched the horizon, we finally made it to a large village. Unlike ordinary villages, there was no road sign here, nor any poorly organized patrol at the entrance. All we had to do was present the Fortress' waybill and we were instantly allowed to pass, without even undergoing a wagon inspection.

"I hope that there's a decent place to stay in this pit hole," muttered the being in the back, indicating that it had awoken. *Analyze* didn't tell me if it was male or female—this particular information was missing. One thing was clear: the shapeshifter was over eighty years old.

"Excuse me, boy. Where is there a hotel or an inn nearby?" I stopped a spirited young fellow and showed him a silver coin. That proved sufficient payment, and the kid ran in front of us, leading the way. He also steered onlookers away from the path so that we could safely pass. Soon, a strong scent of fried onions and sewer hit us. Faux-Karina wrinkled her nose, covering her mouth with a perfumed handkerchief in disgust. The inn was quite large, but apparently sewage systems were a foreign concept here. I handed the boy the coin, tied the horses up at the entrance and went to haggle for two rooms. However, as soon as I got inside, any desire to settle in this pigsty disappeared. There was filth everywhere, and all the tables were filled with pilgrims coming to Hearth. And, apparently, from what I saw, the common folk hadn't yet heard of hygiene.

When I went back out into the street, I noticed that my guide had not gone anywhere.

"Sir, if you don't like the inn, I can take you home to my place. Mom rents out rooms. The price will be the same as here, but you will get clean rooms, a bath and even a good dinner."

I looked at Alia. The girl nodded her agreement with the proposal. Judging by her face, she wasn't fond of the smell either. The boy again ran ahead to show the way, and soon we found ourselves in a fairly well-tended area, by local standards. Some houses were even painted, and the paint had clearly been applied within the last couple of decades. The house he led us to was not the largest on the street, but it was spacious enough. The smiling woman at the door was not surprised to see us—her son evidently hunted out visitors to invite back. Few people liked the inn. In fact, this was how they made their living. We were charged forty silver coins for the night, ten more for food and a bath. After a moment of thought, I handed the gold to the hostess, shelling out double what she asked, with a request to take care of the horses and make sure that no one disturbed us. Faux-Karina settled in the largest room and soon left, declaring that she was going to take a walk. I suppressed the urge to find out where she planned to go in such an ordinary village, and instead went to the backyard to stretch. Half a day behind the reins didn't do anyone any good.

Aliya also left—we didn't even manage to talk. Accompanied by the same brisk boy, she went to meet the local servant of the Light. If she was going to find steel chains, hoops and nets, then this was the place to look. After stretching out, I sat down on a bench and closed my eyes. I had a tough night ahead of me.

"Is the lord in need of any service?" the landlady, a woman of about forty, said, stepping outside. Despite the phrasing, there was not a hint of romantic sentiment behind it.

"Tell me, is there a prison in Verse?"

"Where, sir? We have such a small village, we cannot afford to run a prison."

"What happens if one of your guests starts to fly off the handle? I can't believe you would just let them run amok. You must be putting them somewhere."

"Yes, that is true," said the woman, looking down. "They do get rowdy sometimes. Not everyone is accustomed to keeping up appearances. If one of my guests drinks too much, I call a neighbor. He is our blacksmith, and has unmeasured strength. So he rounds up the ruffians and sticks them in the cellar for the night."

"Even mages?"

"Come now, sir! What would a mage be doing in Verse? They pass straight through to Hearth. And even a tent in that city is better than anything our village has to offer."

"So the cellar, you say. Will you show me?"

"There's nothing to show, there it is." The woman led me over to a shed where, among other things, there was a small, inconspicuous door. As soon as she opened it, however, I was speechless—behind this flimsy little door, there was a powerful steel grate.

"And what's that for?" I asked.

"Well, rowdy folk don't stop being rowdy once they're in the cellar," the woman said, bewildered. "And the neighbors don't always behave proper. Instead of saving their own stockpile, they try to weasel their way into mine. Before, there was only a door—they broke it. Then my neighbor whipped me up this little contraption. At first he wanted to make it from simple iron, but then he got an order for steel grates, so he saved a few scraps for me. Come, I'll show you what's down there."

She held her lantern aloft and started down the steep staircase. To my surprise, there was another grate at the bottom.

"So the guests don't rummage around in the supplies!" she explained. "They'd ruin them. So they sit on the stairs, cool down, and in the morning, I hand them over to the village chief."

"What a system you've arranged here!" I said.

"How else? Everything must be in its place and stored properly. This is where we store the potatoes, cabbage, salads and compotes for the winter," she said, indicating each compartment. I looked at the walls. They were made of solid stone. This wasn't a basement, it was a bunker.

"Is the ceiling wooden?"

"You can't make the ceiling of a cellar out of wood," she said in a tone as if relaying a commonly-known truth. "The boards will all rot.

This is masonry. First, the frame is made with metal, then everything is covered with clay and then it is tempered with fire. It's certainly a chore, which is why not everyone has basements, but it's impossible to build any other way. Mold will eat through everything. Including the supplies. And then what would I serve my guests? By the way, would you like meat and potatoes? Baked in the oven with garlic, dill and lard. You'll be licking your fingers!"

"Of course I would," I smiled as I finished forming my crazy scheme. In preparation for the journey, I'd not only activated the magic stones for myself, but also took a part of the reward I was due for closing the eight-level. I mean the chabre— the resource necessary for activating magical symbols. Alia issued instructions on how to properly crush the crystals and prepare the dye, so all I had to do was prep everything before the girls—we'll call Faux-Karina one for now— came back. The whole trip to Verse, I was puzzling over how to deal with this strong opponent by working out several options, but I could not share them with Alia. Because none of the plans I had in mind adhered very closely to the church's beliefs. There was not an ounce of light in them. But this did not stop me—I saw no other way of dealing with this monster.

The first to return was Faux-Karina. Throwing me a haughty glance, the girl sat down at the table that the hostess had set and started picking at the stunningly aromatic potatoes. After taking a few bites, she placed the fork defiantly aside and got up from the table. It was not proper for a duke's daughter to eat such coarse food. Another red flag, Twinkletoes. The Karina I knew would have gulped down that dinner and asked for seconds.

"I'm going to sleep. We need to get up early tomorrow morning. I can't wait to get to Hearth so I can take a bath," she said. I activated *Analyze* and smirked maliciously—the transformation clock now showed a little less than twenty-four hours. Faux-Karina had met up with the real deal in Verse and updated its appearance.

"I wanted to talk to you," I said before she disappeared into her allotted room.

"What now? You decide to hang yourself and wanted to notify me about it? I don't want to hear another word from you."

"No problem. In that case, the information about Miralda Lertan will remain with me."

"Pff! What could you know about the princess, ex-doomer?" At these words, our hostess blanched and magically vanished into the kitchen. Her guest had turned out to be her worst fear.

"Enough to know who will be declared her fiancé and when the wedding will take place."

"Hogwash!" Faux-Karina exclaimed. "The princess is not getting married!"

"Alright, if she's not, she's not. Apparently, you know better, and the High Priest, who told me of it only yesterday, is mistaken. His job is to make mistakes. Although, as I recall, he met with

Miralda Lertan a few days ago? Just after the Wave and the destruction of the academy."

"Okay, tell me," Faux-Karina returned to the table. "What do you know?"

"Here?" I looked pointedly around the room. "Are you kidding me? As if there aren't enough rumors already. Of course, I have the utmost respect for our hostess, but..."

At that moment, the door creaked—the frightened woman had fled from her own house.

"No, Karina, I'm not going to tell you anything here. That's the first thing. Second is, what do I get in return?"

"Don't even mention forgiving your debt. You owe me for the rest of your days!"

"What's this about a debt? I need gold. A lot of it. Especially now that I'm alive again."

"How much?" the girl grimaced. She'd obviously expected something more interesting from me.

"Five thousand gold," I casually listed off the sum of gold that it would require to hire a mercenary to kill the Duke of Odoevsky.

"Are you crazy?" said Faux-Karina, sincerely taken aback. And, as I understood it, the shapeshifter really was taken aback. "Where are you getting these numbers?"

"The information I have could greatly influence the politics of our empire," I whispered mysteriously. "What would you say if I hinted that we might have a possible change of emperor?"

"What bullcrap are you dragging in here, you

idiot?!" Faux-Karina finally lost her cool. "What change in emperor?"

"Give me an IOU for five thousand gold and you will receive a full report on this matter. I promise, if you're not satisfied, I'll refund your IOU. I give you the baron's word!"

"Is that so?" Faux-Karina said, her interest piqued. "Are you that serious about this?"

"You can't even imagine how serious I am. So serious that I'm willing to cooperate with you. One of the beneficiaries of these future changes."

"What do you mean, beneficiary?" she scoffed again.

"Give me the slip of paper, we'll go to a secluded place where no one will overhear us, and you will find out everything. Do you think the High Priest just shared this news with me for no reason? After all, it directly concerns the Fardi family, which I plan to cut down at the knee."

"Some things never change," Faux-Karina snorted, but less spitefully than before. My thoughts began to spin feverishly as I tried to figure out exactly what bullcrap I was dragging in. "Alright. you'll have your IOU," she replied after a long pause. "You have the word of Countess Fardi! Is that enough, or will you not take my word for it?"

"Well if I don't trust the word of a countess, then who in this life can I trust?" I chuckled. "Come on, I'm not going to tell you in the house."

"What is this?" Faux-Karina frowned when I led her to the cellar.

"A cellar," I responded coolly. "One of the most secure places in this village. Hold the lantern and go down, I'll make sure no one follows us. If the High Priest finds out that I told you about the princess and your family, I will not only be punished, but most likely will be returned to the ranks of the doomers."

"Mark my words, future corpse: if your information turns out to be useless, I'll skin you alive! Do you understand me?"

"Five thousand gold pieces, Fardi," I repeated. "Get ready to cough it up. If you can get over the shock of the news."

False-Karina gave me a contemptuous look and began to descend into the basement.

"There's a grate down here!"

"I know," I replied, closing the door and hanging the huge barn lock across it. It was a good thing I traced our hostess's steps when she hid the key.

"What are you doing, you moron? I'll make sure you rot for this!" Faux-Karina jumped at the grate and tried to open it, but no luck. For the real Karina, who had undergone so many enhancements, this obstacle was ridiculous. For a shapeshifter who was only buffed by his own mana, the steel bars were insurmountable. Given that Faux-Karina had nothing with her to use as leverage, and also that her ability did not deal physical damage, the girl was trapped—if it was even a girl at all. How wonderful it was when you knew your opponent's capabilities and could prepare for them. Although, frankly, I was just lucky that the mistress of the house turned out to be a resourceful woman who had made friends with her blacksmith neighbor.

I sat down on the ground, out of sight from the cellar door, and took out the can of paint I had brought along.

"Karina, do you know who I am?" I decided to pass the time by talking.

"You are dead! If even a hair falls from my head, you will regret the day you were born!"

"No, partner, I'm talking about something else. About the fact that I'm dark. A creature of Skron, hiding under the guise of a man. Just like the Evil Engineer. Did you copy her memories of the dark mentor, shifter? Or was that unavailable to you?"

"What are you on about?" For the first time, notes of another voice broke through Faux-Karina's facade.

"I noticed the peculiarities within the first few seconds. Real Karina doesn't behave like that. You didn't go far enough back when stealing her memories. How far did you go? Two weeks, maybe three? Four, max, if you were pushing it. No more than that. Is it really possible to truly master your victim's mannerisms in this amount of time?"

"Did you hit your head while we were walking?"

"The second giveaway was the food. Try rummaging through your memory—after every training session with the Evil Engineer, Karina wolfed down everything that wasn't nailed to the table. Because otherwise, we simply would have wasted away. Meat and potatoes? That's a delicacy compared to the slop they gave us. So, I have no idea what kind of beast you are, but you are definitely not Karina Fardi. Since this is the case, you too will die. I would like to say that it will be quick and painless, but I can't lie. You will die in agony."

"You chose your own fate, Doomed Max," a male voice said. "Do you think this flimsy grate can hold me back? Let's get out. Let's see what you can do."

"So you are a man. Great, even easier. As I already said, I'm dark. Not a knight on a white horse, not a member of the light who refuses Skron's assistance. I am dark. The real article. And my methods are quite dark as well. Perhaps this is where our conversation will have to be temporarily interrupted. Welcome to my world, shifter."

With these words, I finished forming the 'Worm' symbol on my leg and the messages popped up in front of my eyes:

Would you like to activate the magical curse symbol?
Symbol duration: 24 hours.

It was like being hit with an electrical shock. +1% to all parameters turned out to be no small feat. My eyesight became sharper, I began to hear better, even smells seemed sharper. A muffled curse was heard from the other side of the basement door, after which the space was lit up by a fireball. It crashed into the steel grate, illuminating the courtyard, but the shifter's monstrous magic didn't permit him more. Without the *Elemental Concentration* stone that blocked physical damage, I wouldn't even try to fight such an opponent on my own. But without being able to break through the bars, the creature was powerless. Steel was impervious to magic, and you'd need to be Skron himself to be able to melt that stone. So the shifter was caught in a beautiful trap. I'd have to thank our hostess.

About ten minutes later, when the flow of magic subsided a little, I decided to strike up conversation anew:

"What is happening to you is called the Vampirism curse. I have deprived you of all positive emotions. Joy, happiness, pleasure. I absorb it all like a sponge. After about half an hour, when you have nothing left to absorb, your body will begin to decompose. And your defenses can't do anything about it. Or are you saying that your shield is able to somehow block curses and resist dark magic? Not sure about that. Even we dark ones can't do that, and you're just a human. Strong, dangerous, but still human. And soon, you'll be a dead human."

The conversation proved fruitless—the shifter started casting again, trying to burn through the grate or stone. But the neighbor blacksmith turned out to be a master of his craft. The grated door was built to hold. This went on for another twenty minutes. The stream of fireballs gradually started to fizzle out, becoming less and less frequent. The swearing and striking of the bars also died down. The shapeshifter was clearly losing strength under my curse. A monstrous thing indeed. But efficient.

The door creaked and Alia entered the yard.

"To one side!" I shouted. "Walk around the perimeter. I locked the creature in the cellar! Don't come near me—I had to use *Worm*. In twenty minutes, the shapeshifter will die."

"Max, stop! Aliya wanted to run up to me, but when she stepped into my aura's radius, she abruptly stopped and jumped away as if she'd been stung. "Not this way!"

"This creature has come to kill us. The fact that it considered itself immortal is its own mistake. I'm not going to let such an enemy live."

"We need to find out who sent him! Where did he get the letter from the High Priest? Where is the real Karina Fardi? What was his mission? I got the steel shackles. If he is a mage, we can block all magic, turning him into a normal person. Does he have boosts?"

"Only to mana. He didn't spend any on his body. Hear that, shifter? Mother Alia is offering you life in exchange for information. Are you still alive in there? Your painful death should come within the next ten minutes, but you should be properly writhing by now. What say you, Faux-Karina? What is your priority? A beautiful, heroic death full of pain and torment, or admitting defeat and relinquishing the information we need?"

There was no immediate response, but I didn't rush him. It is clear that the shifter was not acting alone and that he had accomplices in the village, who were dragging the real Fardi along with them, but I was the least worried about the fate of the girl. Even if she was killed, I wouldn't grieve.

"Stop it!" Finally, after five minutes, a pain-filled wheeze rang out. "I'll tell you everything! I was hired by Kimal Sarento to kill the Duke of Turb and make Karina Fardi look like a suspect! That's why we have her with us! If I die, she dies too! Turn off your aura! Let's talk! I surrender, I'm ready to put on the steel hoops!"

I exchanged glances with Alia and walked a few meters away from the cellar. It looked like we had a long night of captivating conversation ahead of us.

Chapter 9

"WHAT DO YOU SAY?" I looked at Alia, who was sitting at the edge of my aura, and thought about how to proceed. The information that the shapeshifter, who introduced himself as Uskal, told us, had radically transformed everything we knew about the chancellor of the magical academy of the Zarak Empire. Apparently, Kimal Sarento was perhaps the greatest villain alive today. He eliminated objectionable competitors, wove intrigues, and manipulated everyone and anyone, and even managed two or three groups of assassins and slave traders. Not a man, but a monster! Why the chancellor needed to destroy the Duke of Turb, the shifter did not know. He had served with Kimal for thirty years, almost from childhood, so he was used to not asking his master too many unnecessary questions. After all, it was Kimal Sarento who gave him all his stones and forced him to remain silent about their existence under pain of death. Karina Fardi had been captured this morning and put to sleep. At the moment, the girl was sleeping in one of the rooms of the inn under the protection of his assistants. In the morning, if the shifter did not visit them to assign a task, the girl would be killed. This was by direct order of the chancellor.

"By the looks of it, we've stuck our noses somewhere they should have never been stuck," she said. Our prisoner's story was impressive. Everything was so smooth, clear and precise, that if it weren't for a few trifling details, it almost would have been believable. But there were those details that simply didn't fit into the carefully crafted story Uskal was weaving. If that was even his real name. According to the shapeshifter, the chancellor had given him the assignment yesterday, when it became clear that Karina Fardi was heading to Hearth. And that he had served with Kimal Sarento from childhood. Little things that most people would never pay attention to.

I nodded and stepped two meters closer to the basement. Immediately, his tormented screams filled the space as the shapeshifter once again became ill. Alia stared into my eyes for a while, then shifted her gaze to the steel hoops, tossed them back into her bag and turned away, silently agreeing with the punishment. This shifter had proven that he would hold his cards close to his chest until the last moment, and then, when opportunity strikes, he would kill us all.

"She will die!" he cried out. "If I don't return on time, Karina Fardi dies!"

The screams continued for another ten minutes. At one point, a neighbor even came running to help end the suffering, but the purple robes of a cleric of the church instantly quashed their motivation. As well as the guards that came to watch the showdown—Mother Alia took it upon herself to hold back the inhabitants of the village while I destroyed the shapeshifter.

"They'll catch you anyway, dark one!" Uskal shouted through his pain toward the end. "My master's will is always fulfilled!"

What can I say...It was good that Alia wasn't around. The explosion that came a second later sent me flying and slammed me against the wall of the house. Stone and debris rained down from above, scorched all the way through by the fire. However, my shield had done its job. My mana bar dropped almost to zero, but my three hundred and sixty points and thoroughly buffed magic stones were enough to save me. After shaking off a few shards of rock, I got up and walked over to where the cellar had formerly stood. Now it was a huge crater. Alia ran up, stopping just outside *Worm*'s range.

"Are you injured?" the girl asked anxiously.

"Don't seem to be. What did he do, blow up his magic stones?" I asked, bewildered.

"He wanted to take you with him. The Last Will. Mages of the Wall believe that even death is no excuse for not destroying a dark creature. The

Fortress does not approve of this. Did you receive anything? Have your stones changed in any way?"

I quickly reviewed my stats.

"I didn't get any messages, the status bar isn't blinking. No descriptions of rewards received, my magic field hasn't changed. My stones are all in place and neither their descriptions nor levels have changed. What was I supposed to get?"

"If the beast remains alive after the explosion, its magic stones are modified. They become stronger, and the creature itself becomes more dangerous. Apparently it only works with monsters. We have to go rescue Karina Fardi, Max. We can't leave her to the shifter's accomplices."

It didn't take me long to understand what she had said. Apparently, I was still a little shell-shocked. However, when I realized what Alia was demanding, my outrage knew no bounds.

"You're joking, right? Are you in shock or something? I'm not lifting a finger to save Karina from the clutches of that shifter's accomplices. Because they will do what I should have done a month ago. They'll finish off one of the Fardis!"

"The Duke of Odoevsky slaughtered your family, but left you alive," Alia remarked calmly. "I don't mind if you destroy all the Fardis, save for Karina. She is part of the Fortress, Max. She could be a future Sweeper. Someone who can close rifts instead of you. We need her."

"The Duke let me live because of the doomed soldier law," I protested. "He made his killer with his own hands. I'm not going to repeat his mistake.

If Karina remains alive, she will avenge the death of her family. Do I need that? I don't think so. I'm not going to do anything to get Fardi out."

"You have a blood debt to Karina. You owe her your life, Max. You can refuse it, you can claim that she is not a doomed soldier, so the promise you made is invalid, you can even shift your debt to me. The meaning does not change. You owe her your life, Max. Save Karina now, pay off your debt, after which you can prepare your revenge with a clear conscience. Or have you forgotten? Do or die. Die, but save. The blood debt is sacred..."

"Weren't you the one who was saying I'm no longer a doomer?" I said, starting to boil over.

"You accrued this debt when you were still a doomed soldier. Or is Baron Valevsky so hypocritical that he is ready to adjust the circumstances to fit his own needs? When it came down to the fact that the Fortress owed you forty thousand ranking points, you were unbothered by the fact that you are no longer a doomed soldier. After all, you earned points on the eight-level as a doomed soldier. But when it comes to the blood debt you gained while of your previous status, you suddenly balk. Where is the consistency, Max?"

My emotions went wild and demanded I act, but my mind took over. Whatever anyone might say, Alia was right—aristocrats, even us lowly barons, must keep to their word and be consistent in their actions. Otherwise, how did we differ from peasants or highway robbers?

"Fine. If she's in the inn, I'll get her out. We

must discuss the reimbursement issue with our hostess. Something went terribly wrong in the cellar."

I felt compelled to say the last thing—a whole crowd of curious villagers had already gathered behind the fence. Including our poor hostess, who had sheltered such dangerous folk that they had turned her whole barn over, destroyed the cellar with all her supplies and almost destroyed her house. Not humans, but monsters in human form!

"I have no gold," Alia replied.

"Me neither. Write her an IOU in my name. No, better in the name of the Fortress. Personally, I think this was a blunder on the part of your security service. Did you know that such creatures even exist?"

"Not a creature, but a stone," Alia corrected me. "And yes, the Fortress had heard whispers. Exclusive stones are singular finds, and ones like that are generally unique. We must write a letter to the High Priest about what happened. He must know that something strange is going on. Who is this master and why does he want you?"

"If only I knew." The shifter's last words haunted me as well. It turns out I was the ultimate reason he had turned up in our company after all. But for some reason, he was playing for time, updating his appearance and in general, behaving completely differently than one would expect from a villain. Or did the bastard decide to throw us off the scent even further by shouting something completely fictitious at the moment of death? What would stop him from deceiving the man who killed him?

Leaving Alia to work things out with the hostess, I went to the inn. *Worm* was still active, so people shied away from me as if I were a leper. Which only really worked to my advantage—my mood had been completely spoiled by the realization of what I must do. I was going to save Karina Fardi. And of my own volition! Not quite, of course, but the outcome was the same—I had the opportunity to refuse, but I didn't, and that annoyed me the most. What a Skron-damned turn of events! My Skron-damned personal attendant! She knew just what buttons to push!

The inn was located just a kilometer from our dwelling, but there were suddenly so many people in the narrow, dusky streets that my parameters had almost doubled by the time I reached the building, which reeked of fried onions. All my senses were heightened, especially smell. The scent of the unwashed bodies sitting inside hit me like a wall a hundred meters from the inn. Twenty meters to the entrance, I doubled over and spilled the contents of my stomach. The smells were just awful. Out of sheer willpower, I went inside and looked around. The pilgrims shied away, hastily trying to crawl out from under the influence of my aura. Even the bartender wiping mugs with a dirty rag retreated. Evidently they'd be telling a new story after today, about how Skron himself visited the village at night. Shit! I needed to go upstairs!

I made my way to the staircase. My

heightened sense of smell did come with a perk: I managed to pick up on the scent of my former partner's perfume. It was light, barely noticeable, but in that fetid cloud of odors that hovered around the inn, it felt like a breath of fresh air. No one dared to stop me, and soon I was standing outside of the locked door. What was the probability that there were two shifters? That the girl was now standing with someone as strong as the mage who had blown himself up? It seemed close to null to me, because what would be the point of sending two monsters to complete the seemingly simple task of catching the dark one?

I kicked the door so hard that it flew off its hinges and into the opposite wall, taking a few fragments of wall with it. I had never had such power before, and for a moment I was taken aback by my own capabilities. *Worm* really transformed me into a monster. A thousand people, and I could feel like this forever…Just a thousand. It's too bad the exploded mage didn't count. He would have been the first.

Shaking my head to drive away traitorous thoughts, I entered the room, ready for anything. But no one dared attack me. Two prominent representatives of the Shurgan Empire looked at me with horror-filled eyes. I would say they were as round as saucers, but their hooded eyes defied this description. Karina lay on the bed. The girl was tied up but unconscious. The bottles lying next to her left no room for interpretation—they were clearly sleeping pills. Fardi was sound asleep, unaware that she had been kidnapped and dragged away to distant lands.

"Who are you?" I asked, but I couldn't get an answer out of the frightened Shurgans. They were shaking with fear, unable to even say a word. I had already decided to activate my new katars in order to deal with the kidnappers, when my eyes caught on a few details—the couple were wearing slave collars around their neck. Almost the same as they used for doomed soldiers, only crafted with great elegance. After unbinding Karina's legs, I tied the ropes to the rings around their chained collars, and then lifted the girl in my arms and, without even stopping to see how the couple reacted, walked out of the room. *Worm* had buffed me so much that I didn't even notice the load I dragged along with me. The Shurgan slaves trailed after me, wheezing, but I wasn't going to slow down to somehow alleviate their suffering. In my mind, I understood that this wasn't the kindest option, but I couldn't do anything about it. Some part of my humanity had evaporated. However, the Shurgans turned out to be quite dexterous fellows—they managed to get to their feet in front of the stairs. So none of them broke their neck. However, they also did not resist, dutifully following behind me on a leash. Again, no one dared to stop me, so I made my way straight home.

"Max, what's wrong with you?" Alia asked frightfully when, unable to open the gate, I lightly shoved it with my shoulder. The door flew off to one side, along with the broken post to which it had been attached. The people now filling the backyard fled in horror.

"These two need to be interrogated. No one can touch me for a day, or I'll kill you all," I said, restraining myself with difficulty from rushing after the fleeing crowd. I had wanted to gain a new portion of gratuitous power that would intoxicate my brain. An omnipotence that both intoxicated and inspired. The fact that I managed to maintain at least some semblance of humanity was a miracle, nothing less. In any case, I had to constantly fight the desire to run around the entire village, using *Worm* to absorb all the inhabitants.

Alia nodded and pointed to the crater. I understood without words, putting Karina on the ground, untying the ends of the rope from her belt and overcame twenty meters in a single bound, hiding from the fearful villagers. But I didn't just sit there motionless—within ten minutes, I was so overwhelmed that I seriously began considering transforming into a true dark one. Gustav had once told me about the phenomenon of withdrawal that some people faced when they were particularly greedy for intoxicating or forbidden powders or tinctures. I never understood this term and was surprised that people could not cope with their own desires and indulged their carnal cravings. What happened over the next hour while the buff was still active could be called nothing but withdrawal. I think I was screaming, cursing the entire world. But I couldn't be certain—this hour became a real test of will. It was all I could do to activate the healing aura, which at least alleviated my suffering a little.

The obsession passed suddenly and with no warning. When I came to, I was lying on my back, gazing up at the starry sky without an ounce left of the power that had so inebriated me. Turning my head, I saw Alia sitting along the edge of the crater.

"What a nightmare," I said sincerely. "The rollback is so bad that I almost died. I wanted to absorb it all. More power, more strength, more than anything."

"But you managed," she replied in a strange tone. "You were able to overcome the temptation. I saw your face when you brought Karina and the Shurgans. You only looked human from a distance. I even had my own doubts, thinking you had become dark. Real dark."

"I had similar thoughts myself," I said. "As I said, the borrowed power didn't just intoxicate me, it suppressed the will, demanding more and more. At some point, I even caught myself thinking that there was nothing human left in me. But I didn't care at all. Apparently today was the first and last time I use this symbol. It has no place in this world. It...it's dangerous. What did the slaves have to say?"

"Are you talking about those two unfortunate souls who are unable to string two words together out of fear of the monster that found them? It took a lot of effort to get them to talk, and Max—we've really gotten ourselves into trouble. You captured the personal servants of one of the nine padishahs of the Shurgan Empire. Not his most trusted servants, but far from the lowest on the list. This kind of mistreatment would warrant sending someone from the Nocturnal Guild. We'll have to release them as soon as they're back on their feet."

"Now I have no idea what's going on. Release them how?"

"Release them, just like that. The Fortress has enough bad blood with the Shurgan Empire."

"I never thought I'd say such a thing, but they held Countess Fardi prisoner! What is this if not a conflict?"

"These two were following their master's orders. You were their target. Faceless, as they called the shifter, received an order from the padishah to bring him an interesting trinket that could close high-level rifts. You were supposed to be delivered to Hearth, from where you would go by caravan to the Shurgan Empire. Sometimes it seems like humans are far worse than the dark ones...At least you know what to expect from beasts."

"And despite all they told you, you still want to release them?"

"When you kill someone who attacked you, do you also break his sword and rip apart his armor?" Alia asked. "They are slaves. Their job is to follow orders. They do not have their own will, they do not have their own thoughts or desires. Only executing their master's orders."

"Let's keep them with us?" I promptly

suggested. "Like a war trophy. When I kill an opponent who has a good sword, I take the weapon for myself. If the relatives of the slain want to see the sword returned, they must pay a ransom. How is this situation different? I don't want to let anyone go. The Fortress, by the way, has nothing to do with this. This is the will of Baron Valevsky. Future Baron Valevsky."

"This is dangerous, Max. A padishah of the Shurgan Empire is parallel to one of our dukes, except that in our country the dukes are appointed, and the padishahs pass their position on through inheritance. Are you prepared to tell one of the leaders of the Shurgan Empire that his actions were illegal? Do you have the strength for this? The resources? The connections, just as a start? Or is it your youthful bravado speaking now? Like, 'I defeated everyone, so the winnings should be mine.' If you are going to lead a clan, you will have to think in slightly different terms than just your own desires. You have to take care of your people. Are you sure the padishah won't kidnap half your people in retaliation for not returning his slaves? Just because he can. And you can't do anything about it. Because the empire won't go to war for the sake of a simple baron. Think about it while you still have *Worm* on you. Don't you want to know how Karina's doing?"

"Couldn't care less," I replied. "From now on, I consider my oath fulfilled, even if Fardi won't admit it. Hopefully this is the end of our relationship. She will return to Turb, we will move on. Without her."

"I'm afraid it's not that simple. According to Karina, she was indeed sent to us by the High Priest. Or rather, his assistant. The Duke of Turb is extremely concerned that you're traveling freely throughout his region. After today, when you almost sent half the village to their graves, rumors about Dark Max will fly throughout the empire. You can't hide it anymore. In a month, the emperor will return your title, and the whole empire will know you as the Dark Baron Valevsky. Something will have to be done about this, because the aristocrats will not accept you into their circle."

"As if I care what they think," I muttered.

"I suppose not. But we must not forget an important detail—many families have children who have died on the Wall at the hands of the dark ones. In you, they see the embodiment of their grief and suffering. Duels, assassination attempts, forgeries and setups. This is what awaits you once you have your own name back. I don't get scared, Max. I warn and prepare. Even when you become Baron Valevsky, I will still stay by your side and follow you to the end. However, until then, you must stay alive. The Duke of Turb will indeed visit Hearth in a few days, and a dinner party will indeed take place. Karina Fardi will take the brunt of arranging your stay in Bishop Zwat's city. Father Urg gave her all the necessary powers. Our mission remains the same. In a day, Karina will travel with us. I understand that you don't care, but I still feel the need to inform you that she does not know anything about her own kidnapping. She just fell asleep and woke up somewhere far from the capital. We can't prove she was kidnapped. The shapeshifter no longer exists, and servants have no voice in the matter."

"We should check their room. There must be something of value there. The servants can be returned, but this does not mean that we must return the property that belonged to the faceless one. It belongs to us, and not a single padishah has rights to it. Maybe there's some evidence that Fardi was kidnapped and held against her will, and we'll uncover it. Although it has already been an hour since I knocked the door down...the locals have probably looted everything."

"But we should still check," Alia said, getting up. "I struck a deal with the hostess, there will be no complaints against you. She said that you fought the dark one and miraculously won. As for your terrible aura, these are the consequences of the dark curse, so you need to lie down while it is in effect. I'll go to the inn, check the room. I'll release the servants. Fardi...She's coming with us, Max."

"Yeah, I got that part already," I muttered unhappily. "And absolutely no killing her."

"Not on this trip. She is now acting as messenger to the High Priest. Try to see her as a representative of the Fortress, not a member of the Fardi family."

I swore, but Alia didn't hear me. She was

already running off to check the room. The *Worm* sigil didn't wear off and had become a part of my body. I even tore at the flesh where the symbol was burned into me, but to no avail. I didn't see any point in staying awake. Since I was stuck in this crater, all I could do was sleep and gain my strength. However, just as I got comfortable, my eyes fell on some kind of glare in the very center of the crater. Gathering the last of my strength, I rolled over and crawled toward the target. It was something metallic. Sweeping the dirt aside, I found myself staring at a metal plate the size of a playing card. On one side was a portrait of a smiling man in his fifties. A handsome face, a neat beard, a turban with a peacock feather. There was also a signature, in case someone didn't recognize one of the nine influential figures in the Shurgan Empire. *"Padishah Bayazid the Third."* On the other side was a line of text that made my heart skip a beat: *"The owner of this card is acting on my will and my behalf. His word is my word. His hand is my hand."*

Well now, Bayazid the Third. Let's see how much weight your word carries in the Zarak Empire. Now I knew how to get back at the man who had gotten the idea to kidnap me. Now there was little left to do but return to Turb. Alive and preferably in one piece.

Placing the plate in my breast pocket, I climbed out of the crater and, under the frightened gaze of the local onlookers who were still loitering around, found a shovel in the rubble of the barn.

Since this metal plate had survived the explosion, it means that something else could have as well. What if one of the shapeshifter's stones didn't explode? I'd have to check everything.

Chapter 10

NEITHER ALIA NOR I found anything of interest—the metal plate ended up being the only thing that terrible monster had dropped, and the room had been ransacked before Alia had gotten there. We were escorted all the way down the street. Accompanied by pitchforks, clubs, and all other manner of instruments of hospitality. Evidently the roads would be closed to us next time around. We traveled on horseback—the wagon had been parked not far from the barn and it was in pieces. And our horses too. Alia had to write another receipt saying that the Fortress would reimburse the cost of the horses. It wasn't the best situation, of course, but there was still a silver lining—Fardi was silent the whole time and dutifully did everything that she was told.

Not even a single attempt at sarcasm or to say her piece. At one point, I even had to go over her with *Analyze* just to make sure we weren't dealing with a second shapeshifter. But everything was in order—the girl was who she said she was. But I understood how Karina was able to bench press one twenty kilos—twenty-eight enhancements, most of which were focused on physical development and body strength. If we were to fight in hand-to-hand combat right now, without magic, the girl would twist me into a pretzel without breaking a sweat. Her strength, agility and speed far exceeded most people's maxed-out stats. I didn't see anything unusual about her stones, so I didn't focus on them.

We only made it to Hearth two days after the fight with Faceless had taken place. We were greeted by huge throngs of pilgrims filling the streets, but maneuvering without a wagon proved much easier. The town itself was quite cozy and humble. While in the capital, most homes, especially those near the center, had three to six floors, in Hearth, people mostly lived in two-story cottages. The only exceptions were the hotels that towered over the city, and the Bishop Zwat's residence. The Red Goose was not far from the central square, and when I saw the picture above the entrance, I guffawed. Only now did I make the connection that in Turb, Alia and I lived in the Silver Goose, which bore nearly the same sign as this one. Goose here, goose there, the only difference was the plumage. Apparently if you didn't know which hotel to pick in any particular city, just utter the word "Goose" and you'd likely find a match.

Check in was no problem—Aleksy had managed to book rooms for us before Count Kupatsky arrived with the invitations. They were handed to Karina along with the keys to the room. As agreed, Fardi went to the fifth floor, while Alia and I found ourselves in a small room with a single bed. Alexy's hands had been tied—in fact, he hadn't been able to find a room for himself at all. Apparently in two days, the bishop would hold his annual meeting in the town square, during which he would distribute alms, perform miracles and demonstrate in as many ways as possible the church's mercy to the common folk in the central region. That was, in fact, the reason for the huge army of pilgrims marching this way—they were all trying to get a piece of the miracle. Alexy had found out everything he could about the upcoming event. It turns out that every year the bishop randomly selected a few people and gave them over to his healers. For the chance at such an opportunity, many disabled civilians were ready to tear other contenders limb from limb in order to prevent them from entering the central square. Conflicts flared up here and there around the city, and the guards were running back and forth trying to subdue the particularly rowdy bunch, but they simply didn't have enough hands. Merchants tried to close up shop as early as possible, and it was better not to wander the streets of Hearth after dark. The poor wretches, unconstrained by any moral framework, wreaked havoc, with not a shred of remorse for the dozens of corpses that the guards had to clear up every morning. This Fortress-organized event proved to be a real nightmare for the empire. But no one could stop the bishop. His power in Hearth was unbridled.

After leaving my things in our room and trying to freshen up from the road, I dragged Alia out for a stroll. She resisted—she was impatient to write a letter to the High Priest about the incident with Faceless, and she did not want to be distracted by such idle things as a walk around the city. Nevertheless, my perseverance eventually won out, and soon we were moving along the avenue. Although truthfully, this took us a while, because as soon as the poor saw the purple robe, a huge crowd of the suffering formed around us. The pilgrims extended their hands to the girl, tried to touch her, prayed for mercy, for help. Unlike Bishop Zwat, Alia did not enjoy excessive attention from the crowd. She was lost and had no idea how to proceed, so we had to go back and change.

"It's here." I sat down on a bench and took out a bottle of water. To any casual observer, we looked like a couple of lovers on a promenade.

"Here?" Alia didn't immediately understand me, but then she turned white and cast a quick glance at the town hall. "You're sure?"

"Absolutely. The map's margin of error is only twenty meters. And there's clearly not an entrance to the rift on the main square."

"Max, this is unthinkable." Alia couldn't believe my words. "The town hall has been standing here for two hundred years, no less!"

"I don't have any answers for you, but the rift is definitely right here. If the map I have isn't lying. And something tells me it isn't. Which raises a rather interesting and topical question."

"How did a rift appear underneath a building that has stood here for so many years?" Alia asked, to which I snorted in reply.

"Are you really bothered by such a small thing? Personally, I'm more concerned about the fact that you are trying so hard to keep me out of the rifts, when it has not been officially confirmed that Bishop Zwat has a ten-level chasm at his disposal. In addition, the High Priest himself said that at one time, he also used the rifts for his own gain. But apparently you are even worthier than these respected gentlemen. A true servant of the church, ready to sacrifice everything in order not to violate the dogmas that have been hammered into your head since childhood."

"What others do doesn't matter," Alia said. She wasn't so easily offended. "What matters is what I do. How I react to the situation. If there really is a rift under the town hall, then Bishop Zwat has no right to hold such a high position. He must resign."

"Oh yeah?" I even raised my brows at such a naive suggestion. "Alia, you're a smart cookie, but sometimes you talk such nonsense, you wouldn't believe. What makes you think the bishop owes anyone anything? Are you sure, for instance, that some of the resources extracted from this venture are not being sent to a particular old man we both know? Yeah, I'm talking about Father Urg. Are you sure he's not in on it? Is it really possible that over the many years that the rift has existed, that none of Bishop Zwat's assistants tried to double-cross their boss and hand over information about the rift to top management? I'd never believe such a fairy tale. What I believe is actually happening here is that the bishop has managed to traverse two or three levels of the rift, and that he controls everything that happens on these levels. And keeps it open just so that the clerics can strengthen their blocking skills. After all, the main mission remains the same—pushing back the darkness. The real surprise for Father Urg was the depth of the rift. We're here because the bishop neglected to share this little detail with the high priest. And there's no need to shout down from your high horse that Bishop Zwat must relinquish his powers and join the ranks of the doomed legion. More likely they'll send us there. Note that he didn't send a spy here. That Phantom that serves Zurgan Shor could easily sneak down to the third level unnoticed. But the Fortress did not send him here, because Father Urg did not need information about the existence of the rift. He already knew about it. He needs dark ones. Those that can descend down to level eight or nine, where ordinary people would stand no chance. So go ahead, Max, go find me evidence of collusion, and I'll just keep on being the High Priest, and you can continue carrying out my assignments like an obedient lap dog. If you have any doubts or balk at the reins, there's always the sweet girl we've trained to follow the church dogma with fanatical devotion. Probably the only one in the whole church. She will instantly convince you of anything and everything. Even to save Karina Fardi's life."

"You finished?" Anger had crept into Alia's voice. I'd hit a nerve. "Now listen to me. We had just left the capital when the personal assistant of the Duke of Turb immediately galloped up with a note of protest. Saying dark ones have no place on his land. Wherever you go, that's the welcome that awaits! The only way to more or less safely move between cities is to travel under the auspices of the Fortress. Or with someone of Karina Fardi's status. Even when you become a baron, nothing will change. So don't blame me for asking you to keep her alive. Without that, you would not have made it to Hearth!"

"So basically you don't care if we close the rifts, just how we do it, right? Then I have a counter-question for you: if we leave the bounds of the empire, will you calm down and let me handle my own development?"

"Leave the bounds of the empire?" Aliya was taken aback. "Beyond the Wall?"

"Nothing so radical. We could go west, for instance, into the desert. I'm sure there are rifts there too, but no one save the local Bedouins, if they exist at all, knows about them. Or, yes, we could look to the north, beyond the Wall. When have people ever gone there? There are huge territories we've surrendered to the darkness. Why not disturb their peace? Why, instead of doing things that are actually of use to us, are we sitting on a bench across from the town hall, too afraid to admit the obvious—that Bishop Zwat is no more a traitor than High Priest Urg. Why should we wait for a meeting with the Duke of Turb? Why in Skron's name can't I enter the town hall right now, find the entrance to the rift and shut it down? Sure, it will take me a couple of weeks to raise my tolerance to the last levels, but I can solve this problem once and for all. It's just that I wasn't asked. On the contrary, they told me not to be a hero and to simply gather evidence about collusion with the dark ones. Why? To me, the answer is obvious—the black market shouldn't suffer just because of a conflict between two churchmen. Surely the higher hierarchs are carefully monitoring the situation. Which raises another rather vexing question. Why are those who are supposed to be fighting the darkness instead grooming and cultivating it? Or am I speaking out of turn?"

"It doesn't matter where the rift is, in the empire or outside of it." Alia was stubborn. As I understood it, she also knew how to cherry pick convenient points from a conversation and focus on them, ignoring everything else. "They belong to the Fortress. If there really is a rift under the town hall, this should be reported to the High Priest immediately. I need paper and pencil. Come on, I don't see the point in wasting time. Nothing will change if we keep sitting here."

Alia's fanatical adherence to the dogmas of the church infuriated me, but I couldn't do anything about it. Persuading the girl turned out to be an impossible task, even when she was confronted with irrefutable facts. Maybe it really was futile? Why did I need to convince my personal attendant of anything at all? If she wanted to believe that Father Urg is so great and infallible, so be it. Personally, I'd learned a lot during this trip. The Fortress was not so different from the empire. People were people, no matter where you went, what clothes they wore or what titles they hid behind. Personal gain was a priority, everything else went out the window like useless garbage. I needed to reconsider my position in life.

Aliya sat down to write her snitch report while I, so as not to interfere, went out into the common room. The festivities were in full swing here. Hotel guests played cards or chess, or simply chatting while drinking wine and eating sweets. But this was all in the VIP zone, where visitors with green cards were allowed to pass. A different area was allotted for holders of simple white cards, such as mine. Here, too, you could play cards, but there was no talk of any wine or sweets. Not complimentary, at least.

Karina Fardi was already in the common hall, of course, in the area corresponding to her greatness. The duke's daughter melted in the spotlight, feeling like a fish out of water. The guests fawned over her, showered mountains of compliments on her, vied with each other in offering her gifts, which Karina refused with a businesslike look. It was not proper for a duke's daughter to accept gifts from obscure barons, and even viscounts. The girl noticed me, but defiantly turned away, pretending that I didn't exist at all. Personally, this suited me just fine—the less we communicated, the less I would have to fight my desire to strangle her. I went to the card table and started observing the hand. Six people were playing poker, the stakes were small, more for interest, and in this case there was no banker or dealer to speak of. The players had to deal their own cards.

"You waiting for the next turn?" said a voice, and I realized it was addressed to me. Spinning around, I saw a fat man with a wide grin. He surpassed even Zurgan Shor in his dimensions. There seemed to be something peculiar about him, and it took me a while to realize that he was a member of the Shurgan Empire. The excess weight masterfully hid the heavily hooded eyelid.

"No, just watching," I replied, stepping aside. The sudden appearance of this Shurganite didn't make me happy. Judging by what the padisha's servants had said before we had, inevitably, left them in the village, Faceless had wanted to take me to Hearth and send me off to his master in a caravan.

"Allow me to introduce myself: merchant from a long line of merchants, master of a caravan of twenty camels, a harem of ten concubines, two magnificent sons and a wonderful garden near the palace of Padishah Bayazid the Third, Hassan Kera—at your service.”

“And what good is your name to me? I didn’t ask for friends or conversation partners.”

“I beg your pardon for my lack of tact. Naturally, you are correct—you are not required to introduce yourself to, let alone extend welcome to an ordinary merchant from another empire. I would like the chance to explain my bold behavior—today, I was an unwitting witness to the fact that you arrived at this worthy establishment with your companion. Now she, as sweet and fragrant as a rose, blooms under the attention of the other distinguished residents of this glorious empire, while I haven’t a single chance of approaching and introducing myself. It hinders my natural modesty.”

“But this natural modesty didn’t stop you from approaching me?”

“Well, you’re a man, you must understand how difficult it is to find the proper words in the company of a beautiful lady. I would be forever indebted to you, O nameless youth, if you could introduce me to the enchanting Karina Fardi.”

“You even know her name, do you?”

“Everyone in the Red Goose knows who resides on the fifth floor. The daughter of the Duke of Odoevsky enjoys too much celebrity to slip by unnoticed.”

“I’m afraid I can’t help you. As you see,

Countess Fardi is in that part of the hall where I simply don't have access. And I don't have a strong desire to go there either. You'll have to find yourself another wingman. All the best!"

"Don't misunderstand me, but no one else in all of Hearth can help me like you can. For my bold request, I am willing to pay you twenty gold pieces. Such a generous sum, just for her acquaintance."

"Apparently, you didn't hear me," I said, simmering. This merchant's obtrusiveness was infuriating. "I will not introduce you to Karina Fardi."

"Young man, you are twisting my arm. I see that haggling is in your blood. Name your price. I'm sure we can come to an agreement."

I turned around and walked outside. Any desire I had to be in the common room had dissipated like smoke in a gust of wind. I have always been irritated by pushy people, especially such unpleasant ones as this fat man. The sun was already setting below the horizon, and the city slowly fell into the hands of the vagrants who began to appear. While there were already quite a few of them during the day, now a whole sea of beggars and peasants of all stripes had formed in front of the hotel. Nobody paid any attention to me. Despite the quality of my clothes, outwardly, they looked like an ordinary hunter's outfit. Casual enough to be lost in the crowd—most of the townspeople wore somewhat similar clothes. I didn't fear for my life. It was unlikely that anyone here would be able to break through my shield. As a last resort, I could shoot off *Dark Spike.*

"I'm sure it was the Bishop!" An excited voice reached my ears.

"You're lying! Our benefactor would never meet with bandits!"

"I bet my right hand!" the voice insisted. "I was huddled under a shelter so I could have a little snooze, that's why they didn't notice me. It was the bishop, I know for sure! You think I wouldn't recognize the man who passed me by last year and didn't choose me?"

"So what, a whole wagon?"

"Filled to the brim! The guys in bandages consulted some list, and then gave the bishop a small package. Didn't look like gold at all. I was lying there, too afraid to even breathe. The ones in bandages had guards. They scared the pants off of me! Nearly pissed myself while laying there. Then everyone left, so I got out of there."

"And the wagon? Where did the wagon go?"

"Skron knows where. I could barely remember my own name, I was so scared, and you're going on about a wagon."

"Oh, he's lying!" said a third voice. "I'm guessing he got drunk and had a dream about it. I can smell the fumes from here!"

"I only drank later, for courage!" protested the first. "It's not every day you stare death in the face. I still haven't gotten over it—it was just an hour ago. The guys in the bandages were really awful. It was as if they exuded something horrible. No, lads, you can do as you wish, but I'm going home. It is clear that I'm not destined to be selected this year. I've already seen the benefactor. Anyway, my luck has run out."

"Go on then..." the second egged on his comrade in misfortune, but I stopped listening. With a quick step, I moved away from the square, going through my options. An hour ago, a wagon had left the town hall in an unknown direction. There were a lot of people in the city, so either the wagon would be moving slowly, or it was standing in one place until the morning. A map appeared before my eyes, and once again I thanked the Riftmasters for such a generous gift. I could survey all the streets and houses here at a glance. And the town hall that Alia and I had visited was already marked. Panning out, I admired the two main roads that led from the town hall. One went toward Turb, the other led all the way to the northern region where the Wall stood. Moreover, as it was, Hearth was only a stone's throw away from the borders of the region. Where had the wagon gone? To the south, the north or somewhere in the city? Something told me that the second option was most feasible.

As I found the path that led north, I broke out into a run. People looked around at me, someone even shouted something after me, and some rushed after me several times, thinking that I was running away from someone, but no one could stop me. Hearth did not have a single city wall, so I ran around the guard post that blocked the road, through the vegetable gardens. Judging by the well-trodden path, I was not the first to get the idea. Once I was back on the road, I picked up my usual pace and ran due north. Soon the sun disappeared below the horizon, and the night began to come into its own. Slowly at first, but every minute the darkness became thicker and thicker, until the stars began to twinkle into existence. The darkness did not impede me, except for the fact that I now occasionally trod on small pebbles. But after the training courses the Evil Engineer had put me through at the arena, something as small as that couldn't stop me.

After about twenty minutes, I realized that I was mistaken—not a single wagon had crossed my path. Apparently, the one the peasant had spoken about remained behind in the city. But I'd gotten a nice evening workout. I stopped and was about to turn around, but then I noticed a light ahead. It wasn't on the road, but a little off to one side. Where those who generally don't want to meet anyone else might go. Mages, aristocrats and, mayhaps, strange people in bandages.

In the end, I decided to check, so I slowly moved toward the fire, but suddenly the light went out, as if it had never been there. It seemed strange to me—who would hide their fire? And how could they hide it? You can't enclose it in the wagon, only with some kind of protective canopy, like what Alia did. So they were mages. Or were they? Curiosity got the better of me, so I decided to move closer— I wanted to use *Analyze* on the owner of this mysterious stone. Maybe I needed one just like it?

It soon became clear that I was mistaken—the fire hadn't been obscured by magic, but rather by the dense fabric of a huge tent, inside which the light source was hidden. The fact that I had managed to catch a glimpse of it as they set up the tent was a real miracle. Dropping to the ground, I slowly crawled closer—it was foolish to think that the rest stop was not guarded. When I was about twenty meters away, suddenly the canopy of the tent opened up, illuminating the space, and a man came out of it. Closing the flap tight, he stepped aside to relieve himself, and at that moment I realized that today I would no longer be able to return to Hearth.

Because *Analyze* had just showed me a rather intriguing message:

"Convert?? 47% probability, additional verification required."

Chapter 11

A CONVERT. A CREATURE that was essentially useless to interrogate—as soon as it lost control of its body, Skron would immediately take control of its consciousness and make the converted sing some sort of dark melody, enveloping everything around with its influence. During my short life as a doomed soldier, I had encountered these monsters twice already, but I had never waited for them to finish their song. In the first case, Father Nor had screamed like a dying man to interrupt the convert's muttering, and in the second case, the creature could not withstand the influence of the elite ousel. Incidentally, I definitely had to visit the local blacksmith and get myself a steel box with a small hole. It'd be nice to have such a thing now—instead of fighting, everyone would either run away or raise their hands to the sky in devotion. That allowed them to be killed relatively safely. But in this case...I'd have to compromise.

I didn't see any more sense in hiding—even if there was a guard here, I'd also have to deal with them somehow. So let's see what I was working with.

"Pardon, good sir, but could you show me the way to Hearth?" I got to my feet, attracting the attention of the man who came out to relieve himself. To his credit, he didn't flinch or draw his weapon. He finished business, then approached me with the gait of a trained fighter. I pulled my sleeves down, thus hiding the katars and crossbow—now I didn't even go to the bathhouse without a weapon.

"No way, are you lost?" the potential convert asked. Even now, at night, his head was wrapped in what looked like a turban. Only his eyes remained uncovered. Dark eyes, exactly like the Evil Engineer's. Of course, it could have been written off as poor lighting, but I couldn't help but notice the black holes devoid of pupils.

"I'm going to meet with the bishop." I kept waiting for a guard to appear, so I delayed my attack. "I thought I could make it through the night, but I was wrong. When I saw your light, I was glad that I found someone. I'd already decided I was done for. Now one of Skron's beasts would leap out of the darkness and there'd be nothing left of me but a memory."

"You saw the light?" came a voice from behind me. I'd been right—there was a guard. The way he had crept up so quietly was frankly alarming.

"Not exactly." I stalled a little longer. Suddenly there were several guards. "First I saw the light, then it vanished. I had nowhere to go, so I walked toward the place where I remembered it had been. I thought, gentlemen, that maybe a mage had put it under some sort of shield that had blocked the light. I approached and saw this tent."

"How did you not get yourself killed in the dark?" asked a voice behind me, forcing me to spin around and back away. My fear wasn't feigned—it was sincere and deep. There was no bandage on the guard's head, which allowed me to see his true face. Not human. Humans didn't have such huge, gaping mouths filled with rows of jagged shark teeth.

"What an apt response," the guard chuckled and flicked his long, pointed tongue, which did not quite fit in his mouth. With a tongue like that, he could easily lick his forehead, and was clearly also not human. "Delicious."

"It seems I've come at a bad time," I backed away from the guard, but stumbled into another guy stepping out of the tent. "The night isn't so dark, and Hearth can't be that far, eh? I'll just leave."

"Where do you think you're going? Aren't you afraid that a beast of Skron will jump out from the darkness and attack you?" The one without bandages grinned. Finally, I managed to control my emotions. Think—wide shark mouth. What hadn't I encountered any creatures like this in the rift? Another monster, except that he can speak.

My mana was already a third gone, but I didn't begrudge myself another third to use *Analyze*. And it didn't let me down this time, listing off exhaustive information on the monster, including, among other things, one interesting line of text. It turns out that this creature wasn't a convert at all, and *Analyze* didn't always show me what I needed to see.

Tarkatan. Dark being.

Physically, the Tarkatan turned out to be much stronger than a man. *Analyze* did not display any enhancements, but most of its physical parameters far exceeded one hundred percent of the person that Skron had chosen to represent the average.

"Come into the tent, have tea with us, and tell us, why does such a strapping young man as yourself need the bishop? I suppose you're hungry from the road? We're starving. We haven't had a decent meal in two days."

"Guys, can I still go? I don't want to disturb you," I decided to take the role of the victim, playing along with the Tarkatans. It seemed like they wanted to devour me, which meant that their whole gang would gather together for such an event in the tent. Then I wouldn't have to chase them around. Because I wouldn't be able to catch up with these freaks at my current stage of enhancements. I'd need to keep my mask up until the last minute.

"What do you have here?" the tent flap opened, spilling out light, and two more came out. Yes, that made four already. The pilgrim whose story I accidentally overheard had not said anything about the number of terrible men in bandages, but there were hardly that many of them. Four? Or was it five?

"He got lost," grinned the one without bandages.

"And still hasn't figured it out?" asked the one who had just arrived.

"His reaction was delicious indeed," said the guard. "Invited him in for a cup of tea, he refused. Says he doesn't want to disturb us."

"Tea is the right choice." The ones who had just stepped out of the tent pulled off their bandages, revealing the same monstrous faces. "Take him to the tent. Let's feed our dear guest. And fortify our own bodies as well. Make sure everything is quiet here, then bring him in."

That was how the commander of the entire group presented himself. So there were still four others. They took me by the arms and dragged me to the tent. I did not resist, pretending that I was barely able to maintain consciousness. There was enough space inside the tent to safely place a fire and a few beds. A pot of water was warming on the fire, as if the Tarkatans really did want to brew me a cup of tea.

"All clear. He was alone, came straight from the road, didn't circle around the camp. He wasn't lying."

"Oh wasn't I?" I muttered. "I came here with my friends. We have a gang of hundreds of people. I am a scout. We wanted to take the city, but we stumbled upon you, and they sent me to scout everything out. A hundred people! They'll all be here soon if I don't leave the tent and say I'm okay."

"Of course you'll leave," the leader grinned nastily. "You will definitely leave. Everyone leaves."

"May I ask a question?" I asked in a groveling tone. The creature smirked again.

"Just one. We haven't eaten properly for two days. I can even promise you, we'll answer before...I mean, I will answer honestly and without concealing anything. What did you want to ask, dinner?"

"What did you give the bishop in exchange for resources from the rift? I never managed to find out what was in that bundle."

I was really a big fan of *Dark Spike,* especially under the *Amplify*s. And I loved my katars. And adored my crossbow with steel bolts. Everything capable of destroying dark beasts. The leader got his bearings immediately, but still not fast enough—as soon as he jerked in my direction, a dark spike crashed into his chest. I did not expect to kill him—judging by the stats I'd read, the creature had a protective aura, something like the one many magical monsters have. But here's what I expected and what I got: temporary chaos. It's hard to keep your cool when a huge spike crashes into you with great force, splattering darkness all around. Aiming my cocked crossbow at the Tarkatan closest to me took only a second. The steel bolt barreled forward and disappeared into the creature's head. Magic protection and amulets could not stop steel. One down. There was no time to reload the crossbow, so I activated the katars and prepared for battle. Strange, but for some reason the creatures did not attack. The darkness dissipated, and I stared in amazement at the three Tarkatans lying on the ground without moving. The leader was pierced through the chest by a thorn, which had swept away his shield like paper. A level six stone outfitted with *Amplify* proved too tough for a simple amulet. The other two were hit by shrapnel. They were still breathing, but unconscious. I didn't hesitate to finish off the one who took the most damage. Only the Tarkatan that acted as a guard survived. I had to fiddle around to find a rope to bind him, but soon I was sitting opposite the creature and trying to bring it back to consciousness, slapping its terrible cheeks. The huge toothy mouth was terrifying and triggered my gag reflex, especially considering the fact that otherwise, the creatures outwardly resembled people. Of course, as soon as one was undressed, the differences immediately became visible: a more slender physique, growths and spikes on the joints, strong sharp claws that could easily tear flesh to shreds.

Soon my actions produced results, and the creature groaned, opened its eyes and immediately twitched, trying to break the ropes. If I did not know the dark one's true powers, I could have mistakenly tied him up like an ordinary person. But since I knew there was nothing human about this one, I approached the process of incapacitating him very seriously. The creature must not escape.

"Where were you supposed to deliver the goods?" I asked.

"Who are you?" I had to hand it to the Tarkatan. He wasted no time panicking or moaning about the difficult fate of a dark beast. Instead he stared at me, trying to understand who I was and how I had managed to take out his group.

"Where were you supposed to deliver the goods?" I repeated the question and switched on *Healing Aura*. The dark one even sighed with pleasure—unlike the monsters of the rifts, the treatment didn't harm this one, but completely healed him, as if he were an ordinary person. Pretending that this was intentional, I held the aura for a few more seconds and cut it off. Pulling a knife from the group commander's belt, I put a dark blade to the guard's leg and raised an eyebrow demandingly.

"Who are you?" The Tarkatan was clearly not timid either. The blade entered the body, but the creature did not even wince, continuing to stare.

"Pointless?" I asked on a whim, and unexpectedly received an answer:

"It is pointless to torture me. We know how to turn off the pain."

"And 'we' is Tarkatans?"

"You know who we are. I don't know who you are."

"You can call me a hunter. A hunter of darkness. Where were you supposed to deliver the cargo, and what was in the package you gave to the bishop?"

"Hunter of darkness...never heard of that."

"So you don't plan to talk?"

"There is no way to get a Tarkatan to talk. That's why we're hired for such dangerous jobs. For we are the strength. We are a guarantee of information safety. We..."

"You're dead," I replied with a swift movement. I wasn't about to listen to this creature's pathetic speech. The corpse fell to the ground, and I proceeded to do a thorough inspection of the tent, hoping to find at least something that could connect the four Tarkatans and Bishop Zwat. But if something like that existed, it was only in the head of the group commander. Not a single document, not a single hint of where these creatures were heading, not a single clue. Just four dark ones who had somehow found themselves in the middle of the Zarak empire. I opened the map again and sighed sadly— we were a few kilometers from the border of the central region. Everything that happened next is a fog in my memory. I needed to persuade the High Priest to give me the opportunity to run through all the regions, no matter what the cost. After all, the Fortress would get much more out of this than me—all the new "resource extraction points."

Having dragged the bodies of the Tarkatans onto the cart, I returned to the tent. Heading back to Hearth at night was a stupid idea. Firstly, the guards wouldn't let us through, secondly, the horses' legs would be broken before we could make it to the main road, and thirdly, I was feeling stupidly lazy. I threw a few large logs to keep the fire burning as long as possible, I lay down on a sleeping bag and fell asleep almost instantly.

When dawn broke, I had the opportunity to examine the wagon. It held mainly nux and chrone—the most common materials in any rift. However, there were also a few rare gems: several blanks for amulets, three magic stones (I never learned to determine the number of facets, and I didn't want to use *Analyze* for something so simple), as well as two barrels stuffed with something. Apparently, a valuable material, since the Tarkatans had hidden it under the very bottom of the wagon. For me, black market prices remained a mystery, so there was no way to even assess how profitable my night had been. The question was instead, 'What do I do with all these goodies?' I had nowhere to put it. If someone noticed the beasts were missing, experienced trackers would easily find the rest stop, as well as a place where I could hide all this until better times. Although, to be honest, the question was bothering me more and more: why were the stones mined from the rift ending up on the black market? They also needed to be somehow processed in order to turn them into elixirs of one sort or another. Mana or recovery. As I understood it, the necessary devices were all hidden away in the Fortress, which had a monopoly on the process, as well as those in the magical academy. Or was I wrong? Who needed rocks? They had been bought for some reason...Take the same chabre that I used to prepare the paint for the symbols. In order for the crystal to be used, it just needed to be ground into dust. With the help of the Fortress's equipment, this was done without any problems, but who would forbid the use of an ordinary mill? Similarly, with other resources, the main thing was to find the right way to process them, and then the church's monopoly would be in jeopardy. Wait, what the hell was I talking about here? After all, the church itself supplies materials to the black market. So, it processes them itself and passes the result along. A good way to fight the black market for materials is to become the leading supplier. But sometimes there were carts like this. Not recorded in the general register, and heading north. To the Wall. Where the vast territories of the darkness were located, almost exceeding all three empires combined in size. Wait...why were the dark ones dragging resources out of the empire? Didn't they have their own? Weren't there any rifts behind the Wall? What was this nonsense?

A map suddenly appeared before my eyes, and I almost smacked myself on the forehead, bringing myself to my senses. A conversation with

Kimal Sarento popped up in my memory, when he had talked about the need to close the rift under the academy. That new buildings were already being built in another place, literally under Turb itself, where a rift had been discovered quite by accident. But my map showed that there was no rift near the capital! None at all! The nearest one was a few hours' from the city at a gallop. Would the empire build one of the leading academies so far from the capital? Never in my life! I thought that the academy wouldn't be built outside the city, but in one of the city parks. So that later, once all the buildings fell into place, an entrance to the first level of the rift would suddenly appear under the main building and the Master would begin his slow but purposeful march into the depths.

My seditious thoughts astonished even me and I plopped down on the ground to consider them. Weren't rifts the brainchild of Skron? Rather, they were his essence and flesh, but not the offspring? Were they run by either the Empire or the Fortress? No, it was too far-fetched—judging by the High Priest's reaction, he had not known about some of the rifts in the central region, as if they appeared by accident. Damn, who would scout all this? Because now it turns out that most of the rifts in the empire were created by the church. And all those human casualties that occur when the creatures crawl out for prey are on the church's bloody hands. I wonder what my little zealot would have to say about this? Would she reject it, or ruminate on the essence of being? Or would she find such cutting words that I would believe that I'd been winding myself up and that everything was completely different from what it really was? Those were the options with Alia.

Okay, the rifts were one thing, but that didn't give me any idea about what to do with all this loot. It was useless. Leaving it here was stupid.

A wicked smirk crept across my face as I realized what to do. Rolling up the tent so that later I could sell some thick fabric to some craftsman, I threw everything I could find in the camp into the wagon, including four grinning corpses of Tarkatans, and then slowly moved toward Hearth.

It was an unforgettable journey. I got to the city without any issue. There were no pilgrims from the north, so no one interfered with the cart's progress. However, once I rode up to the city…

The guards who blocked the road were the first to meet me.

"Halt!" shouted the head of the guard menacingly. "Present your cart for inspection and take out your purse for travel tax. Where are you going? What are you carrying?"

"I'm a hunter of darkness," I introduced myself with a fictitious title. I was starting to like it. "I'm taking my loot to the main town hall."

"Loot?" the mustachioed guard brayed. "What kind of loot could you have there? A hunter of the darkness…Only yesterday he tore away from his mother's teat, but is he already a hunter? From the North? Found some mushrooms in the forest along the way, eh boy?"

"Looks like he had his fill," one of the assistants chuckled. "He's clearly still just a boy. A scrawny one, but a boy nonetheless."

"Show me what's in the wagon!" the commander of the guard demanded sternly.

"As you wish," I shrugged, after which silence fell, broken only by the quiet whispering of the guards:

"What in the love of Skron is that?"

"Eyes! Look at those eyes! It strikes fear in you, all the way to the bone!"

"And the teeth? Humans don't have teeth like that! Three rows! This creature has three rows of teeth!"

"As you can see," I calmly remarked, "I have four dead dark creatures in my wagon that almost ate half of Hearth. Although, as I suppose, such brave soldiers would have dealt with them in an instant, since such a wimpy little boy like me could never cope with them. And the magic holes through their bodies are just decorative."

"So you...are you a mage?" The head of the guard changed his tune in an instant. It was one thing to mock a commoner, it was another thing to mock a mage.

"I am a hunter of darkness," I repeated. "I'm taking my loot to the main town hall. Are there any objections, or do I have to pay a tax for every dark head? I'm not going to stand for that. I'll just toss the beasts out here, deal with them yourself. As if I have nothing else to do but argue with you. Here, hand over the dark ones yourself. Tell them that they tried to get into the city at night. You'll be heroes."

"And they'll ship us off to the Wall," the commander muttered. "The Red Churchmen have broken our spirits. Come on, there's no reason to scare people."

"No, it won't work like that. I need a paper stating that today, I officially dragged the corpses of the dark creatures I killed near the city through the outpost. My actions are very carefully monitored. Every step is verified, so I won't go into the city without a slip of paper. All I need is the patrol stopping me and sending me to prison without a trial. So either write me a slip, or take the cart and do whatever you want with it."

"You'll have your slip," the commander said gloomily. "Who should I write it out to?"

"Max, Hunter of Darkness," I made a small addition. "Yeah, just Max, no titles or other regalia. I'm in Hearth incognito. And do not indicate that I am a mage."

"Yes, I understand." The commander became even more gloomy and retired to a small booth, which acted as resting place, shelter from the weather, and, as it became clear, the commander's dwelling place. "So, is this wording suitable for you?"

On the official travel letterhead, there was a clumsy inscription that Max, Hunter of Darkness rode into the city of Hearth, carrying with him four dead dark creatures killed not far from the city. I had a hard time holding back a smirk. The first part of my plan was complete.

Then came the onslaught of civilians and pilgrims that filled Hearth. I did not close the wagon, allowing everyone to enjoy the views of the scary monsters. It was amazing how quickly word spread that something unusual was happening in the city. The first poor people and peasants whom I met on the edge of the city didn't even think about moving, but as soon as they saw my cargo, the color left their faces and they quickly scattered. I drove up to the town hall without delay—everyone, including city patrols, gave way to the terrible wagon coach. Moreover, at the entrance to the main building of the local church, they were already waiting for me. Not the bishop— his position did not permit him to meet strangers. It was one of his assistants.

"The news has reached me, my son, that you have brought us a terrible cargo," boomed the servant of the Light, dressed in a white robe.

"That is correct, Father...?"

"Father Pithr," the attendant introduced himself. "Manager of the city hall."

"I am Max, Hunter of Darkness," I introduced myself in turn. "Loyal servant of the Fortress. Arrived in Hearth at the behest of High Priest Urg, who was concerned that dark creatures were seen near the city. Actually, you see the result of my travels—four dead Tarkatans and a whole wagonload of resources extracted from the rift. I have yet to figure out where the creatures got these resources from—it seems unlikely that the dark ones would drag resources back over the Wall. I have nowhere to put all this, Father Pithr, so I will donate both the bodies and the resources to the church of the central region. I ask you to conduct an audit and provide me with a complete inventory of the property—I will need to notify the High Priest about what was transferred to your diocese and in what quantities."

Judging by the way Father Pithr turned white, he was fully aware of the situation and recognized not only the cart, but also the four lying on top. Of course, I didn't show it, but I had taken the second step toward achieving my goal. Now there were too many witnesses in the square in front of the town hall, so they wouldn't do anything to me, and would even provide the necessary inventory list. But then, on a dark night, a villainous wretch would come to visit me in order to finish off the overly zealous hunter of darkness and destroy the compromising slip of paper. The local clergy still didn't know I had a hall pass from the head of the guard. But I had other plans for it.

"It will take time to count everything here," Father Pithr stammered.

"I am in no hurry, holy father," I shrugged. "My mission has been accomplished—the dark ones have been found, killed and delivered to the church. I'll be happy to wait for you in the town hall. I have long wanted to see such an interesting building from the inside. I'm sure it's not only beautiful, but also quite majestic. Besides, I would like to quickly enter into a place of the Light so as to rid myself of the feeling of the dark influence, may the Light be merciful to me. I can smell these creatures from hundreds of meters away."

Father Pithr blanched even whiter.

"I'm afraid we won't be able to receive you now," the cleric said. "The town hall is closed to prepare for the upcoming event. Wait here, Dark Hunter Max. The inventory list will be ready as soon as possible."

The way the clerics were bustling around made me smile. Like ants. Father Pithr brought a whole team with him, which quickly sorted out the contents of the cart into several piles while he himself carefully wrote everything down on a piece of paper, which he then handed to me. I even had to give away the tent—I only remembered it when I saw it in the general list of the act of transfer. An act of transfer! This wasn't a church, it was a building full of bureaucrats! If only they fought the darkness as enthusiastically as they filled out paperwork.

"Thank you." I slipped the folded paper into my breast pocket. "If you have any questions for me, I am staying at the Red Goose Hotel. Perhaps I will stay in Hearth for a couple more days to make sure that the dark ones are truly finished off. And the event may prove interesting. It's not every day that a bishop blesses a crowd of people. All the best, Father Pithr. May the Light be kind to you."

Leaving the churchman, I went to the hotel with a clear conscience. There was no doubt that they would try to kill me tonight. The only thing left to do was warn Alia and prepare. The High Priest wanted proof? No problem—I'd get it, even without seeing the rift. It was unlikely the Bishop of Zwat had his own Faceless. That would just be too much.

Chapter 12

"COUNTESS KARINA FARDI, daughter of the Duke of Odoevsky, with her companions!"

All the eyes in the hall were suddenly riveted on our group, which no doubt looked a little peculiar. First of all, there was Karina, all sparkling and gorgeous. Incredibly, in two days she had managed to find a decent dress and jewelry, as well as hire servants, and was now constantly the center of male attention. Alia followed behind, attracting as much attention as the countess. The thing was that, contrary to my advice, the girl had donned her purple robe, displaying her high rank within the church. Translated into the language of the empirical hierarchy, Alia was an equal to the Duke of Turb and Bishop Zwat, who was expected to appear at any moment. And finally, a lowly student of the magic academy. I couldn't find anything better to wear than my familiar jumpsuit, demonstrating that I belonged to the best educational institution in the empire. The best, according to its teachers and students. There was also a very simple reason I was in such common garments—I had run out of gold. Of course, I could have sold something or gotten a loan from the Fortress, but I didn't see the point in spending a ton of gold to buy a suit that I would wear at most two or three times in my life.

Incredibly, in the two days that had passed since my triumphant return to Hearth, absolutely nothing had happened. Not the first night, when I didn't sleep a wink, waiting for the killers to arrive, and not the second either. For some reason, Bishop Zwat decided to delay his response to my actions, which was significantly more unnerving. Alia could barely stop herself from screaming at me when I got back. She spoke in a dry tone, but it was clear that she could barely contain her rage. The fact that I had disappeared without warning nearly undermined her faith in me. It even crossed her mind that I had decided to run away. I had to apologize and explain that there was no opportunity to warn her. I didn't want to fight or somehow aggravate the situation, despite the fact that we had never discussed the consequences of me disappearing suddenly for an undetermined amount of time. So we did, and agreed that from now on, I was permitted to be out of her presence for twenty-four hours. If it became clear that I would need more time to complete my mission, then I must do everything I could to warn Alia about this. Actually, those were the only two moments worth noting in the last couple of days. I didn't even go to the bishop's event—hanging around the unwashed masses didn't particularly appeal to me. I devoted all my remaining time to conversing with Alexy—I was sorely lacking knowledge about the geography of the Zarak Empire, and the teacher was happy to help me sort out the details. So now my map had labels of all the major cities, rivers, and even some of the more remarkable villages.

"Countess Fardi, you are magnificent," said some pompous dandy as he approached us. First came the cloud of his sugary-sweet perfume, then he appeared.

"I thank you, Viscount Lukinsky," Karina replied, wrinkling her nose. Apparently, she had already made the acquaintance of everyone who was anyone in this city.

"Would you permit me to invite you to a dance?" the delighted dandy grew bolder, to which Karina, with a smile that could freeze blood, replied:

"You should find a dance partner more suitable for your status, Viscount. I beg you, do not hound me with your company. It makes me uncomfortable."

I had never seen such a perfect "Fuck off, or you'll regret it" in my life. Moreover, Karina didn't try to veil her intentions with sugar-coated phrases. She told the dandy in no uncertain terms that he was not welcome here.

"Are you like that with everyone, Your Radiance?" I chuckled as the red-faced boy stepped aside.

"Only with provincial aristocrats who, due to the lack of any worthy competition, imagine themselves to be the center of the universe. I can't stand these types. He's used to all the locals kissing his ass just to earn the attention of such a valuable person, his head was inflated. Of ten such viscounts who ended up in the capital city, only two or three of them were still alive after a couple of weeks. The fact that he approached me after I openly declared yesterday that I no longer wanted to speak with him would be grounds for a duel. Do I need to explain what the metropolitan viscounts do with little upstarts like him? To say nothing of the counts."

The first dance began, so we had to step aside. Judging by how few couples made their way to the center of the hall, the entertainment was clearly wearing thin. Everyone was waiting for the heads of the region to appear, and finally the herald loudly proclaimed:

"Count Nikitin, Duke of Turb!"

The music faded out, and everyone turned toward the door, through which a man of around fifty, nearly a head taller than me, emerged with a quick step. Something about him reminded me of Gustav—his tight suit showed off his well-developed form, several scars slashed across his face made him look even more courageous as his tenacious brown eyes instantly took stock of the people in attendance, picking out the most important figures. I liked the Duke—he felt like a man with the right and ability to command. Viscount Kurpatsky, as well as several other men in his entourage, moved like shadows behind their master. The whole hall kneeled, with only a few remaining on their feet. In fact, there were only three who didn't kneel before the head of the region: Karina Fardi, Mother Alia and one particularly crazy dark human. This did not go unnoticed—the Duke of Turb changed direction and approached us with the same quick step.

"Your Radiance." Karina curtsied in greeting. Now that the man had approached us, it was appropriate.

"Countess Fardi," nodded the duke in reply. He had a pleasant low baritone that matched his appearance.

"Allow me to introduce you to my companions, Your Radiance. Fortress representatives, Mother Alia and Max."

"Dark Max," the duke corrected, prompting whispers in the hall.

"Dark Max," Karina agreed lightly. "A Fortress-recognized servant of the Light."

"Who has no place in society," the duke turned his hard gaze on me. "A dark one who appeared in Hearth without my consent. A dark one that frightened half of Verse. A dark one who, in violation of all Fortress treaties, strolls around the city scaring folks left and right! A dark killer."

"Forgive my tactlessness, but I must

intervene," Alia paid no heed to manners at all. "Max acts in strict accordance with the rules established and agreed upon between the Fortress and the Zarak Empire. I, his personal attendant, one of ten who have the right to vote within the Fortress, am his guarantor, here to assure that all regulations and laws are being adhered to. When you accuse Max of not observing something or of murdering someone, you are blaming the church as a whole. Don't make false statements, Duke. You have no right to punish or reproach us for anything. We respect the law. As for your words, Max was doing his direct duties. He destroyed creatures of the darkness. Can you call him a killer for that? I do not think so."

Not a single muscle moved in the duke's face. Looking at Alia as if she were a little girl, the duke clarified:

"Creatures of the darkness? Mother Alia, I recognize your right to stand in my presence, but I will not allow you to blame the central region for not properly handling the dark ones! There currently are no, and never will be dark humans in my region. This is carefully monitored by those who are loyal to me, ready to lay down their lives for the sake of the inhabitants of the central region. Or do you mean to suggest that the Duke of Turb is unable to cope with his duties as defender of the region?"

"Apparently you aren't," I said, and a heavy silence hung over the hall. "So I had to intervene."

Once again, the Duke of Turb took the high

road. He did not yell, swear, blush, or reveal a single emotion. He just turned in my direction and calmly said:

"An accusation of this kind permits me to disregard a person's status within the Fortress. You have one minute, Dark One, to prove your words, otherwise you will be arrested as a slanderer and punished in accordance with the laws of the Zarak Empire!"

"I've read the law, Duke of Turb," I said, also seeing no point in getting emotional. "My task in the Fortress is as simple as a simile—seeking out and hunting down the darkness in all its forms. I have been in Hearth for three days. In a protected area, according to you. Purified of the darkness. However, on the first day, I came across four dangerous dark creatures. They were Tarkatans, human-like creatures with shark teeth. By some monstrous misstep of the region's defenses, the creatures got into their paws a whole wagon of rare resources mined from the rift. I managed to stop the monsters, destroy them, and also deliver the stolen valuables to Hearth Town Hall. And only now do I find that the Duke of Turb considers my actions to save the city and its inhabitants to be wrong and to somehow discrediting the honor of the region. I had to sit in a hotel for two days and try not to think about how many children and women had fallen to the darkness during this time it took me to find them. How much havoc Skron's beasts can wreak. But in all honesty, I complied with both the laws and your demands. My only mistake was that in Verse, I was unable to save at least a scrap of the dark one I destroyed. That creature was too strong. In Kostrishche, I managed not only to save the bodies, but also to deliver them to the town hall for identification. So that you don't consider my statements unfounded, I ask you to acquaint yourself with these documents. The first is the city guards' report, which says where and when the dark ones were killed. The second is a complete register of resources delivered to the town hall, which the dark ones were hauling through your territory. I don't throw out groundless accusations, Duke of Turb. I don't need to. Because I'm a hunter of darkness."

"Get Sergeant Stoltz here, immediately!" the Duke ordered after reading the documents. Two assistants instantly flew out of their seats, as if their lives depended on it.

"Are you saying that the four corpses you brought to the town hall weren't human?"

"This is indicated separately in both documents signed by two different hands. The creatures that I destroyed were nothing close to human. If you were given other information, it means that you were deliberately misled. Or that one who gave you this information is mistaken. There are dark ones in the central region, Duke of Turb. And I just proved it to you."

"You haven't proven anything yet," the duke said. Turning around, he saw that the whole crowd was standing and listening to our every word.

"Music! Continue the festivities!"

The music started playing, but no one went to dance. The hall was like a buzzing beehive. Everyone wanted to urgently discuss what they had heard. The duke stood and studied the documents, as if he was trying to find evidence of a forgery or a fake. But it was all too true. So we stood there next to each other for fifteen minutes, until the duke's breathless assistants rushed into the hall. Behind them, barely keeping up, ran a flushed and sweaty sergeant. The same cordon commander who had written up my pass.

"Do you recognize him?" The duke handed him the paper without further ado. The sergeant wiped his sweat with his sleeve, glanced briefly at the contents, and nodded.

"Yes, indeed, Your Radiance. I personally wrote this document two days ago. A man who introduced himself a hunter of darkness was bringing four dark creatures into the city. Terrible creatures, your grace, I have never seen anything like them, even on the Wall."

"Could it have seemed to you that they were dark beasts, when really they were human?"

"No, Your Radiance!" The sergeant spoke with confidence, without flushing. "The whole guard saw those monsters. We are ready to undergo any sort of questioning—the things in that wagon were not human."

"Well, could this person have stopped somewhere in the city, thrown the monsters out of the cart, and killed four ordinary citizens to turn them in to the church?”

"Not a chance, Your Radiance! I could not personally accompany the hunter of darkness, because I had no right to leave the post entrusted to me, but I sent my deputy, Corporal Edarge, after him. He escorted the wagon all the way to the town hall and returned, saying that the hunter of darkness did not stop or turn off anywhere. Near the town hall he was met by a churchman, a conversation took place between them, after which the churchman disappeared into the town hall and left with a huge group that began removing the contents of the wagon. The corporal did not wait for the end results, but rather returned to his post and reported to me. You can send for him—he will confirm my words.”

"Write a report on exactly what happened. You are free to go,” ordered the duke, dismissing the sergeant. Examining the documents once more, he handed them over to Viscount Kurpatsky. "Order the clerks to make copies. Return the originals.”

For a while, the duke continued to stand beside us, contemplating what had happened. Finally he said:

"Mother Alia, I will await you in my office tomorrow at ten in the morning. The address will be given to you by Viscount Kurpatsky. As for you, Dark Max...Dark Hunter Max, you are permitted to move freely around the central region. Tomorrow you will receive the appropriate documents. Countess, have a lovely evening.”

With that, the duke finally left us alone and moved on to greeting the other guests.

"I see you must have gotten your hands on some courage elixir," Karina noted without turning to address me. "After what you said, the Duke of Turb had every reason to declare you an undesirable person and cart you out of the central region in a prison wagon. But no—he recognized your right to be in Hearth and wants to see Alia tomorrow. Our good duke is disturbed by something, and deeply."

"I had the same thought," said Alia. "However, Max acted in strict accordance with the laws of the empire. The duke had no reason to exile him. Yes, he was a little harsh, a little brazen, but overall not bad. The result has been achieved."

"So you're dark, are you? I despise dark beasts!" said the same dandy whom Karina had snubbed, suddenly popping up beside me. The inexplicable Viscount Lukinsky, who fancied himself the center of the universe.

"Any attack on Max is an attack on the Fortress, Viscount," Alia immediately stepped in. "Watch your tongue."

"What, your old lady does all your talking for you? I suppose you'd shit yourself in fear if a real man ever talked to you?"

"Are you publicly declaring the Duke of Turb a woman?" Karina said loudly. The hall immediately turned their attention to our group. Fardi continued: "So Viscount Lukinsky doesn't consider Count Nikitin a real man, since he permits himself such remarks?”

The dandy turned pale and backed away, but then, to his misfortune, Viscount Kurpatsky approached us.

“Viscount Lukinsky, as a defender of the honor and dignity of the Duke of Turb, I challenge you to a duel! Today, in an hour, in the courtyard of the estate. Weapon or magic?”

“What?” the viscount mumbled. All his arrogance had vanished, revealing his true colors. A pale-faced, yellow-bellied little man.

“Do you choose weapons or magic?” repeated Kurpatsky.

“I have never insulted the Duke of Turb!” Lukinsky insisted. “Not even close!”

“So you also accuse me of lying?” Karina Fardi was not going to step down. “Me, Countess Fardi, daughter of the Duke of Odoevsky! This won’t be a duel, it will be an execution! You will fight me! I can defend my own honor and dignity from nasty, sniveling little freaks like Viscount Lukinsky! Weapons or magic, dead man?”

Such anger emanated from Fardi that the people around us involuntarily took a step back.

“He is mine, Countess,” Kurpatsky tried to defend his own, but Karina was not the girl who had accompanied him on his journey there. Now she spoke with the voice of a real countess—one who would not tolerate any transgressions.

“Do not interfere, Viscount!” Fardi’s voice was cold. “Otherwise, I will be forced to relinquish your right to duel this villain! No one accuses the Fardi family of lying!"

"He is yours, Countess." Viscount Kurpatsky stepped back, but remained nearby.

"Have you made your choice?" Karina returned to Lukinsky. "Weapon or magic?"

"Weapons." It was painful to watch. The dandy hunted around, trying to find an ounce of sympathy or support, but everyone diligently averted their eyes, not wanting to provoke the wrath of the offended countess.

"Let's go. I don't want to delay another minute. The insult inflicted upon me can only be washed away with blood."

"Alia, do we really need to watch this?" I asked as the whole crowd rushed after them. No one dared to stop the countess, who was burning with righteous anger. Even the Duke of Turb. He and his entire retinue also trailed behind the offended parties.

"Do you have another suggestion? Personally, I have no desire to see Karina slaughter this unfortunate soul. I have a rough idea of the discrepancy between their classes."

"I can't even imagine," I sighed. "She's right—it's not a duel, it's an execution. Viscount Lukinsky won't even make a scratch. I propose we run away from this celebration of life before another miserable wretch approaches us."

"Am I counted among the ranks of the miserable wretches as well, Dark Hunter Max?"

"Hunter of Darkness," I corrected the stranger as I turned around, then immediately fell to my knees. This was a man to whom I should pay my respects. For whatever anyone else might say, there was a possibility that he would soon be the new High Priest.

"Mother Alia, I did not expect to see you in our area. What brings such remarkable company as yourself to Hearth?"

"Hunting darkness, as usual," Alia grinned.

"Yes, so I've heard," the bishop nodded. "I even saw the documents that the sergeant of the guard issued for you. I hope this will help clear up the little misunderstanding that my brothers in the Light have made. Imagine, they forgot to indicate in their report that the four corpses brought to the town hall by the dark one two days ago belonged to Tarkatans. Couriers of darkness. An unforgivable oversight—someone must be punished."

"Is that why the Duke of Turb was so surprised by our papers?" Alia asked. "He was informed that the hunter of the darkness turned over four human corpses to the town hall?"

"Everyone makes mistakes," the Bishop said pointedly. "However, I didn't come up to you to tell you of the errors committed by my brothers in the Light. Viscount Lukinsky is a respectable inhabitant of our region, a true representative of the Light. Like any young man, he is sometimes short-tempered, hot-tempered, perhaps even irreverent, but does he deserve to be killed for it?"

"I also think that Countess Fardi should not execute this young man," Alia agreed easily. "But

I have no way to influence her decision. Rather, you should approach the Duke of Turb himself about this issue. I'm sure he can put an end to the duel."

"Count Nikitin will not interfere," the bishop sighed. "The only ones who can prevent this irrevocable act from happening are you, Karina Fardi's companions. Please, speak to the countess. Persuade her to accept an apology and a worthy compensation for the viscount's transgressions, and Bishop Zwat will be in your debt."

"We'll try, but we can't make any promises," Alia said and began to scope out what direction the crowd had gone.

"Let us go, I will accompany you," Bishop Zwat said and offered Alia his hand. My attendant accepted it and the two purple-robed clerics strode majestically toward the exit. I looked after them and in all seriousness thought about running away from the whole nasty situation. No one had asked me personally to negotiate with Karina. So I wasn't going to.

"Has Dark Max reconsidered?" sounded a voice. One of Bishop Zwat's assistants approached me, pointing toward the backs of the departing clerics. They clearly weren't going to let me escape.

The duel was being held in the courtyard of the estate. The guests formed a large circle, in the center of which stood Karina with a knife in her hands and the pale Viscount Lukinsky, a sword in his. Fardi did not begrudge her offender even such a small thing as a dignified death. To go out with a sword against a dagger was the height of dishonor. This was usually done only by those who were suicidal or overly confident. Karina was neither.

The Duke of Turb was personally overseeing the affair. He walked to the center of the circle and addressed the duelists:

"Have you agreed on your terms? No? In that case, Viscount Lukinsky, as the person who was called to fight, you have the right to choose the first condition."

"We fight to first blood!" the pathetic man blurted out immediately in an attempt to save his own life. But this little trick might not work with Karina. She wasn't looking to nick him across the cheek. She'd kill him with a single blow to the heart. For some reason, that's how I saw it happening.

"Accepted." The duke turned to Karina. "Countess Fardi, your terms?"

"I have no conditions, only a clarification— you can't spill your own blood," she answered angrily. Her mind was already in the battle, and all these sidebars only pissed her off more.

"Clarification accepted," said the duke. "In that case, the duel will be carried out in adherence with the standard rules of the Zarak Empire. And, in adherence to these rules, I want to address the assembled guests: does anyone wish to speak in defense of the participants?"

The crowd was silent. Defense did not imply a speech. Defense meant that whoever spoke up would be the first to meet the opponent, and if he lost, would step aside, allowing the original duelists to fight. And given Countess Fardi's mood, no one would be stepping aside. Karina would kill anyone who came between her and her opponent.

"Well, if there are no people willing to act as defenders, in that case, I announce..."

Suddenly, a loud cry filled the space:

"Viscount Lukinsky has a defender! I will stand up for him and fight Countess Fardi!"

The crowd parted, and a strapping young man of eighteen entered the circle. Karina grinned wickedly and drew her blade. She had no disdain for the new enemy. She knew his strength and capabilities, she understood full well that a difficult battle was ahead. Especially in such a magnificent dress, which she did not have time to change. Because even without magic, I was already not so inferior to the girl in strength.

Yes, 'twas I who stepped up to defend Viscount Lukinsky. I didn't see any other legal grounds for killing Fardi with impunity. All I had to do was make sure she didn't bleed before I could lodge my katars in her heart. And somehow prevent the Countess's sword from ending up in my body, of course. Because fighting without magic meant that I'd be forced to switch off the *Golden Dome of Protection.* Strength against strength. Steel against steel. Valevsky vs. Fardi. Everything I'd been dreaming of for the past month.

Chapter 13

"DUE TO THE FACT THAT a defender has stepped up, the parties have the right to set additional conditions," the Duke of Turb announced. "Countess Fardi, you are given the right to be the first to indicate an additional term that does not contradict the original ones."

"I have none." Karina didn't take her eyes off of me.

"Hunter of Darkness Max, do you have any terms?"

"No. I am satisfied with the previously discussed terms."

"In that case, may I remind you: you can only fight with the weapons that you took with you into the ring. The use of any magic is forbidden. Please affirm that you understand the terms and agree to comply!"

"Affirmed." I deactivated my protective dome

and pointedly removed both rings, placing them in my pocket. Let Bishop Zwat ponder where objects of such value came from and why he knew nothing about it. Maybe he would be tempted and send more dark ones to snatch them from me? That'd be just peachy.

"Affirmed," Karina said. The girl didn't remove anything, as she had already prepared for battle with the viscount. To any outside observer, it might seem that the gown she was wearing was not suitable for a duel, but not to me. I knew very well that Fardi could still put up a real fight, even in this magnificent garment.

"To first blood. Please comply with the terms and respect each other. Fight!"

Karina took a standard fighting stance, ready to defend herself. A month ago, she would have destroyed me without any strain. Now, after all that I had been through, she couldn't guarantee herself an easy victory. As such, Fardi finally started taking me seriously. She, like everyone else, was counting on a beautiful fight, with pirouettes, lunges, blocks and other attributes of noble swordsmanship. But I had other plans. Gustav, my old mentor, taught that the best opponent is a dead opponent. And while the enemy is busy with their flaunts and flourishes, your task is to strike a single blow. Because you don't get second chances.

I activated the katars and, extending my right hand forward, aimed the blade at the girl, as if beckoning her to attack. I raised the second blade close to my head, as if preparing to parry a devastating blow. Quite an effective battle pose on its own, but there was one more thing—as soon as Karina began to move, smoothly flowing to one side, I activated another one of my weapons.

The crossbow I never took off.

My hand tremored. Although the recoil was slight, there was a kickback. The steel bolt flew forward at such a speed that even Magister Hwang probably couldn't track it, let alone react to it. And what else can be said about the monstrously enhanced, but simple girl? At the last moment, Karina's eyes widened when she realized what I was doing. She even waved her sword to beat off the flying steel, but she was too slow. The steel bolt pierced through all her defenses without resistance and crashed into the forehead of the woman whose father destroyed my entire family.

One Fardi down.

The onlookers froze, not believing their eyes. There was a frightened cry from Alia, a muffled swearing from the Duke of Turb, even a joyfully hysterical exclamation from Viscount Lukinsky. But all this was overshadowed by the fact that the crossbow bolt, capable of penetrating steel chest armor from such a distance, crashed into Karina Fardi's forehead, but did not come out the other side, but rather splashed sparks and shrapnel around the area. My opponent staggered, retreated a couple of steps and grabbed her shoulder. Thick dark smoke came out from under the girl's fingers, and an unexpected message appeared before my eyes.

**You have learned the symbol "*Az*."
3 enhancements available.**

"Stop the duel!" The duke's voice filled the courtyard. "Countess Fardi was dealt a fatal blow, but a magical amulet stopped the damage, saving her life. Countess Fardi, please explain why you neglected to comply with the terms of the duel, which you yourself approved? Why use a protective amulet?"

"I'm not explaining anything," she hissed through her teeth. She removed her hand, revealing to everyone present a huge burn on her shoulder. The symbol there had managed to not only wound her hand, but also burn through her dress. The Duke stared at Karina for a while. Judging by his shifting expression, he was trying to cope with some overwhelming emotions. Finally, he spoke in a heavy voice, as if every word was a great struggle for him:

"Countess Fardi is declared the loser due to a gross violation of the dueling code. Countess Fardi, and through her the whole family of Fardi, is obliged to compensate for the reputational, moral and physical losses of Viscount Lukinsky in the amount of one thousand gold pieces. Information regarding this decision will be delivered to all interested parties of the empire."

A dumbfounded whisper went through the rows of spectators. For many families, a thousand gold was not just a significant amount, it was completely out of their reach. From what I remember, the annual budget of the entire Valevsky clan was one and a half thousand gold pieces a year. This included the salaries of staff, guards, the purchase of provisions from neighbors and castle maintenance. What a fool I was to ignore such tedious issues as accounting before. All I did was wave my spear and cuddle my twins. That's what I liked to do, and I spent all my free time doing it.

But the Duke of Turb didn't stop there. After waiting for the roar in the crowd to subside, he continued:

"Countess Fardi is considered an undesirable in the central region. She must leave my lands within twenty-four hours. I don't care how Countess Fardi gets to the region of her father's domain. She no longer has the right to roam freely on my lands. In the event that Countess Fardi needs to travel to the capital, she is obliged to notify me and obtain my permission. In no other case is she allowed to be in the central region. Do you have something to say about this?"

"The use of a crossbow is not provided for in the dueling code," the girl said, also struggling to contain her anger, directed, as I understood it, at me. "My opponent must be declared the loser!"

"Did you know that Hunter of Darkness Max had such a weapon?" the duke asked.

"I knew. But that doesn't change the essence of the point—you cannot use crossbows!" Karina shouted the last words, unable to restrain herself.

"The dueling code does not prohibit the use of ranged weapons. This must be stipulated in the terms that the parties agree to at the beginning of the duel. You knew that your opponent had a crossbow. However, you did not forbid him to use it. Max, Hunter of Darkness entered the ring with a crossbow. He didn't get it after the fight began. Your claims are baseless, Countess Fardi. Do you have anything else to say? No? In that case, by the right given to me by Emperor Devalon the Sixth, I affirm my decision! Let it be so! Viscount Kurpatsky, see to it that Countess Fardi leaves my lands within twenty-four hours."

Kurpatsky approached Karina and gestured for her to leave the estate, but the girl ignored him. All Fardi's attention was focused on me. She looked at me, I looked at her, and there was an empty space between us. Even the viscount stepped aside, the situation seemed so electrified.

"You killed me, you bastard!" Karina Fardi snarled. "You killed me!"

"Not all the way, unfortunately." Unlike her, my voice remained calm. "The next time I get a chance, I'll remember to take into account that you disregard all the rules and regulations adopted by your own society. I will act as is customary in mine. I will kill you, and then go back several times to make sure I finished the job. And it won't just be you. I'll do the same to your entire family."

"That was your chance, dead man! I swear that I will do everything in my power, I will use all the resources available to my family to ensure that you don't live to see the end of the month! I will destroy you, and the Fortress cannot protect you now. Do you hear, Mother Alia? I don't need your handouts! I don't need your training! I don't need the Fortress anymore! I'm leaving you! Stick your dark ones where they belong! Up the ass of your great High Priest! From now on, everything I want, I'm taking myself, everything that is my birth-given right! And you can't stop me! He will get his, or I'm not Countess Fardi. Just try to put a finger on me, Viscount! Your master gave me twenty-four hours, so I'm not going anywhere just yet."

Shooting me another look, Karina Fardi turned around and left the manor at a quick pace.

"This is a bit different from what I asked for, but this result is still more than satisfactory." Bishop Zwat and his retinue of faithful assistants magically appeared at my side, despite the huge seething crowd that had been there as the drama unfolded. "Viscount Lukinsky, please come here."

The emboldened dandy with a new taste for life approached us and immediately collapsed on his ass as the bishop smacked him with all his might right in the nose. Bishop Zwat dealt a mean right hook—the viscount's nose was a bloody pancake.

"Next time you decide to harass a representative of the Fortress, I will recognize you as a dark beast and burn you in the center of Hearth." The bishop's voice was calm, but by the way the buzzing crowd receded sharply from us, it became clear that something out of the ordinary was happening. "You owe Dark Max your life. Your worthless, stupid, vice-ridden life. Because of you, fool, the Fortress has just lost one of its strongest warriors in decades. And you will pay for it. You will definitely pay. Duke of Turb, I am of the opinion that Viscount Lukinsky is eager to gain glory for his family. I think three years on the Wall will turn this brainless bastard into a real citizen of the Zarak Empire, fit not just to piddle away his family fortune, but also to bear at least some responsibility for his life. What do you think?"

"I think that three years is not enough time to gain the wisdom and experience he lacks." The duke looked at the Viscount, sitting there, swallowing his own snot like a piece of shit. "As the duke of the central region, I believe that Viscount Lukinsky should serve for the glory of the empire the maximum allowable period for his class. Viscounts serve for five years, inspiring simple warriors and petty barons by their example. So our compatriot will not disgrace the glorious name of the central region, standing shoulder to shoulder with the doomed soldiers at the edge of the Wall."

The Duke turned to another of his assistants.

"Viscount Haben, in an hour I should have a paper to sign that Viscount Lukinsky is going to the Wall to defend the Zarak Empire from the encroaching darkness for a period of five years. After that, I ask you to see that this young man begin his service immediately. I give you four days to accompany him to the Wall and return with a report back. Move!"

"Have mercy, Your Radiance!" The man had forgotten all about his broken nose and tried to fall on his knees in front of the duke, but Count Nikitin's assistants jumped up to intervene. The Viscount was dragged away.

"I hope, Hunter of Darkness, that you understand what you are doing and what kind of enemies you have acquired. The Duke of Odoevsky is one of the most influential people in our empire. Becoming his enemy—his true enemy—is a rather dangerous idea."

"The Duke destroyed my family," I replied calmly. "On a completely fabricated accusation. I will not stop until every single member of the Fardi family has been wiped from the face of the planet. Today I took the first step toward my goal. It is a pity that the death of Countess Fardi turned out to be falsified. I'll be more careful next time."

"If you get a second chance, that is," the duke said and left the courtyard. Soon other guests followed him. The party was clearly a success, and everyone hurried home to talk about what had happened. It wasn't every day that a countess was expelled from the region.

"The duke will be waiting for you tomorrow at ten at this address," one of the duke's assistants handed Alia a piece of paper. "Security will let you through."

"Us? Or me?"

"You both. The Duke specifically indicated

that he required the company of the dark one. All the best."

Soon we were alone. The owners of the estate attended to the few guests who had not yet gone home, the servants ran around as if pursued by bees, putting the main halls in order, while the duke, the bishop and their retinues went on about their business. Alia sat down on one of the benches and sighed heavily. The girl seemed to be looking at me, but at the same time through me, off somewhere in the distance, her mind in the clouds.

"Was it worth it?" Alia suddenly asked.

"It was." I sat next to the girl. "And it was so worth it that I have a question for you. Do you know about that symbol?"

Alia was silent.

"My personal attendant, the Radiant Mother Alia, did you know about the existence of the *Az* symbol on Countess Karina Fardi's left shoulder?" I asked pointedly. I'm glad I was looking at her, as all she could do was give a small nod, unable to confess aloud.

"Did you know how *Az* can be imprinted on a body?"

Another small nod.

"The Evil Engineer? His work?"

This would be it for me. If my mentor was the one who gave her the symbol, then from this moment on, he was as dead to me as if he never existed. The reason such thoughts occurred to me was in the symbol's description:

Az. *The symbol of life. Applied to the body. Grants the wearer a one-time absolute protection against lethal damage. After use, the symbol burns out. Duration: indefinite. Requires chabre powder and 10 human souls to use.*

Ten people! Ten people lost their lives in order for Karina to survive today! Anyone who exchanges ten human lives for one is not fit to be called my mentor. I understood that the Fortress had no other options, but suddenly Alia shook her head:

"The Evil Engineer has nothing to do with the symbol. Karina Fardi received it from a special magister, who is invited by the Fortress once a year to renew the symbols of power of the highest hierarchs. It happened two weeks ago when you passed the eight-level rift. The High Priest made the sole decision to secure the would-be Sweeper from an accidental death. She almost died on the third level of the rift. She was nearly devoured by an armored krona. She almost fell at the hands of the princess. The former incident was the reason why the High Priest decided to take such action, you missed it because you were in the rift. The magister was invited, the Fortress allocated ten of the lowest-ranking doomed soldiers, and Karina Fardi was offered protection."

"So likely the same protection is held by the High Priest, ordinary bishops, the entire top echelon of the Fortress, probably on Father Nor and..." I looked demandingly at Alia.

"I can roll up my sleeve—there's nothing

there. Symbols are the essence of Skron," the girl replied. "They are contrary to church dogma. As for the others, I cannot say. I am not privy to this information."

"I don't need to know. If the symbol was given to Karina, then the others also have it. And after all this, will you continue to assure me that the Fortress, and the Church as a whole, is the very essence of goodness?" I asked, trying to keep the tremble out of my voice. I wanted to scream in anger. "Ten people, whoever they were, were killed, just like that! Ten, Alia, ten! Just think about that! Sure, doomed soldiers are no innocent lambs. Many of them deserve to die, but not like this! People don't agree to fight the darkness on the front lines so that they can be sent to slaughter like cattle, just to grant someone an extra life. How could the Light have anything to do with this? Let me guess, the master who paints the symbols comes to the Fortress from behind the Wall. Is it some high-ranking dark being who, instead of being killed, is being fed, cared for and cherished? They also get paid for a job well done. Tell me, am I wrong?"

"No, you're not wrong," Alia whispered, staring at a point between her feet.

"Then what's the point of the church, personal minister? What is the point of fighting the dark ones, if even the highest hierarchs of the Fortress cooperate with them? With those whom they swore to destroy in all their manifestations! Rifts are remaining open because they help the

Fortress maintain its financial position. Not only that, rifts are being generated in order to get even more profit in the future. Who cares about random civilian casualties? Resources are important. Us dark ones are not killed because we are useful. You know, I wouldn't be surprised if it turns out that the Wave under the academy was sanctioned by the very top level of the Fortress itself. Just to remind the empire how important the Fortress is, and that it's a force to be reckoned with. And must be shared with."

"I don't have answers to your questions, Max," Aliya continued to look at the point between her feet. "Everything that has happened to me in the past few weeks is radically different than anything I ever prepared for. I thought long and hard about your words. About the dark, about the rifts, about the black market. When it gets difficult, it is much easier to close your eyes, hide behind the usual dogmas and assume that all people adhere to them. But as soon as you open your eyes, the real world hits you in the stomach, knocking your spirit from you. I don't like everything that's going on with the Fortress. With the people that are in it. Everything is not as it should be. Everything is completely different. Sometimes I have the heretical thought that I don't even want to be a part of this church. It disgusts me. And the more time I spend with you, the more often these thoughts arise. One thing I know for sure is that as long as I'm by your side, we'll do what we have to do. Destroy the dark in all their manifestations. Both in the form of beasts and people. Because Skron has no place in our world. Whatever decision you make regarding how to proceed, I will stay by your side and support you in all things. I think it's time our trip to Hearth comes to an end. Tomorrow, after meeting with the Duke of Turb, you can go to the rift. Max, I ask you one thing—please don't descend below the eighth level. You're just not ready for it yet. Let's solve our problems as they come."

"Will you stay with me even if I refuse to cooperate with the Fortress? Refuse to be their obedient lap dog on a short leash?"

"You and I are bound together until the end of one of our lives. Even if you become the leader of the darkness, even if you replace Skron himself, I will stay by your side. Because that is my calling. This is my path."

* * *

(Office of the High Priest. Turb. The next morning)

"Father Urg, urgent news from Hearth! Countess Fardi has left the church!"

The winded messenger entered the High Priest's office without knocking. Such a right was granted only in cases where the news could not be delayed.

"We need details," Father Urg said and looked at the other participants in the meeting. Father Dvar and Father Gron. Father Urg's closest associates, with whom he began his journey in the church in the southwestern region. The messenger recounted the duel and its consequences, and also handed over the letters to Alia. When there were once again three people left in the office, Father Urg handed over her note to the others.

"Dark couriers," said Father Dvar thoughtfully. "That alone is enough to keep the Bishop of Zwat out of the upcoming elections. I think that Max completed his task and that my time has come. I need to visit the Bishop of Zwat with an unscheduled inspection. And to personally ensure that he does not bribe any of my brothers in the Light. I have faith in them, of course, but sometimes even a rock can crumble with the right approach."

"I'm more concerned about something else," Father Gron said. "Will Max figure out how Fardi survived?"

"I assume that Alia has already told him about *Az* and how it is applied," the High Priest replied in his unfailingly cool tones. "There's no need to rush things, Father Dvar. I believe that in a few days we will receive some interesting news regarding the Bishop of Zwat."

"You do understand that this will turn Max away from the Fortress, don't you?" Father Gron was clearly nervous. "If he really is who you want him to be, he will soon come for answers. And I have the feeling we won't like his line of questioning."

"I sincerely hope he does just that. And when

Max comes with questions, in my last moments I will rejoice, my brothers. Rejoice, because this world still has a chance to climb out of the steaming pile of shit into which we have plunged it."

"Alia will follow him," said Father Dvar. "The girl is too pious to put up with what is happening around her. We will lose a valuable source of information."

"What's important is that she stays with Max and provides him leverage. Even if this leverage no longer works in our favor. If Max is at least half of who I think he is, difficult times await the Fortress in the very near future. But I charge forward, knowing full well that I will lose everything, including my life. Because this is the only way we will be able to rectify all we have done in the name of the Light. Father Dvar, prepare an incriminating report on Bishop Zvat. I need to demonstrate to any other contenders to the throne the dangers of the path they tread."

Chapter 14

"HAVE A SEAT." The Duke of Turb indicated the chairs that had been set out for us. Count Nikitin's residence was located not far from the hotel. The duke did not have his own official estate in Hearth, so he had to turn to a few local counts. There were only two of them in Hearth: the Belovs and the Durnikovs. And in fact, Nikitin was staying with the latter. The spouses Ilya and Helena, relatively young persons, warmly welcomed the head of the region, providing him and his retinue with decent accommodations. The hospitable hosts even temporarily found other living arrangements so as not to disturb Count Nikitin with their presence.

"I'll say up front that there will be no consequences from my side for refusing my offer," the duke said. "However, before I get up and leave, I want you to hear me out. Can I count on you to do so?"

"Absolutely," said Alia, but I tried to take a stab at what this could all be about. What might make us stand up and walk out of the office of the head of the region? Us, representatives of the Fortress? Only something that might violate the laws and principles the Fortress holds dear.

"You want to close the rift without the consent of the Fortress?" I guessed, to which I received a kick from Alia and a gaze from the duke. "Is that why you came to Hearth? To personally assess the situation and determine how bad it is?"

Instead of answering, the duke gestured, and one of the assistants laid out a map of the central region across the table in front of us. A fairly large area just a few hours from the city was circled in red pencil. It was set apart from the main roads and settlements. Just a bare steppe that could and should be used to grow food.

"For five years now, this territory has been forbidden to any inhabitant of the central region," the duke explained. "Once there were several large villages there, but the dark creatures plundered them all. Several of the squads sent to cleanse the area vanished without a trace, as did the three groups of mercenary mages that I had to hire in order to deal with the creatures crawling out of the ground. Bishop Zwat claims that there is a ten-level rift in those places and the Fortress has no way to destroy it. In addition, behind the scenes, it was announced to me that the church has its own long-term plans for this rift, so I should not set my ambitions on it. The resources you have obtained were extracted from this rift. The creatures that crawl out of there have destroyed all life in a huge radius around it and have no plans of stopping. I've been receiving more and more reports of missing people in nearby areas. Where until quite recently, there were no dark ones. If things carry on like this and that red line continues to grow, it will soon reach Hearth. I cannot allow this. Bishop Zwat continues to assert that this rift is valuable to the Fortress and that it's absolutely impossible to close it now, and the people who vanish there are to blame for staying behind in places marked as a quarantine zone. The emperor does not deign to involve himself in such affairs as closing a rift, so they won't send me an army. The groups I've sent there haven't come back. I have lost a trusted friend. The situation, in my opinion, is extremely critical, however—and this is astounding to me—for some reason, no one wants to deal with it. That is why I came to Hearth before acting and seeking out specialists capable of coping with this scourge. I wanted to have a one-on-one talk with the bishop for the last time. The result of our conversation was predictable—the interests of the church in this regard have not changed. The rift is important. But then suddenly, someone unexpectedly appears in Hearth, someone who will appear before the emperor in a month. He who was able to close the rift under the magic academy. The whole empire is already talking, asking, 'Who is this Dark Max?' It's not every day that a former doomed soldier gets the opportunity to meet the emperor. I've made inquiries and am aware of the strange status the High Priest has given you. It seems like you have dealings with the Fortress, but are your own agent. Just what I need. I had to issue a note of protest to the Fortress in order to detain you in Hearth and evaluate your qualities. I understand that the church is in charge of the rifts and I have no right to send people there. But I don't want to lose territory after territory just because the church, for whatever reason, doesn't want to fulfill its obligations. I want to make you an offer. This rift threatens my region. If you destroy it without the consent of the Fortress, I will be in your debt. I cannot offer you any money or other material goods, all I can give you is my favor. It's worth a lot in the central region. What do you think?"

"Max?" Alia looked to me.

"There is no rift here," I frowned, once again consulting the map. "None whatsoever. Not a single-level and certainly not a ten-level. Zilch. I thought this would be about the rift under town hall, which we came to investigate. There are no other rifts in the vicinity of Hearth. This is verified information."

"There's a rift under the town hall?" the duke frowned, as if this was the first he'd heard of it.

"Yes," I nodded. "Today, right after this conversation, I was going to go down there to test its depth. But this hole in the ground is nowhere near the territory you have circled. Whatever is there, it's definitely not a rift. I understand that you have no reason to believe me, and there is nothing to back up my words. Consider it the knowledge of the dark ones. Like it or not, I really am one of them."

The duke leaned back in his chair and thought, occasionally glancing at his assistant. I was tempted to check him with *Analyze,* but I had too few mana elixirs left to mindlessly waste a third of the bar on random people. I needed a solution to this mana problem, but at the moment I had no idea how to approach it. Maybe Kimal Sarento could help me with this? I thought the chancellor at least owed me that.

"Let's say there really isn't a rift there, despite what Bishop Zwat says. As yesterday's events demonstrated, sometimes there are moments when even he cannot be trusted. I assume you already know that they wanted to accuse you of killing four citizens? But, if it's not a rift, then what is it? What could destroy several villages and armed groups? Including one of my strongest assistants?"

"The bishop spoke directly of these lands?" Alia asked. "And said that the rift was precisely there?"

"That is correct. Around three years ago, on the recommendation of the bishop, these lands were declared uninhabitable and placed under quarantine. The churchmen posted their patrols on the two roads that lead there. Here and here. The bishop's power in Hearth is practically limitless, so no one was going to argue with him.

And I've been occupied with other things for quite some time. I had enough problems."

"So it's not a rift," Alia began to think aloud. "At the same time, this is something that Bishop Zwat does not want to destroy, noting that it's important to the church. Have you spoken to the High Priest?"

"No, what's the point? Do you turn to the emperor when the river overflows and your lands are flooded? This is why they appoint dukes to be in charge of the territory. I know more than enough to understand the Fortress' stance on this issue."

"I see." Alia looked at me. "There really aren't many options. The first is that it could be a dark creature sent there from behind the Wall. Placed here for the purpose of...whatever it is. The second is that the bishop's secret residence is located there and all the missing people were simply unlucky enough to be in the wrong place at the wrong time. The third is that it's the bishop's military base."

"There is a fourth option." The events of recent days told me that all options should be considered, even the most unrealistic ones. "That it's not just a base, but a base where dark beasts are stationed. Like those Tarkatans I killed. A stronghold of darkness in the Zarak Empire, just a day's drive from the capital. And the base is constantly expanding, as the dark ones need more and more room."

"A dark base under the Fortress' patronage?"

The duke frowned. "That's a pretty serious accusation."

"It's not an accusation, it's a suggestion," Alia corrected. "We're just throwing out options, it could be anything, right? But there's definitely no rift. And you shouldn't be sending specialists. You need spies. People who can covertly enter the territory and scout things out."

"My assistant, who never returned from his mission, was a specialist in that very field," the duke admitted after a pause. "He had a special magic stone that allowed him to dissolve into the shadows, but apparently it wasn't enough. The dark ones sensed him."

"Then a force operation," Alia suggested. "The Fortress had no right to organize a base on your territory without agreement. Even if we omit the possibility that it is a base full of dark ones."

"So you refuse to help me?"

"I specialize in the dark ones. If there are humans there too, my strength will not be enough," I replied. "I need insurance. I will deal with the dark ones if someone else can take care of the people. If there are any, of course."

"Viscount Kurpatsky can accompany you," the duke suggested. "You won't find a better fighter in the entire central region. Unless, of course, you take the capital into account."

"Yes, the viscount would be an ideal companion," I agreed, remembering this seemingly unpretentious man's beefed-up stats. "However, we have not yet decided the most important issue.

What will I get for helping you? You suggest that we go against the Fortress. If there really is a stronghold of darkness, the church will not be very happy that we destroyed it. Along with everyone inside."

"I feel like I made myself clear," the duke began to simmer, but managed to keep it mostly under wraps. "I have no opportunity to reward you with any material benefit. I'm not going to budge on this point. All I can offer you is a personal favor."

"I don't need rewards, I need something else. You know, in four weeks the emperor will recognize me as a hero who saved the capital. With a high degree of probability, he will return my former name to me. I will again become Baron Valevsky, but such a lowly title will oblige me to take an oath of vassal to one of the dukes. I don't want anything to do with that."

"I understand your meaning completely, Hunter of Darkness," the duke nodded. "Are you prepared to spend three years on the Wall?"

"Better that than falling into the hands of the Duke of Odoevsky. If he really is such an influential person, it would be easy for him to arrange things in such a way so that I had no choice but to return to the southeastern region. A favor for a favor, Count Nikitin. And no one owes anyone anything."

"Apparently I missed something," Alia turned to me. "What's the Wall got to do with it?"

"All ten dukes will be required to attend the

meeting hosted by Emperor Devalon the Sixth. Darkness Hunter Max, as soon as he becomes Baron Valevsky, will kneel before me, pleading for mercy. He wants to become Viscount Valevsky. According to the code of laws on ranks and titles of the Zarak Empire, any change in the status of an aristocrat imposes an obligation on him to serve on the Wall. Even if this aristocrat has already served his duty earlier. Thus, if Baron Valevsky becomes Viscount Valevsky, thereby gaining the opportunity to serve the empire directly, without intermediaries in the form of dukes, he will have to spend three years on the Wall. I have the right to promote particularly distinguished families from barons to viscounts. Which would be more than appropriate at an event dedicated to the heroic deed of Maximilian Valevsky. The only question is what the Duke of Odoevsky will say to this, but I am ready to confront him. I need to resolve the issue of this territory and really get down to the bottom of this.”

“In that case, agreed. The rift under the town hall can wait until better times. Nothing will happen to it either tomorrow or in a couple of months. But the meeting with the emperor will take place quite soon, so I’ll visit this territory first. Let’s find out where those people are disappearing to. Is your proposal to send Viscount Kurpatsky with us still on the table?”

“I need trusted eyes and ears on this campaign,” the duke confirmed.

“There is still one thing left to decide, and

much depends on it," Alia said as soon as the main points were settled. "We were barely introduced a few days ago. I mean no offense, but we do not know at all what kind of person you are, Duke of Turb. My first impression is positive, but can you really trust your first impressions in such difficult times? I'm talking about how we will cement our agreements. Just a handshake, and Max goes off to risk his life so that in the future, you can go back on your words? Circumstances tend to change. Perhaps the Duke of Odoevsky will set a condition that no one recognizes Baron Valevsky regardless, or something else. The Fortress has taught me one thing—people, for the most part, are only true to their word as much as it serves them. When they want, they give, when they want, they take. You don't need to give me that look, you know I haven't the faintest thought of offending anyone. I'm worried about the future of my ward. About what will happen to him after his meeting with the emperor. Including the fulfillment of your current obligations."

"You clear the area first," the duke said in a dull voice. Alia's words proved not just offensive—if she were under the empire's domain, Count Nikitin would challenge her to a duel, despite the fact that she was a girl. The code did not forbid challenging persons of the opposite sex, except that they were allowed to call for those to fight in their honor. For both men or women.

"So we still just shake hands and hope that everyone fulfills their obligations?"

I really wanted to kick Alia under the table. It seems as if my personal attendant had taken a grave misstep. However, suddenly the duke smiled:

"The Fortress education leaves its mark, right? Every action must have a paper trail, otherwise you can never prove anything to anyone later?"

"It was the paper trail that saved Max's life," Aliya remarked calmly. "If he hadn't taken a slip at the entrance to the city indicating that he was bringing in dark beasts, and not just corpses, I think that at this moment my ward would be sitting in a damp dungeon awaiting Bishop Zwat's sentence. Because someone got it wrong. It happens."

"I cannot argue with that," said the duke. "When I went to meet you, I could barely hold back my anger. On the one hand, I needed you, on the other hand, I was informed that the dark one had killed four people. Later, however, the Hunter of Darkness added fuel to the fire by declaring the region incapable of fending off the darkness. There were a lot of things going on. But in general, you are right—putting it down on paper prevents anyone from going back on their word. Not me and not you. Even if the High Priest personally forbids you from visiting this area."

The duke made a gesture with his hand, and the assistant who had been standing in the office with us this whole time suddenly approached.

"I need two copies of an agreement drawn up

with all the terms just agreed in ten minutes."

"Yes, Your Radiance," the aide bowed and disappeared through the door.

"A game of chess while we wait for the documents?" The duke pointed to the blackboard on the table.

"With pleasure," Alia smiled. "I love chess. Max?"

"I know the rules, but I haven't really played," I admitted honestly. "My older brothers were the chess champions. I preferred swinging my spear around."

"I see," Alia sighed. "Another gap in your education that we will have to urgently address. Black or white?"

"As the host, I choose white. Let us see how good the Fortress' educational system really is..."

Alia had lost spectacularly even before the assistant brought back the two copies of the agreement. To be honest, I didn't understand what happened at all. Black's position seemed unshakable, but a few unexpected moves by White, a few, it seemed, thoughtless sacrifices of pieces, including the queen, and soon the black king had to concede. It was a shame to watch Alia lose. As soon as Count Nikitin went on active attack, she was thrown off, not expecting such agility. A few moves before the finale, when it became clear where everything was going, the girl's eyes were shining, but she did not allow herself such weakness as shedding a tear. Toppling her king, Alia found the strength to smile:

"Bravo, Count Nikitin. Among my peers, I was the best, I even beat many older brothers in the Light, but I have never lost so thoroughly as this. You are a strong player."

"You just lack practice," said the duke. "If you start training up your ward, you'll train yourself up too. A piece of advice: read the literature. The chess school has made significant strides over the past decades, but you still play by the old rules. Apparently, the Fortress does not want to accept the new, and for some reason insists on clinging to the obsolete, but tried and true."

"Are we still talking about chess?" Alia frowned.

"What else? Chess and nothing more. Here are the agreements. You will sign, as I understand it?"

The duke read the prepared contracts and put his signature on them. The assistant brought sealing wax, and he stamped the seal of the Duke of Turb next to his signature.

"So the question now is, how long will it take you to start the task? Viscount Kurpatsky will be ready in an hour."

"I can leave right now. My attendant is staying in the city." I looked at Alia. After thinking, she nodded, recognizing my right to leave for an indefinite period.

"We will provide you with transportation and provisions," the duke stood up, indicating that the conversation was over. "Hopefully, by the next time we meet, my lands will be free."

An hour later, I was riding out of Hearth in the company of the slender man who looked more like a teenager than a confidant of the duke and one of the most dangerous people in the central region, according to the duke's words and what *Analyze* had revealed. What really betrayed his age was his eyes. I have never seen such deep blue eyes in my life. They could easily compete with rift crystals in terms of purity of hue, however, as soon as they met your gaze, you had the immediate feeling that you were small and insignificant. Of course, the viscount was no Father Nor, but he moved confidently towards this goal. Unsmiling, silent, he showed with all outward appearances that my company was unpleasant to him, and that he had been forced to fulfill the duke's orders. Although perhaps he was just solemnly saying his goodbyes to life as he set off on a dangerous journey to an area inhabited by unknown beasts. I had already noticed in myself a relative disregard for danger. The *Golden Dome of Protection* was so firmly ingrained in my essence that I could not imagine any situation in which I would put it down. Even when I was spending some time with a girl from an elite brothel, the dome remained in place.

In fact, we rode like this for several hours, immersed in our own thoughts. First, the villages petered out. Then we were in farmland. At one point the vast fields stretched out on both sides towards the horizon across the untouched steppe, speckled with the rare scrubby forest.

"A large detachment passed through here most recently," Viscount Kurpatsky unexpectedly offered. "A carriage and a dozen riders on horseback."

Judging by the fact that my companion was looking at the road, he had learned this all from the tracks, but no matter how hard I examined them, I could not make out anything. Except that the road, unlike the lands, did not look abandoned. Trampled, smooth, it looked like an ordinary country road found everywhere throughout the empire.

"So you don't see anything at all?" Kurpatsky interpreted my confusion correctly. "What were you taught as a child? You're a baron's son, even if you are the youngest! Isn't tracking a mandatory part of the training program?"

"Spearwork, more spearwork, and quite a bit of swordwork," I replied. Being embarrassed because I didn't know how to do something was stupid. No, I couldn't read the tracks. But did that make me any worse than a viscount? I don't think so.

"And evidently, despite the fact that these lands are under quarantine, someone is actively using them," the viscount continued. "The churchmen's cordon is a few kilometers ahead."

"If you're proposing we go around through the fields so that no one sees us approaching, I'm all for it. I haven't the slightest desire to shoot the breeze with fanatics, and no one else would agree to be stationed in such a place. Right or left?"

"Right. There is a hilly area, we will not be visible from the road."

We slowed down significantly. We didn't want to lose horses due to a hole or pebble. But it didn't get us very far. As soon as we drove up to the first hill, which was supposed to hide us from the churchmen, my soul fell to my knees. Which was what usually happened during close contact with dark beasts.

"Stop!" I ordered and jumped off my horse.

"What's the matter?" Viscount Kurpatsky also dismounted.

"You don't feel anything?" I was surprised. "There's a dark beast nearby."

"Nothing," the viscount frowned. "You're certain?"

"Absolutely. I can't see the creature, so I can't tell what it is. A monster or something more sentient. I don't know what the range of my ability is on the surface. I've never used it outside of the rifts. But there is a dark one somewhere nearby, I am certain of it."

"I don't feel anything," Kurpatsky said, still a little incredulous.

"Even now?" I took the reins so that the horses would not rush away from fear and put up my mirror, appearing before the viscount in the form of a dark beast."

"Even now what?" the man asked, almost giving me a panic attack. Was my mirror not working? The horses snorted a little, but stayed put, the viscount himself did not even twitch, as if his defenses against darkness were even better than mine. That didn't happen. Did it?

"Do you have your block up against the darkness?" I asked just in case.

"Up? Are you saying there's a way to put it down? I learned how to block creatures at the academy and have been blocking ever since. Both there and on the Wall."

"Then I have a question. Do the rift creatures or those that climb over the Wall affect the animals in any way?"

"None whatsoever. The darkness only spreads its corruption to rational beings. I don't like having to tell you common truths. What kind of a hunter of darkness are you if you have no idea how the dark ones behave?"

"I hunt a very specific type of prey," I replied, feeling the creature approach. "Stay where you are."

With these words, I ran towards the monster, and as soon as I broke over the top of the small hill, I finally caught sight of it. It was dark. But this monster was nothing like a rift beast. Outwardly, it resembled a wolf, which, by some horrible whim, had grown until its hackles reached my neck and a huge number of spiky growths had broken out all over its body. It turned its dark gaze towards me and growled angrily, filling the space with its monstrous voice. Ordinary beasts couldn't scream like that.

"Get back!" shouted Viscount Kurpatsky. There was pure panic in his voice. "It's a khorib!"

The name alone didn't help me much. The khorib crouched down, bristled, and with a menacing growl began to move towards me. I started getting worried. It felt like for some reason the mirror wasn't really working, so now I was just an ordinary guy. But I wouldn't admit the obvious until the very end. Even as the creature lunged at me, trying to tear out my throat. Sparks flashed off of the *Golden Dome of Protection,* and both katars entered the creatures belly. Correction: should have entered. The monster's thick skin easily deflected my blades. It was thrown aside, but the nimble creature immediately oriented itself and began striking the dome with its clawed paw, methodically depriving me of my mana. But no matter how nimble the monster was, it could not dodge *Dark Spike.* The dark icicle crashed straight into the creature's forehead, causing it to recoil, and while it was shaking its head, I was already nearby, slamming the blade of my katar, now in the shape of a spike, into the creature's eye. No matter how thick its skin was, the eyes are always a weak point. This proved no exception. The steel easily penetrated all the way to the hilt. Pulling my hand away, I prepared to leap back, but this was no longer required. The khorib was dead. The spike had pierced the creature's brain. After making sure that there were no other dark ones in the area, I grabbed it by the leg and dragged it back to the viscount. The way he was looking at me, you'd think something incredible had happened.

"What?" I frowned as I looked around. Had

the monster slashed me and I didn't notice? I felt fine.

"You just killed a khorib," the viscount said in a strange tone.

"Well, yes. It's my job to destroy the darkness. But my tracking skills do leave something to be desired."

"You don't understand—you just finished off one of the Wall's most dangerous creatures!"

"An ordinary wolf, slightly oversized, really. What's so special about it?"

"Apart from the fact that it is almost impossible to penetrate his skin, nothing. Of the ten that it usually takes to bring a beast like that down, two or three come out of it alive, if the Light is merciful. If these creatures were not loners who destroy their competitors, the Wall would have fallen long ago. Even during a Wave, the khorib is always alone. Because the two khoribs start duking it out amongst themselves, even against Skron's own will. And you just finished off one of those creatures…I think I'm starting to believe that you really are a Hunter of Darkness."

"You know, Viscount, before we go any further, we have to make a short stop." I looked at the butchered khorib. "I need to know what other creatures are crawling up the Wall and how people are killing them. Because, as logic dictates, there won't be any monsters from the rifts here. Monsters have been brought here from beyond the Wall. And for some strange reason, they don't attack the clergy's post, which is only three hundred meters from us. It seems that we still have to visit the brothers in the Light. If they still hold the fort. We must find out what creatures of Skron do not devour churchmen."

Chapter 15

"STOP! YOU CAN'T COME any further! This is a restricted area!" The road across the steppe was blocked by the most ordinary barrier that you might encounter at the entrance to any settlement, but not in the middle of the barren plain. It would take nothing to turn to one side and bypass this obstacle, but we didn't do this, purposefully continuing our advance.

"Who restricted it and on what grounds? My name is Viscount Kurpatsky, confidante to the Duke of Turb, the master of all these lands. Introduce yourselves!"

"This is church territory, your duke has no power here," one of the clerics replied.

"Then maybe I might have some sway?" I smiled. "Max, Hunter of Darkness, former doomed soldier of the Fortress, and now ward of Mother Alia, an independent bishop of the church."

I had to give it to these two—they didn't even blink an eye, as if groups like ours passed through this area on a daily basis.

"This territory is under the jurisdiction of Bishop Zwat. If you need to pass, you must obtain his permission. The powers of Mother Alia do not apply in these lands."

I drank a mana potion, restoring my blue bar to its maximum level. There were only four bottles left, so I had to ration them carefully. But now was an instance where I simply had to use *Analyze* twice, so as to make sure I wasn't mistaken. This pair had nothing to do with the Light. The data *Analyze* gave me on each was a single line of rather upsetting text:

Common convert. Probability: 100%

"In that case, gentlemen, explain to us why...What are you doing?!"

The viscount's outburst was quite natural—a through hole appeared in the head of one of the men standing in the road.

"You move a muscle or start muttering your weird song and there'll be a bolt through your head too," I warned the second. "Viscount Kurpatsky, allow me to introduce a convert. A dark creature that sold its soul to Skron in exchange for additional benefits. This particular subject received superhuman strength at his disposal. For some reason, most creatures choose either strength or magic stones. As if nothing else in this world exists. Until we bind or otherwise restrain this body, Skron will allow it relative freedom. But as soon as the dark god realizes that his puppet has lost his freedom, he will immediately take control, burning out his mind and starting the dark melody. I hope you have a good block. If you pass out, I'll have to kill you."

"I know what converts are," Kurpatsky said with malice, never taking his eyes off the white-faced man. "Their song isn't so terrible—my amulet will protect me."

"So I'm not talking to you," I also did not take my eyes off the false churchman, pointedly reloading the crossbow. While he was trying to figure out what was going on, the steel bolt was already in its place and was ready to break into flight. "I'm telling this to our new acquaintance, who understands perfectly well what threatens him if we tie him up. Burning out the brain is not the most beneficial thing for the body. However, there is always a way to strike a deal."

"A deal?" asked Viscount Kurpatsky, dumbfounded.

"A deal?" the false churchman asked hopefully.

A deal," I confirmed. "I have no fundamental requirement to kill every convert I meet along the way. If I get the information, you can be free. Run, hide, get lost among the crowd. Because I won't kill you just now. But I will when we meet again, and sooner or later it will happen, your age will end. If you behave well, you'll end up like your partner. If you get sloppy, I'll capture you and make Skron burn your brains out. So, I would like to hear your answer, convert."

'What do you want to know?" stammered the churchman. This was clearly not the most mentally stalwart man, ready to sell his soul to Skron. Apparently, he had very few real supporters, since he had to settle for guys like this. Or did they work fine as puppets?

"What is held within these lands? Who has been here recently? Why are the creatures that roam the area not attacking you?"

"They don't attack because of the protective circle," the convert readily offered. "It was formed by one of the dark masters. Creatures run around the district, but they do not see us. Inside the lands is the residence of the dark ones. Bishop Zwat was passing by with his bodyguards. These lands are under his protection. I can go?"

"Where? What does 'residence' mean?"

"They don't let us in, so I don't know how to describe it more precisely. There is another cordon over there. Of the true dark ones. It was set up to keep people like us out. The main territory is fenced, patrols are constantly patrolling, dark creatures are running around. You don't want to go there."

"And how does one get there? What do you need to present to pass the cordon?"

"A special pass issued by Bishop Zwat. How many creatures are inside, I don't know—there are three roads, and the bishop mostly rides through ours. If any dark pass through, it's only once a week, not more. Basically all northern and southern ones use this route."

"Only two roads lead to this area," Kurpatsky corrected.

"Before, maybe. Now there are three. Why make a detour if you can immediately move straight toward the capital?"

"Besides the bishop and a few dark ones, does anyone else move in or out?" I continued my interrogation.

"Yes, once a month provisions are brought. Two dozen cows, three carts filled with all kinds of food, twenty or even thirty humans."

I distinctly heard Kurpatsky's teeth grit.

"When is the next caravan?"

"Not anytime soon. There was one only a couple of days ago. Huge, a hundred people rode through. Scrawny little buggers, of course, but the creatures there do not care who they eat."

"This is how the annual rally of the poor from all over the region turns from 'become the chosen one and get cured' to 'become the chosen one and give your soul to Skron.' If you think about it, the bishop is kind of like a housecleaner. He makes the area prim and tidy for others. Mostly myself, of course, but who cares? Viscount, do you have any more questions for our new friend? Or can we let him run free?"

"Let him go," Kurpatsky spat. "If you think you can get away with this, you are wrong. The duke will find out that you...Are you completely insane?!"

My partner could not finish his fiery speech. A neat hole from a crossbow bolt had appeared in the forehead of the convert who was starting to smile.

"Did you seriously think that I was going to let the dark creature roam the region and infect innocent citizens?" I said, surprised. "Who do you need to be to do something like this? These freaks have no place in this world, and I will destroy every last one of them that I can't drag to the bonfire."

"You promised him life! Who cares who he is, you made a promise! What you have done is vile. Not only unworthy of an aristocrat, even a common civilian!"

"First of all, how wonderful it is, then, that I am neither an aristocrat nor a common civilian. Secondly, I let him go. It was his own fault that he didn't manage to escape. Sluggishness is punished. Thirdly, I don't care about your opinion at all, to be honest. I'm doing my job. If someone thinks that there is no Light in what I do, that it contradicts all the norms and rules of secular society, all I can say is that's his problem. I'm not going to live up to anyone's expectations. Or do you have some special opinion about the way dark ones should be destroyed?"

"The wall discourages dissenting opinions," the viscount remarked calmly. "Nevertheless, I want to warn you: the duke will know about your deed. The ability to keep one's word is the basis for the existence of an empire."

"Do what you must," I answered, and looked up at where the road wound into the distance. "We have two options. First, we go through the fields, destroy the dark creatures that we come across, and hope for a miracle that we will not miss the residence. Whatever one may say, the lands allocated to this area are extensive. The second is that we don these robes and walk along the road, leading the horses beside us by their reins. As if they came out of the fields somewhere, so we're going to feed them to the monsters. I'll say right off the bat that I prefer the second option."

"It's more dangerous. No one knows how the dark ones manning the second cordon will react to our masquerade. They must know the converts on sight."

"Nobody said it would be easy. In fact, there is another option, a third. And it is no worse than the second. You mount your horse and return to Hearth to report to the duke about what happened. You can even take the dead creature with you as evidence. Why is this option good? Because the empire will know that lawlessness reigns in Hearth. If something happens to us, as with the previous groups, Bishop Zwat will go unpunished. It's good insurance."

"There is a guardpost in the neighboring village, stationed there in order to provide at least some protection. Your idea seems rational, but I'm not going to leave you. The duke gave me clear instructions: witness everything that happens here with my own eyes. Is there any way to tell that these two were converts?"

"If you kill them before Skron burns out their brains, then they are no different from ordinary people at all. For everyone else, these are just servants of the Light, who fell at the hands of the monstrous dark one. That is me."

"Understood. The khorib must come along— its skin is worth its weight in gold."

"Half and half?" I promptly suggested. "That would be fair."

"That would reduce the price by about fifty gold. Are you willing to part with half the amount?"

"Gold comes and goes," I remarked philosophically. "Good favor is more important."

"After what you did," the viscount nodded towards the murdered convert, "you can't even dream of good favor on my part. I'm not going to turn a blind eye to betrayal. Even for twenty-five gold pieces."

"Oh, whatever," I said, waving him off. "I made my offer, mull it over. Will you help me remove my vestments, or does your high position prevent you from doing physical labor?"

"You know, Hunter of Darkness, a tongue like that will give you trouble when you become a baron. You'll get dragged into all sorts of duels, and sooner or later there'll be someone you can't shoot down like Karina Fardi. If you haven't forgotten, I'm a viscount. And I would like to be addressed in accordance with my status. I turned a blind eye to the familiarity with which you allow yourself to communicate with me, but I will not deign to respond to your dismissive tone."

"I am well aware of your status and who you are. If we were in a city or any other place where the empire has power, I would behave as prescribed by the rules. However, we are in my territory, Viscount. Dark territory. In the rift, your title does not matter to me. Sorry for the harsh words, but despite all your enhancements, you will only be a burden to me during the battle with dark beasts. And I'll clarify that I only mean beasts. Not people. Here, you could give me a huge head start and you'd still pass me on the first level. As soon as we leave this place, you will become Viscount Kurpatsky, and I will be a person of uncertain status who must respect yours. But now you are completely and utterly in my...Freeze and don't move, no matter what!"

I don't even know how I managed to miss the small creatures that had appeared nearby. Four small balls soared serenely above the ground, moving towards us. A magical ousel, accompanied by its retinue. I put up my mirror and prepared to fight, but, having reached an invisible border, the balls stopped and, turning around, flew in the other direction. Judging by the viscount's whitened face, he knew perfectly well what this was. We weren't so easily dissuaded. But these are rift beasts, what were they doing on the surface, and during the heat of day? Or was the Wall also attacked by such monsters? The suppressive aura the beasts exuded, for example, was insignificant, almost imperceptible. But as soon as these little freaks found a human…"

I stepped out from behind the protective circle and immediately realized why I hadn't felt the monsters before: the circle of stones we were standing in somehow not only protected us from the dark ones, but also protected them from their harmful aura. The ousel paid me no mind, mistaking me for one of their own. Which greatly reassured me—the mirror worked perfectly. khoribs were just dull, stupid creatures that did not tolerate competition. I, in his eyes, was a competitor who should have been destroyed. But I couldn't leave these ousels alive. My katars had been set as spikes since the previous battle, so it wasn't too hard for me to catch up with the balls and activate the blade three times. I placed the magical ousel in a steel box that craftsmen made for me in Hearth. Of course, this was not a creature from the rift, capable of destroying half of the region with its aura alone, but, as they say, beggars can't be ch-ousels. I needed to test it just in case. Those unaccustomed to blocking the creatures' influence, as well as the converts hiding behind in human disguises should still react.

"You didn't say anything about ousels. Are they on the Wall?" I asked my partner.

"Very rarely. So rare that many shifts never even see them. Flying death. Monstrous creations of Skron, undeserving of life. Only crossbowmen and special archers are able to cope with this threat. What did you do with the magical creature? Why didn't you kill it?"

"This is a filtration cube," I showed the viscount a steel box and even let him hold it in my hands. "With it, I can weed out the converts. For a short period, I can harness the dark aura and transfer it to others."

"Those who didn't pass the test will die," the viscount frowned.

"No, they will fall down in fear and shake until I turn off the aura. No one will die, we tested it in the capital at a reception held by the Barons of Chescony. There, I was able to locate the convert and force him to reveal himself."

"That's right, I heard about that!" remembered Viscount Kurpatsky. "Baron Dahlem, if I'm remembering correctly, very clearly expressed his negative attitude towards the Fortress and the dark one who made half the guests of the event faint. Including him."

"What happened to the baron should be called a different word, something less cultured, but you described the overall picture correctly. Dahlem's assistant turned out to be a convert and I had to pursue him...and the rest is Fortress business. The object I used to reveal the convert is in your hands."

"And everyone can use it?"

"Not really. To do this, a person must have a special skill. I'll say right up front that it's trainable, but dark. Actually, the fact that I have this ability is precisely why they call me dark. Although I have nothing to do with Skron or his creatures. But who cares? Once you have been christened dark, you can never wash it off."

"Okay, but why did you capture another ousel? As I understand it, you already have one."

"They took it. After active public outrage broke out, and Baron Dahlem demanded my blood for insulting him, my curators seized the cube and declared the experiment to find converts a failure. Although in my book, this is one of the best ways to deal with hidden beasts. A blacksmith in Hearth made this box for me. I thought I'd find one in the rift, but I never imagined I'd see the little floating orbs calmly whizzing around the middle of the central region. Apparently, I'll be here for a while before I catch all the monsters. If they get out of hand, there will be a mountain of victims. Both among the peasant population and those who come to destroy this rubbish. Ready to get going? We must inform the duke about what is really happening in his lands."

The viscount nodded, and soon we were moving confidently away from the terrible area. Due to Kurpatsky's slim physique, the khorib fit on the horse with him. I carried my own luggage, including the dead converts. We removed their robes so that the peasants would not have questions about what frightful event caused the duke's confidante to kill two churchmen. For everyone else, this couple would look like bandits from the main road, who decided to profit from the forbidden territory. For everyone else, but not for the duke.

The way the commander of the guard looked

at us made us proud of our work. He was a man of a certain age who knew perfectly well what a khorib was and what it could do. When I pulled out the three punctured spheres, the poor fellow almost jumped aside, grabbing his sword. Ousels inspired fear, even dead ones. Viscount Kurpatsky wrote a note to the duke, sealed it and demanded that someone urgently deliver to his master the irrefutable evidence that Bishop Zwat was a traitor to the interests of the church. That is, until it turned out that the bishop was working with the top tier of the Fortress all alone. What I'd do if this was the case, I hadn't a clue. As an option, they might try to hush up the incident and finish off all the participants. For, whatever one may say, the Fortress was a bulwark of stability and confidence in the future. If it turned out that it was collaborating with the darkness, the stable foundation of world order may begin to crumble beneath our feet.

Soon, we once again returned to the first cordon. According to the viscount, no one had passed through here in our absence. Putting on the mantles, we led the horses into the interior of the territory. I sincerely hoped that our movement would interest some other dangerous creature, so that later we would not have to chase after them all through the district, but either the khorib ate them all, or the monsters had begun to fear us. No matter how hard I probed, I did not feel any negative sensations. Finally, a long and high fence appeared ahead, running almost to the horizon in both directions. The road led to the checkpoint, where even from a distance some movement could be seen. Soon, three creatures headed towards us. Judging by the fact that these creatures moved on four limbs, and rather briskly, if they were people, then they were somehow extremely modified.

"Werewolves," I heard my companion explain. "The basis of Skron's army. If we take into account only the sentient part, creatures with minds. These ones are fast, strong, dangerous, but extremely stupid. They may stop in the middle of a battle and start eating. Simply because it is in their nature to do so."

They were standing in front of us within a minute. The horses, not expecting such a crowd, began to nervously snort and twitch. Werewolves in some ways resembled people with overgrown fur and disfigured faces. In fact, they turned out to be essentially a mixture of a human and a dog. Hairy body, thin, overly elongated limbs and a wiry form. The only hint of intelligence was in their eyes. Those were all too human.

"Why did you leave your post?" one of them snapped. The speech was quite understandable, but one could tell immediately that it was not a human voice. It was too low, too drawn out, too unnatural.

"Two horses rode in from the steppe," my partner began first. "We took them for feeding."

"Horses from the steppe?" the werewolf scratched himself with his paw amusingly. When these creatures weren't running, they stood on their two hind legs, using their front legs as hands. With such tiny, fat and terribly ugly fingers. After today, these beasts were at the top of my list of most disgusting creatures.

"The khorib ate the riders but did not chase the horses," Kurpatsky continued to explain. "How many of you are at the checkpoint? Can we leave and you deliver the horses to the authorities? We must return."

"There are five of us," the creature replied, taking the reins. "We'll take the horses. Or we'll eat them. Haven't decided yet."

"Well, decide quickly. We have already reported that we are delivering two horses. If something happens to them, they will deal with you. We have completed our task."

"How did you report them? To whom?"

"I reported it to whoever needs to hear!" Kurpatsky answered sharply. The viscount generally behaved as if he had been dealing with such creatures all his life. He headed north.

"Alright, stop filling my head with all sorts of nonsense. They're your horses, aren't they? They are. So take them to the base yourself. As if we have nothing better to do but mess around with barn animals. No matter how delicious they may be."

"We cannot leave our post," Kurpatsky looked back, where the barrier was.

"If someone comes, we will greet him," the werewolf remarked carnivorously, but immediately became sad. "It's just that no one comes here anymore. What are you standing there for? Take your horses and follow me. You still have a few hours to trek to the base!"

The two remaining werewolves met us with loaded crossbows. However, seeing their comrades, they lowered their weapons and opened the gates.

"Do you have amulets for mindless animals?"

"How? They don't let us inside," I replied. "I was just about to ask for four of them."

"Take them." His stunted hands with stubby fingers poured four pebbles into my palm. "Put them around the horses necks. There will be no khoribs inside, but there will be a lot of broxies. Everyone, get lost! Grab a couple of runty humans on your way back. I'm hungry."

Perhaps he shouldn't have said that. Viscount Kurpatsky was suddenly a bolt of lightning and in a flash, he was next to each of the five werewolves in turn. They collapsed to the ground and scrabbled at their necks with their paws, trying to staunch the blood from the huge woulds that had appeared there. Kurpatsky had slit everyone's throats with such skill that I involuntarily clenched my stomach. I finally had first-hand evidence that Kurpatsky was not just dangerous on paper, but in practice. Moreover, he moved so quickly and carefully that not a drop of blood fell on his white mantle. Like the rift creatures, the blood of the dark surface creatures was also black.

"So the fact that I finished off the convert is

base villainy but the fact that you slaughtered five werewolves who were already letting us through the gate and weren't expecting an attack—that's just fine and dandy?" I couldn't resist commenting. Kurpatsky looked at me like the enemy of all mankind, but still replied:

"I didn't make foolish promises to them. My conscience is clear. What are you doing?"

"Pillaging, what else? We were given four amulets against dark creatures. This means that there are a sufficient number of them at the checkpoint, and leaving them..."

"Quick, drag the bodies into the booth! Someone's coming!"

Leading by example, the viscount grabbed two werewolves and, despite his willowy physique and the weight of the creatures, quickly ran to the small shed they had been using as a dwelling. I did not argue—Kurpatsky had already managed to prove his usefulness and adequacy. Like him, I would not be able to communicate with werewolves. Soon the creatures were safely hidden behind a flimsy door, and we, remaining in church robes, stood near the passage, playing the role of monitors.

The rider only showed up a full minute later. I wondered how the viscount could have even heard the sound of hooves from so far away. However, all these thoughts disappeared when I saw who it was.

"Take him alive. He must be alive," I said, calming my body's trembling with difficulty. It seemed that the High Priest's task would be completed without going into the rift. From the dark lands, Father Pithr, manager of city hall, galloped in our direction. And, judging by the satisfied look on his face, his trip to these lands had been a success. As if he'd gotten something he'd been dreaming of for a long time.

Chapter 16

"OPEN THE GATE!" commanded Father Pithr as he approached. He seemed to pay no mind to the fact that there were two churchmen standing there. It looked like he couldn't be distracted by anything now. The euphoria the man was exuding was palpable. He was in seventh heaven. *Analyze* gobbled up another thirty percent of my mana, and my heart sank when I saw that nasty little line in the cleric's stat sheet:

Convert. Probability: 100%

The disappointment I felt was so vivid, so deep, that when I looked at Viscount Kurpatsky, he immediately understood everything. Under no circumstances could we block Father Pithr.

"Amulet!" demanded Viscount Kurpatsky, changing his voice. The hood hid his face, so that the churchman could hardly recognize him. Especially in its current state.

"Choke on it!" Father Pithr said as he threw two stones to Kurpatsky, but they fell short and landed in the dirt. "Open the gate, already! I need to go to the city!"

"Orders come first," Kurpatsky continued. "The Bishop's orders are not to let anyone out without an inspection. Even himself. We were clearly ordered that if we don't want to die, we are obliged to inspect everyone, even if they start yelling that we have no right. The duke is now in Hearth, so nothing of value can be taken from the estate. You don't have any contraband, do you?"

"I have a right to it!" said Father Pithr and instinctively put his hand on his pocket. "The duke would never hassle a bishop!"

"Get down and show us what you're carrying!" I joined the conversation. My initial wave of emotion had passed, and I had to give it to the viscount—he once again proved his worth. If the convert couldn't be caught, we could try talking to him. Especially since he was clearly in some sort of excited fervor. "As a supreme convert, I have the right to search any creature."

"Supreme?" Father Pithr was taken aback. "At the gate?"

"This has been clearly explained to you—the duke is in Hearth. He came here to deal with the estate. He already appealed to the bishop, but once again came back empty handed. Times have changed. The duke is gaining strength and has begun to undermine anyone who might threaten his position. Including the bishop. I was personally stationed here by the dark master to ensure our security."

"So you are close to Magister Meram?" an expression of astonishment mixed with some kind of reverence broke across Father Pithr's face.

"Not just close," I answered, but immediately stopped short, pretending that I caught myself in time. "It doesn't matter. Orders first. Show what you're carrying."

So I had a new name: Magister Meram. Who could that be? Just another name in the highest echelons of darkness? Then why was there such reverence in the cleric's voice? He clearly knew who Meram was, and he was clearly practically awe inspiring. Take a chance? Why not, it couldn't get any worse. Waiting for Father Pithr to get off the horse, I, still hiding my face in a huge hood, asked:

"What symbol did the master gift you?"

"Gift?" he was surprised, and I very nearly aimed my crossbow at him. Was I wrong to think that there was a dark master who drew enchantments on the top members of the Fortress? But then Father Pithr continued: "Can you call something you had to pay for a 'gift?' And it wasn't cheap."

"Any one of the master's creations is a gift. Especially to those like us. You didn't answer. What did you get?"

"*Firth.* He restored *Firth.*"

"Show me where you got it? I need to check that no one may accidentally discover the symbol."

"Here?" the clergyman asked dumbfounded. "Shall we step into the booth?"

"Here," I insisted. "I don't have time to play games, going over here, going over there. Either show me or we're done here. You can return with the bishop. Let him take responsibility for letting you through."

Father Pithr grimaced in displeasure, turned around and lowered his pants, showing the symbol painted on his ass.

"Certainly no one there will notice," I nodded, barely hiding my displeasure. I saw a new symbol but it didn't appear on my list. Why not? Damn, how I missed the normal education system!

"For a year?" I nodded towards his behind.

"About that," the churchman sighed. "For a full year, the master asked for more than I, even with all my ambition, was able to give. And the bishop carefully monitors his goods. Only three months. But even that is enough to get some good use out of it. It's no joke—the ability to take anything with no consequences! Powders, alcohol—anything! The bishop has already signed off on my leave, and here you are detaining me!"

"So, you are still carrying contraband?" I nodded to his pocket, and again Father Pithr made a reflexive move to protect his property.

"It's a gift from the bishop, don't even give me that look! I won't give the oblivion crystals to anyone!"

The name meant nothing to me, but Viscount Kurpatsky twitched as having a full-body cramp. It was good that the clergyman didn't see. He seemed to see nothing at all, continuing to hover somewhere in the clouds.

"So this was a gift from the bishop? Then yes, we have no right to take it away. Is there anything else? Stones, amulets, elixirs?"

"Where?" Father Pithr was surprised. "I am a simple servant of the Light, admitted by the grace of the bishop to certain sacraments. I don't need stones."

"Do you know if anyone else is coming our way? I've been on my feet for three days already, I want to sleep, but how can you rest here when people are constantly running back and forth?"

"No, I don't believe so," the churchman said pensively. "Master Meram and his assistants are leaving tomorrow for the Wall by the northern road, you must know that yourself, you must be going with them. The mercenaries who are now resting on the estate aren't going anywhere, the bishop is also on leave, he will return only tomorrow, and there is no one else on the estate."

"What do you mean, what about security?" I asked.

"What occasion would they have to leave the estate?" Father Pithr gathered himself and focused on me. "Wait, why are you standing over here? You should stand on the outer perimeter, and the beastmen are usually monitoring things at this station."

"Because, Father Pithr, the beastmen are no more," I said as I threw off my hood. The churchman's face lit up in a moment of revelation, then scowled, unable to ascertain how I had gotten here, then contorted into a grimace of horror. Father Pithr's eyes rolled back, foam came out of his mouth, and the churchman raised his hands to the sky. Skron had taken control of his puppet, burning out at least some of his mind. Viscount Kurpatsky acted with lightning speed—the first mutters had barely left the convert's lips before his head was on the ground. His dark-filled eyes clearly indicated that he was a convert, and not just an unfortunate churchman who fell under the passionate hand of the Duke of Turb's confidante.

"What are symbols?" the man asked, as soon as we hid the newest body in the booth and kicked dirt over the traces of blood on the ground.

"External enhancements or curses, depending on how you look at them," I explained. I saw no point in hiding this information from the viscount. I didn't understand at all why the Fortress made so many things into terrible secrets? After all, if the aristocrats knew about the existence of, for example, the *Yat* symbol, the Fortress would have no end to customers who wanted to quickly apply reinforcement symbols to themselves. Which required nothing but mineral resources to produce. But for some reason, the church pretended not to know anything about it.

"What I'd rather know is, what are oblivion crystals? By the way you reacted, I'd wager you're familiar with them." I tossed a small pouch around in my hands, full of small green crystals the size of a coarse grain of salt, then threw it over to Kurpatsky.

"Do you know how much these cost on the black market?" asked the viscount, shaking the pouch appraisingly.

"Listen, enough already! Just like you get upset that I'm supposedly disrespecting your title—which I'm not, by the way, because I recognize your skills—I am infuriated by your eternal reproaches about how much gold I just lost or gave away. Gold is meaningless, especially for those who have been in the doomed legion for nearly a month. We were well paid, for one break you could earn from twenty to fifty gold per person. But what the hell would a doomed soldier do with this gold if he was devoured by a dark beast in the next rift? So they spend it left and right, without even thinking about its true value. Because we are used to living in the here and now."

"Oblivion crystals are a powerful drug. It gives people unprecedented pleasure, but consuming them has monstrous consequences. Someone who tries it once cannot stop. They need more and more. The body begins to dry out, rot from the inside. But that doesn't stop those who are addicted to it. Crystals are banned in all three empires, but somehow they're constantly cropping up on the black market. The churchman had clearly already taken a small dose. He didn't look normal."

"The dark ones are part of the delivery process," I said, recalling the package that the Tarkatans had given to the bishop. Directly into his hands, no intermediaries. "I believe that our esteemed bishop is directly involved in creating a channel to infect the Zarak Empire with this stuff. It remains to be seen whether it's just him or the entire Fortress is behind it. We need to go in and find out everything there. Do you think there are many people inside?"

"Mercenaries, a Magister and his assistants, a bishop with twenty soldiers and guards," the viscount began to list our opponents. "Plus a ton of broxies crawling around between the wall and the estate. And there are only two of us."

"Two is better than none," I said to the viscount, trying not to think about the fact that a dark master specializing in symbols was quite dangerous. Skron knows what he painted on his own body. He certainly had a lethal damage blocker, but what else? Would the Magister, accustomed to the estate being relatively safe, paint himself with various symbols? Only in one case—if we went into open battle. In which, as usual, we would heroically lose without even reaching the main building. Because the viscount was right—there were indeed only two of us.

We needed a plan.

"What plan?" the viscount asked. Apparently, I had spoken the last thought aloud.

"I suggest moving through the fields. We leave the robes and horses here, they have played their role. I protect us from the broxies, you deal with the mercenaries and guards. Preferably as quietly as possible."

"How many crossbow bolts do you have left?"

"Seventeen. Reload time is ten seconds, but twenty is optimal. It's in an awkward position."

"Do you have any other weapons besides katars? Magic?"

"I do. It looks like this," I directed my hand towards the house where we stored the werewolves and the convert and activated *Dark Spike.* The already flimsy building could not withstand such outrageous treatment and shattered into small fragments. Kurpatsky looked at me, demanding an explanation, but I just shrugged my shoulders:

"It just looks menacing and scary, in fact, it's quite harmless. I slammed it right into the khorib's forehead and it shook it off. Any relatively decent shield can block the explosion. So, entertainment for the poor."

"A controversial statement," the viscount turned his gaze to the ruined house. "I thought that we would deliver the body of Father Pithr to Hearth as proof of his cooperation with Skron."

"He's still here," I said, approaching the crumbling house. The destruction really wasn't as terrible as it looked from the outside. "But the question remains: how will we deliver it? Go back now, then return? I'm not interested in that—we need to move on. We can't let this Magister slip through our fingers. This dark one, who trades people's lives to draw sigils on the bodies of the privileged, must die."

"Trades lives?"

"Some symbols require human lives to inscribe. Didn't it seem strange to you the words of Father Pifra that he could not fully pay for the year of happiness, since the bishop carefully monitors his goods? As I understand it, he meant people. The same poor souls who make the annual pilgrimage to Hearth from all over the region. And, from the looks of it, not just the region. From all over the empire, people rush here in the hope of being cured, but some of them fall under the knife of a dark master. If they're lucky. Many lose their souls…"

There were no objections. Kurpatsky took one of the amulets so that the broxies would consider us one of their own, and we began cutting through the prairie. Soon the first dark creature appeared, causing me to break out in a fit of uncontrollable laughter. The terrible broxy looked like a huge bald hedgehog. I had once seen this happen—a hedgehog got sick with something and all his needles fell out. Gustav advised me to kill the animal so that it would not suffer, as it wouldn't survive the winter anyway. Broxies looked just the same: stubby little legs dragged along a massive body while an elongated muzzle with long teeth easily ground down both grass and shrubs. Only then did it strike me how well groomed the territory inside the wall was. I thought that servants had been running around for days, cutting every blade of grass, but it turned out to be a herd of dark beasts scuttling back and forth. They were not able to mow all the grass, so it appeared as if there was a beautiful, even grass carpet laid down around the estate. By the way, the broxies died spectacularly. Kurpatsky told where their weak points were, so I left a trail of dozens of the creatures behind me. At some point, we even had to stop—new ones hurried to the smell of fresh blood and, without even paying attention to us, immediately pounced on the bodies of their companions. An unpleasant chomping sound filled the space, and I had to return to finish off the crowd. The speed with which they dealt with the bodies was frightening. It looked like their mouths were small, but the jaws and teeth turned out to be so powerful that they easily tore through not only flesh, but bone.

We spent quite a while here—about half an hour. The result of this purge was almost a hundred dead bald creatures. The last ones I slaughtered I already felt a twinge of regret for. The fundamental purpose of broxies began to dawn on me: they were used as perfect little cleaners and landscapers. Grass, branches, small shrubs, trespassers—they could easily handle them all. If I ever got myself an estate as vast as this, I'd have to find myself some of these little bald freaks for both aesthetics and security. And I'd give the servants amulets so that they wouldn't get accidentally chomped.

"Look at the interesting trim job on this one," Kurpatsky said, pointing to the tree. We had reached a small forest. Again, everything here turned out to be well-groomed, trimmed, not a single twig was lying anywhere. I looked closely and grinned—each tree was equipped with the same amulet as the one that the viscount now had. Judging by the paved path, people passed through here from time to time. We even found a couple of benches! And hanging on them, as well as on the other trees, were amulets. It turns out that everything you didn't want the broxies to eat needed shielding.

"I have a plan," said Viscount Kurpatsky, sitting down on one of the benches. "Right up your alley. Have a seat."

"Up my alley?" I asked.

"Reeking of madness."

"Since when is madness up my alley?"

"So shooting a crossbow at the head of a duke's daughter is, in your opinion, perfectly sane? Or going one on one with a khorib? Or catching an ousel and putting it in a steel box? All this hints at a touch of madness that makes me sincerely concerned about your mental state."

"You don't know Karina," I muttered. "And what I'm going to do to her."

"What's wrong with Fardi?"

"This is not the kind of information that I am prepared to share with strangers," I smiled. "Especially for free."

"So you continue along your path of complete inconsistency," Kurpatsky frowned. "Who was just going on about the fact that gold meant nothing to him?"

"Firstly, not nothing, but rather a means of paying for necessary things. But I'm not talking about gold. Information, protection, safety—those are my priorities."

"I understand, we'll talk later," the viscount nodded. "Let's get back to my plan. You and I will stroll through the garden, periodically stopping near one or another beautiful tree, walking along the path and not touching anyone, even if someone comes towards us. If anyone asks who we are, we arrived today with the bishop and while he is meeting with Magister Meram, we are exploring the surroundings under the protection of our amulets. After all, spies that can penetrate this territory have no protection against broxies, and these, I tell you, are extremely unpleasant omnivorous creatures. We reach the estate, look around and then play it by ear."

"So the 'playing it by ear' part is where my touch of madness and I fit in?" I surmised

"From what I managed to learn about you, yes," Viscount Kurpatsky smiled sincerely for almost the first time since we met.

"Okay, let's go. I'm in for any type of madness where we act on the fly. I've never had a well-thought-out plan work properly."

And so we transformed into idly strolling mercenaries, pointing out various interesting sights to one another. And these became more and more frequent the farther we walked away from the fence. The broxies continued to scurry back and forth, but I vehemently ignored them, although my hands itched to finish off the creatures. There were too many of them. There, at the entrance, I had killed a hundred creatures, but here they were in the thousands! I even wondered how the dark ones had transported so many bald little freaks.

We only caught sight of the estate a couple of hours later. Accustomed to a certain asceticism in the appearance of the houses, I could not restrain myself from whistling with admiration. Stretching up before us was not not an ordinary estate, but a real palace! The high spires of the towers reached up to the sky, all kinds of stucco figures adorned the facade, huge glazed windows delighted and inspired. Everything sparkled, shone and looked incredibly luxe. And I wasn't the only one who was impressed. Viscount Kurpatsky walked in stunned silence, only periodically shaking his head as he noticed this or that detail. Around the palace was an enchanted circle of stones, beyond which the broxies could not stray, which made it possible to set up a neat garden, in which hundreds, if not thousands of different varieties of fragrant flowers were blooming.

"Lost?" A voice called out, making us turn around. Two creatures whose faces were hidden by bandages. I didn't even need to use *Analyze* to identify them as Tarkatans. Evidently, these toothy beasts were the palace guards.

"Just enjoying ourselves," I answered honestly. "We hadn't seen the estate from this side. It is beautiful."

"I agree. There's a wonderful view from here. And who are you?"

"We are the bishop's companions," the viscount replied. "Our lord is now in a meeting with Magister Meram, so the commander said that we could take a walk through the park. And that's what we're doing, enjoying the views."

"And, in my opinion, your flower garden could use a little work," I remarked. "Three different varieties of roses can't be placed next to lilies. They have a different kind of buds, different bloom yields."

"Are you a florist?" the guard asked.

"What don't you have time to study while idly waiting for your masters? There, see: if you look from here, you'll see what I mean. The absurdity of the color scheme will become apparent. But who am I explaining this to? Are you security? Of course, who else? You will defend this garden to the last."

"What are you seeing?" one of the Tarkatans couldn't help himself and came closer. "Where is this absurdity? Where am I looking?"

"Over there," I extended my right hand towards the other, and put my left hand on the back of the guard, as if directing his gaze. "See, between the oak and the maple?"

"What's there?" the guard looked closer. These were his last words. Two things happened at once: I released a steel bolt into the head of the second guard who had turned away to see what I saw there between the trees, and I activated a katar, piercing the heart of a creature that come closer to me. The guards collapsed as if knocked down, and I crouched behind them, hiding behind tall bushes. If we were being watched from the side of the manor, it must have looked to them like the three beings had suddenly decided to take a little nap.

"Sixteen bolts left," Kurpatsky counted for me. "Are these those Tarkatans that were pulling the wagon with resources from the rift?"

"Those are the ones." Without standing up, I managed to drag both bodies off the road into the bushes and even covered them with branches. Now the corpses wouldn't be seen, as long as no one was looking too carefully.

"There is an open door ahead. Shall we?"

"We shall." I got to my feet and looked around. There was no one nearby. No one running toward us, weapons raised, no one summoning fire or lightning to destroy us. The murder of two guards had gone unnoticed.

It hit me as soon as I entered the palace. A strange sensation, as if someone was trying to wriggle into my brain and burrow deep into it. But this "someone" did not succeed, thus the repeated attempts, over and over again. Kurpatsky followed me in and froze as if rooted to the spot. His eyes turned glassy and saliva flowed from his mouth. Without really understanding why, I crashed into the viscount and we both toppled back out of the door, rolling down the steps straight into the bushes. The unpleasant sensation disappeared.

Whoever had tried to get inside my head could only operate inside the manor.

"What... what was that?" Panic crept into the Viscount's voice. "It was like someone was trying to suck me out of my own mind...this...these thoughts...an obsession."

"You alright?"

"Seems like it now." The viscount blinked several times and rubbed his temples. "Now there's no one in my head. I had the feeling that someone had climbed in there and was trying to rifle through my mind with their grubby paws to figure out who I was and what I was doing here. It was madness. Things like that don't happen."

"They do," I turned my gaze to the palace. "It's called a mental attack. Possessed by beasts past the eighth level of the rift. One of these almost killed me, until I figured out how to deal with them. Don't ask, I can't teach you. To do this, you must become dark, and accept all the other shortcomings. Wait here, you can't go inside yet. I'll try to find this freak and finish him off. If a creature like that broke free, it could shut down the entire central region."

I did not elaborate on the fact that the exclusive ring allowed me to block the mental attack of an unknown creature. Imperials can be told about various mechanics and features of the dark ones, but I prefer to keep my abilities and possessions to myself.

When I re-entered the house, I felt those same grubby paws trying to penetrate into my consciousness. Now that I knew what to expect, I was able to identify the source. No, not the source—the direction from whence the influence came. The creature itself was somewhere on the upper floors. Nearby, I noticed a wide staircase and a bloodthirsty grin cracked across my face. Wait there, you bastard, I'm coming to you!

* * *

(Palace of the Duke of Odoevsky, Odoevsk, 3 days after Karina's expulsion from the central region)

"Karina, calm down. Your behavior is unworthy of a countess."

"I don't care! He must die!"

"Emotions, my daughter, are extremely counterproductive in this matter. You're wasting your energy."

"Dad, Max killed me. In cold blood, without warning, he went and finished me off, like some piece of low-born trash he found under a bridge somewhere and decided to have a little fun with. He didn't know about the symbol. Didn't know that I would survive. How am I supposed to not explode when, instead of handing him over to me so that I could tear him to pieces, the Duke of Turb expelled me from the central region? How do I get to the academy?"

"You repeat yourself, my beloved youngest daughter," the duke answered patiently. "As for the Duke of Turb, the question is already being decided. There is a council of heads of regions, where our coalition has an overwhelming majority. In about a month we will meet, and I will raise the issue of your reinstatement. It's too bad that you left the Fortress, the protective seal could be connected to their secret, which you had no right to speak about. Emotions, my daughter, are a dangerous and unacceptable thing. Especially when there are too many of them. I don't recognize my beloved girl. Where is the prudence of which I have always been so proud?"

"He killed me!" Karina stubbornly repeated, staring at a single point on the wall. "He deserves to die! The Fortress won't give him up to me. He's too valuable to them. But I need him, father! I want to personally rip his heart out and shove it down his throat! While he's still alive! And keep him alive for as long as possible. So that he suffers up to his last second of life!"

"I'm afraid it's not that simple, daughter mine. This kid is too valuable to be killed so flippantly. There are certain forces in the empire that want to take him for themselves. And I have no way to resist these forces. When the emperor proclaims him a hero, his former title will be returned to him, and I or another duke who is connected with this power will have to take him as a vassal to use for his own interests. Maximilian Valevsky has flown too high for us to snuff him out so easily."

"Dad," Karina walked up to her father and looked him straight in the eyes. "Can't we be the ones to do it? Can't we snuff him out?"

"We can't, my love. We should! First, he attempted to kill my daughter. This kind of insult to the Fardi name cannot be forgiven. Secondly, I do not like his ambition. Sooner or later, he will find our entire family. We must destroy him. I have a question for you, daughter mine. What are you willing to do to achieve your goal?"

"Everything," Karina said fervently. "Up to and including selling my soul to Skron himself, if I can finish off this scum with my own hands."

"I hope that this is not just bravado," the duke said cryptically. "Rest. It will take me some time to organize everything. The Fardi family will not rest until those who threaten it are destroyed."

Chapter 17

THE ATTEMPTS TO PENETRATE MY MIND continued non-stop, as if the creature that made them was not a living being, able to learn from its failures. Rather, I felt there was some kind of mechanism behind it, soulless and unemotional, doing its job with no concern for the result. It was told to protect the house by delving into everyone's mind, so it worked tirelessly to perform its task.

The interior decoration of the estate-palace was fully congruent with the outside. All the surfaces were plated with marble, there was Shurgan porcelain everywhere, beautiful sculptures, massive wooden furniture that inspired envy—I would gladly take some of these tables for myself. I'd find a place for them. The second floor was not much different from the first—all the same beauty and wealth, multiplied by the boundless desire to spend money. In my immodest opinion, it must have taken a sum nearing the empire's annual budget to create such a house. The order of magnitude of these figures were completely unknown to me, but my imagination suggested the comparison.

The first person I met was on the second floor. A servant, or someone dressed like one, was busy dusting. I was very tempted to cast *Analyze*, but I needed to save my mana. Considering that there was a brain-burning creature in the house, there were unlikely to be any outsiders, so I quite calmly opened the door and entered. The servant ignored my appearance and continued to work. I came closer and, feigning a guilty look, said:

"Can you tell me where they're doing the enhancements? Somehow I got myself all turned around. I was ordered to accompany the bishop, but apparently they thought I knew where to go. I've been here for half an hour now. I don't even seem to be able to find a way out."

The servant straightened up, and I finally saw the oddities in his appearance. This creature was not a man. Black, abyssal eyes stared back at me, and the deathly white skin was so transparent that it did not conceal a terrible network of bluish veins. It gave the impression that this creature was a drowned man who had climbed back out of the water, pulled on his Sunday best, and started cleaning the house. His appearance made everything inside me want to jump out. I had the instant desire to flee from this house and never come back again. Even the tables no longer looked so attractive after being wiped down by a hideous creature like that. Struggling with my desire to bolt, I nonetheless remained standing. I finally caved and cast *Analyze*. Skron damn the mana. Information was more important.

Inferior zombie. Dark undead. Total time in existence: 3 days. Remaining: 1 day.

I felt my jaw fall all the way to the basement, break through, and keep falling. To depths where no living soul has ever been. Undead...horror stories that mothers used to frighten their children, but that no one ever believed. It was much easier to believe in dark altered creatures than in the idea that a corpse could stand up and start walking. Even if only for three days.

Realizing that I was not going to do anything, the servant turned away and returned to his dusting. Only now did I notice that his movements were mechanical, unnatural. Realizing that this move could get me into real trouble, I drove the steel blade into the base of the servant's neck, interrupting his work. The body collapsed to the floor and stopped moving, but nonetheless, killing the undead wasn't part of my duties. Throwing it on its back in disgust, I began to unbutton its clothes, trying to find whatever was giving the body a second life. I found the source on its chest: a huge unknown symbol, similar to a spider but with six legs. And good thing that I started my search immediately, because a few seconds later, the symbol began to fade until it vanished entirely. The undead man had finally found peace.

Again, as was the case with Father Pithr, I did not receive any notification of new knowledge gained. I even opened the list of characters available to me to make sure of this. *Az, Worm, Yat.* Three sigils, only one of which was actually feasible to use. *Yat* and *Worm* I had received when I saw the drawn pictograms. *Az* I got when it activated and disappeared on Karina Fardi's shoulder. But now the symbol has also vanished. Why didn't I have time to capture it? Or was some other condition not met? Karina's was triggered and lost its power. It turns out that in order to receive a symbol, I had to witness how it works. I should have forced Father Pithr to devour all the green crystals, and as for the undead...I didn't even know, watch how the transformation from a dead state to an (in)animate one takes place? How annoying it was to figure everything out on my own!

After dragging the servant behind the curtain so as not to attract too much attention, I moved on. The source of the "radiation" was above the second floor, so I needed to find a ladder. The previous one led only to the second floor, leading me to a certain realization. It wasn't a palace, but some sort of rift, just flipped upside down so it climbed up into the sky. Even dark creatures could be found here. There were undead servants in every room I went through. I no longer bothered to kill them. Why, if they would die on their own tomorrow anyway? Let them work.

The third floor brought new surprises. As soon as I climbed the stairs, I found myself in a large corridor stretching straight ahead. There were doors on both sides of the corridor, located some distance from one other. Finally, a place that wasn't so lavishly luxurious that it made me ache with envy. This corridor was very similar to the hallway of a hotel, but even hallways at the *Red Goose* were more presentable than this one.

The brain-burning creature was on this floor—I felt it clearly. But that was as far as my intuition led. I had no idea which room it was in. Going up to the nearest door, I listened—no sounds reached my ear. Deciding that I should continue to act as if I were at home, I opened the doors and entered the room. Just to immediately run back out, nearly slamming the door behind me. After gathering myself, I went inside again, swallowing hard. The room was small, a little wider than the closet that Alia called her home in the Fortress. All the walls, except for the one with the door, were strewn with hooks, from which people were hanging. Already dead. The blood from the wounds rolled down special grooves to the center of the room, where there was a chute that delivered the life-giving fluid somewhere else. Judging by their faces and physique, they were the same poor and crippled people who had come to meet Bishop Zwat. The chosen ones who were carted away to be cured.

I counted eight in the first room, then started

opening door after door. Six more. Seven. Five. Eight again. The rooms were similar to one other, differing only in the number of dead people inside. Opening the last side door, I finished the count at one hundred and seventy-three. I have never seen so many bodies. And they looked terrible, in pain. They had been hung on the hooks while still alive. Someone must pay for this, and I knew exactly who it was.

Only one door left. The one at the end of the corridor.

I stepped inside, completely devoid of feeling. Any emotions I'd had left me while I was checking door after door. This room turned out to be much larger than the others, and the furnishings were decidedly better. Various cabinets, tables, flasks, mechanisms and alchemical equipment made the room very similar to the one where Kimal Sarento first tried to add stones to my magical field. Of course, there were differences, but it was more than enough of a first impression to go on—the transformation sacrament happened in this room. But it was not the surroundings that attracted my attention, but what was in the very center. The thing that made me clench my fists into white knuckles and distorted my face with hatred.

In the center of the room was a two-meter cube, consisting of only ribs and a central heart the size of my head held in the center by thin threads. Here, in the secret residence of the dark ones, on the third floor was a Riftmaster. And it was performing its primary duty: a broxy was manifesting beside it. The dark ones didn't need to send a huge army of beasts out here. One Master was enough. The broxy quickly gained density and, guided by the will of his master, rushed to the far wall, where there was an opening. The creature wriggled out without hesitation and disappeared, and a new projection appeared next to the Master. Somehow, the cubic monster knew that the number of broxies had decreased and hurried to restore the population.

The invisible hands probing into my mind were coming from the Riftmaster. On stiff legs, I came closer. Who would you need to be to drag a monster like this to the surface? Not even dark—soulless. I couldn't think of another word. Those behind this did not deserve to live. Even if they were in the highest echelons of the Fortress.

The blade pierced through the creature with ease and the building shook tangibly. The pressure on my brain was gone, and something else left with it. Apparently, the Riftmaster had not only restored the broxy population and guarded the palace, but also performed some other important functions. I looked around—the alchemical materials were interesting but I could not find the strength in myself to touch them. They looked dirty to me. Not physically—spiritually.

Shouts and quick footsteps were heard from the corridor. My spirits had sunk so low that I didn't even think about hiding. Stretching out my hand towards the door, I waited for it to open, and immediately activated *Dark Spike*. A mob of something was rushing towards me, which meant that it was definitely not Viscount Kurpatsky. I didn't care about anyone else.

The explosion was magnificent—the door was torn off its hinges and carried into the depths of the corridor. It seemed that I still underestimated my attacking ability. There was a heart-rending cry of pain, several bodies collapsed to the floor, and before any of them began to move, I was already there. Tarkatans. Toothy creatures that acted as ideal couriers and, as I now understood, security guards. Two creatures were lying motionless, one was still moving, but with one movement I stopped short any attempt to get up. The blood-curdling screams continued, but I couldn't see where they came from. The whole space was shrouded in darkness from my shot. The spike icon blinked again, and I held out my hand, roughly estimating from the sound where the screamer might be. A dark icicle flew forward, and the cry ended abruptly. There was an unpleasant crack, the noise of falling blocks, and stone chips hit my shield. When the darkness dissipated, I looked blankly beyond the demolished corridor. The walls and ceiling collapsed, completely blocking the passage. From the other side of the blockage, muffled screams could be heard—a new batch of guards had arrived, but I did not see the opportunity to reach them. If I could just...

Another spike crashed into the wall, sending out a wave of crackling, rumbling, and pain-filled screams. Someone else had been crushed. I did not wait to see the results. The position I had was perfectly suited for defense, but there was no way I was going to miss Dark Magister Meram.

Turning around, I ran to the hole through which the broxy had vanished. It was wide enough to accommodate my body without any issues, but I was perturbed by the slope of the descent. Once again looking back at the rubble-strewn corridor, I dove into the hole feet first, tucking in to make myself compact, like going down a slide. It gave me a tingle in my belly button.

I flew out of the pipe like a bolt from a crossbow. I rolled as I landed, then immediately jumped to my feet and prepared to attack any potential opponents, but there was no one nearby. Except maybe a couple of broxies running around. Here, near the "exhaust" pipe, the stone barrier protecting against the creatures went right up to the house. The broxy spawning process was perfectly automated—no one even had to touch the nasty little things.

The palace was full of screams, but everything outside remained relatively calm. Trying to stay behind the bushes, I slowly walked to the place where I had left Kurpatsky. From now on, we were sticking together.

"Your handiwork?" came the viscount's voice, and I nearly jumped with fright. Turning around, I saw my temporary partner and, without thinking twice, activated the *Healing Aura*. How the viscount remained on his feet is a miracle. His clothes were torn to tatters, his body was slashed apart, the face was one big bruise, the left hand hung limp, but even with all this, the viscount stood straight, held a saber blackened with dark blood in his right hand and, on the whole, looked generally quite satisfied with himself.

"So you're also a healer," he chuckled, gulping down the recovery potion I offered him. "I'm done with my part. Twelve Tarkatans. At one point I didn't think I'd be able to cut it. You're right—they really are fast and dangerous opponents."

"Can you move? Run? Fight?" I tried to assess the viscount's condition. "I stirred things up a little inside."

"A little? The house shook so hard the glass from the windows nearly fell out. This, by the way, is what saved me—two opponents were nailed with shrapnel."

"There are so many of them...I think I killed a couple, but it's just a drop in the ocean. But I managed to squash that creature that was putting pressure on our minds. Do you know what a Riftmaster is?"

Viscount Kurpatsky nodded.

"There was one of those bastards here. It was the thing making all the broxies, which then flew down this pipe...wait! Play things by ear...Does the duke have any plans for this place?"

"What plans could he have if he doesn't even know it exists?" Kurpatsky seemed to feel noticeably better. The blue tint had left his face, his left arm had started to move again, the cuts on his body were no longer visible. Yes, the viscount still did not look very good, but much better than a couple of minutes ago.

"It's a pity, of course, to lose such valuable items, but better them than us, right?" I looked around and, making sure that there were still no detachments of Tarkatans rushing at us, I ran to the protective perimeter of stones. They were carefully dug into the ground so that they would not interfere underfoot and someone would not accidentally knock them over, so I had to tinker a bit while I uprooted a few pebbles. The broxies who were running nearby at that moment, stopped abruptly and twitched their noses in a funny way. They were detecting a new scent.

Five stones were enough to let the first one through. Immediately there was a chomp as the broxy rushed to eat the flowers that grew in abundance around the palace. Kurpatsky looked on, smirking and not interfering. He obviously did not want the dark ones to blame him for the destruction of such a culturally important monument. The first broxy was joined by a second, a third, and soon a huge avalanche of ever-hungry creatures rushed into the narrow passage, burning with the desire to fill their belly as soon as possible and immediately empty themselves in order to continue the process of consumption. Broxies shat almost as much as they ate.

"I think we'd better get out of here," the viscount said as the first broxy reached the wall and chewed off a huge piece of stone without stopping. Then came a second, the third, and soon a whole crowd of bald freaks was methodically chewing through the wall, not caring that it would topple and crush them. The speed with which the broxies destroyed everything in sight inspired awe and fear. I wouldn't want to get caught on the road without my mirror or protective amulet.

"Are you ready to fight?" The viscount adjusted his grip on his saber and turned towards the crowd of people running in our direction. Yes, they were people—their faces were uncovered. Most likely, these were the mercenaries Father Pithr had warned about. They held weapons in their hands, on some of them I noticed crossbows, which they hastily cocked, as others ran towards us, arms outstretched, ready to use magic. But we were still out of range.

"You don't think we'll be able to fight off a mob like that?" I asked, stepping closer to Kurpatsky. He wanted to move away so that there was more room for maneuvering, but I delayed him sticking my hand up in the direction of the oncomers. The pictogram flashed and I sent *Dark Spike* flying. The golden dome hiding me and the viscount flared up and sparked as crossbow bolts flew at us.

"Get down low and don't stick your head up," I ordered, running towards my opponents. Despite my buffs, *Dark Spike's* range was significantly smaller than a crossbow shot.

There was an explosion ahead as the first spike hit its target. I sent the second one right after it and it nearly overtook the first! That's how eager I was. My shield flashed periodically, reflecting the enemy's attacks, my mana was running dry all too quickly, and there was some sort of Skron-awful nightmare all around me, but none of this mattered. There was a second explosion, followed by a third. I took care of the hesitant crossbowmen and ran further, activating my katars and splaying my arms out to the side. If the mercenaries had any sort of protection, I failed to notice it. Turning around, I sent the fourth *Dark Spike* at the mages and finally stopped.

None of the opponents remained standing. Some twitched, but Viscount Kurpatsky, who had been hiding somewhere, quickly finished them off. He lingered only near the mages—my spike didn't destroy them, only stunned them. The viscount's steel sword came in handy now, easily piercing through the amulets' protection. But even this was not enough. When trying to skewer another mage, the viscount stared in surprise at how his blade was deflected to one side. An amulet flashed on the chest of the unconscious opponent, and the man groaned, starting to come to his senses. The mage's eyes widened, he wanted to scream, but could not. With a second blow, Kurpatsky finished off the man with the lethal damage-blocking amulet. What a group of mercenaries the bishop had found himself!

"You know, Hunter of Darkness, I'm starting to wonder why you even needed my help? From what I can see, you're just as good with humans as you are with beasts.

"Have you seen my katars? They're too small for what you just did. Spending a crossbow bolt on every underdog is more than they're worth. I was furious when I couldn't break through the defenses that the creatures that caused the Wave under the academy had put up! If I'd had the equipment I have now, there would have been no Wave at all!"

"What's next?"

"Stable." I pointed to a small building nearby. "We need to let the animals go before the broxies eat them. And it gives some of the more cowardly churchmen a chance to escape."

It was my own fault that I said all of my plans failed. I jinxed it! As soon as we entered the building, it became clear that if this was once a stable, then only in the first days of its existence. Now the huge warehouse had been transformed into a corral for other livestock. Human. There were...a lot of people here. An inordinate number. The whole space turned out to be lined with cages with humans inside. Judging by how emaciated they were, no one was bothering to give them food. In many cells, the poor souls were already simply lying on the floor, unable to get to their feet.

In order to prevent the terrible stench that hit the nose from spreading to the palace, the same blocking stones were placed around the building. Only this time they weren't blocking broxies, but human odor."Who do you have to be to do something like this?" I whispered.

"Dark," Viscount Kurpatsky replied calmly, looking around. The people in one of the cages looked much better than the others, some even managed to stand on their feet. The viscount walked up to the cage and kicked the lock off. A nice trick when your body is enhanced and the locks aren't made of steel. The people in the cage stirred. Kurpatsky opened the door and pointed to a tank of water standing at the very entrance. Here, as I understood it, was where rare visitors to this pen washed their hands after touching the captives.

"Get some for yourself and then give some to the rest. If I find out someone was drinking more than their share or someone else went dry, I'll finish you off right here. My name is Viscount Kurpatsky, a confidant of the Duke of Turb. We've come here to get you out. But we need help."

"Viscount! Kurpatsky!" A muffled scream came from one of the cages. The viscount bolted over, knocked off the lock, and without a hint of disgust, entered the cage and carried out a skeleton of a man in his arms. The lack of food and water had taken its toll, but there was still a glint of sanity in his eyes.

"Viscount, I didn't expect to see you alive," Kurpatsky said, sitting the man up by the entrance. "Max, do you have an elixir?"

"I don't think one will be enough." I handed over the restoration elixir and assessed the scale of the tragedy. The people in cages needed not only water, but also urgent treatment. I activated

Healing Aura and walked back and forth several times, trying to help. "Viscount, we have a problem."

"What now?" frowned Kurpatsky, never leaving his friend's side.

"The broxies. They will soon reach this building. The stones at the entrance won't stop them. If we don't immediately surround the perimeter with amulets from the trees, the captives will be devoured."

"Skron's wounds," Kurpatsky swore. In fact, the longer we were together, the more humanity I saw in him. The viscount who brought me the false Karina would never have allowed himself such a weakness as swearing in front of strangers.

"I'll take care of the house, you deal with the amulets?" I suggested. "I think it's time we put an end to this. Save them."

Kurpatsky nodded and, once again checking that his order was being carried out, ran out of the warehouse. I also left, restoring my mana and preparing for the final battle. At that moment, one of the corners of the palace cracked sharply and collapsed, burying a dozen broxies underneath. But this did not stop the others, and a whole crowd of bald monsters rushed forward, itching to satisfy their eternal hunger. Running around the building, I went to the main gate. Just in time! Accompanied by guards, Bishop Zwat and some old man were running out of the building. A carriage was already at the door, and about half of the guards were on horseback.

"It's him!" The bishop's finger pointed in my direction. The wide-eyed churchman saw me first. "The dark doomer from the Fortress! The chained dog of the High Priest! Kill him! He must not leave the manor! Nobody must know what happens here!"

Chapter 18

THE GUARDS REACTED TO THE ORDER instantly, honing in on me for a coordinated attack. Crossbows, magic, darts, one particularly dextrous mercenary even threw a knife. But this was just the start of it—immediately after they attacked, the guards rushed at me, taking out their sabers as they went. If I was an outside observer, I would definitely admire the smoothness of their operations. But when it's aimed at you, there's not really much time for admiring. My shield flashed, parrying blows. There were so many sparks that for a moment they hid my opponents from me. I stretched out my hand, ready to attack, but I couldn't see anything. One of the disadvantages of my dome was unpleasant visual effects, which I couldn't get rid of. I didn't want to shoot at random—even a two-second rollback could feel like an infinity in the heat of battle. So I waited for close combat, and as soon as the next wave of sparks hit, I shot *Dark Spike* directly in front of me.

The blow was so powerful that even I was thrown back. My mana dropped by a quarter. *Dark Spike* at close range always gave me trouble. The space around me was filled with darkness, but the wind quickly carried it off to reveal twenty guards left standing. Twenty!

No one was lying on the ground, no one was writhing in agony, no one was moaning in pain. Some were shaking their heads, trying to drive the unpleasant ringing from their ears, some were clutching at their chests, wondering where their necklaces had gone, some continued to attack me, as if nothing had happened. Amulets! The mercenaries had death blocking amulets! Sparks began to appear again, but this time there were not as many of them as my opponents might have liked. Extending my hand towards the group that was still standing, shaking their heads, I once again activated *Dark Spike*.

Now that produced results. Such spectacular results that a smirk broke across my face. Of the bishop's twenty guards, only half remained on their feet after the second explosion. The one I'd shot, those whom I had stunned with the first blow, as well as some of those who were still searching for their missing amulets, went straight to Skron. I was pretty sure the Light wouldn't take these assholes.

Engaging my katars, I rushed towards the

remaining opponents. These men had no chance against the monster that the Fortress and level fifteen had transformed me into. They tried to resist, someone even ran at me, wanting to crush me and throw me to the ground, but the dome prevented such impudent treatment. The enemy was thrown five meters to one side where he lay there, motionless.

I only realized something was wrong when I heard the long cry, "We're off!" I struck again, drenching the blade of the katara with blood, and turned to see the bishop and the old man leaving the estate in the carriage. While I was busy with the guards, the main guys hadn't stuck around to find out who won, in a hurry to get out of this place as soon as possible. The four horses in the harness immediately picked up a decent speed, so there was no point in even trying to run after them. Stretching out my hand to shoot down the coachman with a crossbow bolt, I only sighed—I couldn't hit them from this distance, no matter how much I wanted to. My dome flared up again— five Tarkatans joined the guards. More creatures were running out of the continuously collapsing building, unwinding the bandages on their heads as they went. Their teeth were as good as weapons.

I snarled, releasing a spike in the direction of the fleeing churchmen, then ran at those who remained nearby. All my adversaries could do was to detain me and allow the bishop and the old man to escape. Of course, I could pursue them as I fought the others off, but in this case, a huge crowd of people, who were already on their last legs, would die. No matter how strong Viscount Kurpatsky may be, he alone couldn't do anything against this crowd.

Shot! Punch, blow. Kick, kick. Shot!

I acted like a perfect machine. Yes, I was down to my second-to-last mana vial—the damage I'd absorbed in the first few minutes was crazy. Unaccustomed to such treatment, my shield, although it coped, was spending an inexcusable amount of mana holding back my opponent's attacks. So I had to not only attack, but also spin like a snake in a frying pan, dodging especially strong enemy attacks. I was lucky that there were no mages among the guards and Tarkatans. Or, if they were there, they did not possess stones with combat abilities. If a dozen fireballs flew at me at once, my shield would, of course, deflect them and send them back, but it wouldn't be able to save me from the heat. I'd bake under the dome like a roast beef in an oven. And without any seasoning.

Once again turning to attack the opponents behind me, I froze when I saw a guard next to me with a saber blade sticking out of his mouth. The other end was held by Viscount Kurpatsky. Pulling out the blade and allowing the corpse to fall to the ground, Kurpatsky, with incredible calmness, began to walk between the opponents lying on the ground, piercing them all through to be sure. Even those who had a huge hole gaping in their chest from the *Dark Spike* received a poke.

"The bishop?" I looked hopefully at the

viscount.

"Escaped. And the magister. Catching up with a carriage drawn by four horses is beyond my abilities."

"Did you notice where they went? We must chase them down."

"To Hearth," Kurpatsky pointed with his hand to the road winding through the trees. "Those two went to Hearth. Max, we have no right to leave these people. They need urgent help. You are a healer. Your aura can save them."

"The bishop and magister are getting away!" I nearly cried out.

"Let them. But we have no right to become like the dark ones and leave people to their fate. The broxies aren't going anywhere, and once they're done with the palace, they'll start eating everything else. I've draped amulets around the building, but I'm not sure if that will keep the hungry creatures out. We need to save them. Bishop Zwat won't go anywhere—information about what he did will spread everywhere. Even if we don't manage to personally finish him off, there's a fire being stoked for this bastard. As for the magister...I know what he did. If I had the opportunity, I would personally tear out his throat, but we have people, Max. And they need help. I can't force you—you don't obey the duke. I can only ask. Being dark is not having special skills. It is a state of mind. It is the ability to leave others to the mercy of fate, caring only for your own interests. It is important to kill the bishop and the master, but it is much more important to save the unfortunate survivors of this whole nightmare. The choice is yours, I cannot make it for you."

I once again looked up at the road where the carriage had sped away, then back at the palace, which was already half destroyed, cursed obscenely and then went to the shed where the poor fellows had been kept. I'd have to spend the rest of my mana healing people. Convinced that I'd made the right decision, Viscount Kurpatsky mounted the other viscount on a horse and rushed off with him for help. I had a difficult task ahead of me—not just healing people, but also carrying water to them, further strengthening the perimeter against the broxies, and, when the building was at least two-thirds caved in, starting to cull the herd of little beasts. My mana was depleted completely—I didn't even have enough to use *Dark Spike*. I used my katars to handle the broxy, which had miraculously retained their mobility and independence after the Riftmaster that spawned them had been destroyed.

The huge procession arrived only a day later. The Duke of Turb personally came to see what the dark ones were doing on his territory, hiding behind the Fortress. Thirty steel-clad warriors patrolled around the area, searching for any broxies that I had not finished off, mages and healers began restoring people, and several carts with food disappeared within just a few minutes. Kurpatsky returned with the saved viscount, who became much more handsome after a good treatment, as well as Alia. Where was I without my personal attendant? I sat down under a tree and wearily closed my eyes, not responding to the girl's questions. All this time I had spent on my feet, and, despite all my valiant strength, I felt overwhelmed. Even the treatment and the recovery elixir that the duke's healers gave me did not help. I was practically a vegetable, not seeing or hearing anything at all. As Magister Smalog said, total exhaustion of the body. Or critical...I couldn't remember his exact words, but the meaning was clear.

"Max, you must see this," the stubborn Kurpatsky forced me to open my eyes. I really wanted to tell the viscount to go take a hike, but the current situation did not allow for this. No matter what else had happened, the empire had regained control of these lands, and that came with all the rules and etiquette of interactions between servants and aristocrats.

"He can't," Alia tried to protect me, but I stopped her.

"Of course, Your Radiance," I nodded, making no attempt to get up. Hearing such unexpected words from me, Kurpatsky grimaced.

"You know, that's not necessary. From your lips it sounds so fake that it's even disgusting. From now on, I grant you the right to call me Leonid. It's better to just write you off as a friend than to explain to everyone why I have to put up with your antics. Get up, ex-doomer! You really need to see this."

The viscount held out his hand to help me up. Grunting like some old grandfather, I got to my feet. Amazingly, they held my weight. They could even move my carcass from one point to another. Leonid Kurpatsky brought me to the ruined building. The broxies had gobbled up three floors, leaving behind mountains of a very peculiar feces that looked like dirty sand.

"Follow me." Kurpatsky began deftly jumping over the rubble, descending into the basement floors. The broxie's hadn't gotten there yet. Remembering with a swear all the elixir-pumped people I'd recently mowed down, I cautiously moved after him. I couldn't jump briskly over the stones, as Kurpatsky did. I made the descent and looked around. The basement was almost completely undamaged. Mages were already scurrying about here and there, pulling out some kind of flasks and apparati. Leonid led me past the cages where the bodies of the victims hung, and stopped at a massive wooden door plated with thick sheets of metal.

"The Duke has ordered that no one be allowed in there until you have a look," the viscount said and stepped aside. The lock on the door had already been broken, so all I had to do was remove the jam and enter the small broom closet. Maybe more of a walk-in. The room was one large rack containing hundreds of different vials, amulets, powders and other alchemical muck. Assuming that I wasn't brought there just for fun, I carefully examined the contents. My attention was immediately drawn to a huge open box full of small crystals, similar to salt, but green. Oblivion crystals, a thing forbidden in the empire. I continued my inspection, and my eyes rested on a small magazine that looked very much like a barn book. Opening it, I gulped—from the very first page I was looking at a map of the area with a habitat of dark creatures lined with different colors. There were even explanations and descriptions of where the creature was located and how much food it needed weekly so that it wouldn't run away in search of food. Scrolling through, I saw the schedule—the local bookkeepers had carefully monitored and documented their nutrition. The khorib I had killed covered a significant part of the territory, but there were two of them. The one in the east, which was already dead, the other in the west. Where there were deserted forests and small mountains.

"That's right," Kurpatsky stood next to me. "You have a little job to do. Our guys can handle the broxies. But the ousels in the north and khorib in the west are too tough for us. We'd kill them, there is no doubt about it, but how many people would we lose?"

"The Hunter of Darkness doesn't work like that," Alia said, reminding us that she was here too. "This has already exceeded the scope of the agreements he made with the duke. What is the central region ready to offer for the destruction of the dark ones?"

"While I was in Hearth, there were

knowledgeable people whispering that Max's subjects were looking after an estate in Turb. The initial payment was even made, but the seller is awaiting the duke's decision. You can't just find and purchase an estate in the capital. Everything requires approval. Don't frown—you'll get approval anyway. I'm referring to a different issue. This is a completely empty estate. There is no furniture, no kitchen, even the building itself needs a thorough renovation. The only thing this place is famous for is its vast lands. This estate is one of the twenty largest in Turb. The duke offers a trade. Max destroys the khorib, preferably today, while it still hasn't caused any trouble, the region provides a complete restoration of the estate, including furniture, within a month. The furnishings won't compare to here, but they won't be the cheapest stuff on the market either. Something suiting a future viscount. Yes, I know about the arrangement with the duke. Don't forget, I'm his confidant. Will this payment be sufficient, voice of the Fortress?"

"It will," Alia agreed after I nodded. However, that wasn't the end of the matter for me. I pointed to a small inkpot.

"If I understand correctly, this is chabre powder. I want it."

"Why?" The question came instantaneously from both Leonid and Alia.

"Symbols are all different. Some of them do not require human sacrifice and are quite useful. You never know when you'll need paint to make a symbol. There's not much of it here, only enough for three or four applications. And yes, Leonid, I know how to inscribe symbols."

"This is not the kind of information we should be sharing with third parties," Alia said, barely stopping herself from covering my mouth with her hand. "Before making any statements, everything must be carefully discussed and agreed upon."

"Discussed with whom?" I chuckled. "Ourselves? Or the Fortress? I won't have anything else to do with it. Alia, you saw with your own eyes what is going on here. Saw the dark creatures, prisoners, the bodies of Tarkatans that the broxies hadn't eaten yet. I have a lot of witnesses, including the viscount, that Bishop Zwat was in charge here. And that Magister Meram was here too. And I really want to pose the question to the High Priest: is he not the dark one who inflicted the symbol on Karina Fardi?"

"The countess had a symbol?" Leonid asked.

"Max, I understand, you're tired, your emotions are talking right now, but you don't need to flog a fever. You can't blame Father Urg just because one of his bishops turned out to be so rotten that he set up a dark beast amusement park out here. You can't throw information around like that. Later, when your emotions subside, you will regret your indiscretion. When they told me what was happening here, I sent a dispatch to the Fortress. I think that already tomorrow, two days at most, Father Dvar will come here with his inquisition. Maybe even Father Urg himself. There is a process that must not be neglected. We need to give the Fortress time to deal with everything the bishop has done here. Only then will we be able to consider what information should be conveyed to the imperials, and what is better to keep to ourselves. Especially when this information directly concerns you directly."

Some of what Alia said was nonsense, of course, especially about the Fortress, but there was a grain of truth in her words. Why had I opened up to Leonid Kurpatsky? What difference did it make to him why I needed the chabre?

"I'm taking this," I grabbed the inkpot without any further issue, as well as five elixirs each of mana and recovery, which went into special compartments on my belt. "And these. Viscount, do you still need me? Or can I go hunt beasts? My attendant will sign all the necessary papers regarding our new arrangement."

"No one is stopping you. The only thing I'd like to mention is that in five days the duke wishes to make a public statement regarding what has happened here. We would like you to attend the event. Mother Alia?"

"I have no objections. I believe that in five days we will have reached a consensus, taking into account the opinions of all interested parties."

"In that case, Max, have a look at these vials as well. Strength Elixirs. Strength, agility, speed, and so on, vital skills for anyone."

"I have already been enhanced within the past six months," I answered.

"You don't understand—twelve bottles, ranging from five hundred to ten thousand gold apiece. The duke will give you an official paper, where he will indicate that the elixirs were transferred to you by winner's rights, that you did not steal them anywhere, did not forge them. What you do with them is up to you. If you want, you can stretch them out over six years and use them yourself. Or you can give them to your people. Or sell them. And at an exorbitant price. The elixirs will be officially registered. This is your additional reward for helping save people. Even though we lost the bishop and the magister, you still did an astounding amount of work."

"Did we really lose them for sure?"

"The duke ordered all checkpoints to be closed, each and every one to be carefully examined, and he sent a note of protest to the Fortress, an informational letter to the emperor. Yes, Mother Alia, we too have been busy, and moving in all directions The bishop cannot escape. As for Dark Magister Meram...I can't say anything about that. We are afraid that we have lost him. Let's see what the High Priest says."

"I'll make sure the papers are in order," Alia said, and hastily hid the twelve vials in her bag. That was the right move—they were useless to me now and they'd be safer with her.

I wanted to take the map I'd found in the book with me on my hunt, but there was no need. When I opened my map, it had miraculously refreshed the data—the territorial boundaries of the khoribs and ousels were highlighted. Moreover, the zone I had already cleansed of creatures was marked in gray. No point going there. I chose a horse for myself and once again assessed the scale of the insanity that was unfolding. People were scurrying around like ants. The captives were being pulled from their cells, and laid on the grass, healers and mages walked between them and performed miracles of self-sacrifice. Some mages were already staggering, one was completely unconscious under a tree, but this did not stop anyone. A separate group of interrogators was combing the remains of the building, pulling out everything that had survived. Mostly from the basement, where the bruxies hadn't reached. Incidentally, I hadn't come across a live one in a good long while. The duke's personal guard did a fine job of dealing with them. Several more food carts rode up, and the former captives were slowly carted back to the nearest villages. It was quite a system, but one that I was radically opposed to participating in, even despite my healing aura. The only thing I regret was that such a beautiful house had to be demolished. I would have gotten good use out of it.

It took two days to complete my part of the bargain. The ousels showed up pretty quickly—they were hovering near their feeding location, waiting for their next meal. But that trick didn't work on the khorib. The freedom-loving creature was somewhere prowling around its vast domain. It had been ignoring the feeder—the previous bodies remained intact. Of course, I had a glimpse of the hope that the khorib died of old age, but I no longer believed in such fairy tales.

As a result, I only found the creature the next day. I was in such a dispirited mood that the battle against the dangerous beast felt terribly tedious. I put up my mirror, the monster could not resist finishing off a competitor, everything else was a matter of technique—a blow to the dome, *Dark Spike* and the final prick in the eye.

Like last time, the spike was unable to break through the creature's defenses. Despite the fact that even amulets did not help the dark ones in the estate. I have no idea what kind of people served on the Wall. Not those who go there only to fulfill their duties on paper and sit behind a wall somewhere, waiting to return home as soon as possible.

No, I meant the ones who served on the Wall for ten or even twenty years. Veterans who have survived more than one Wave. Capable of destroying a whole horde of dark creatures with just a glance. I was sure they'd eat packs of khoribs for breakfast!

Throwing the carcass of the dark beast on the horse's hindquarters, I slowly made my way back to Hearth. By my calculations, I would reach the city just in time for the churchmen to arrive and the duke to arrange the public event where he announces Bishop Zwat's betrayal.

But my journey back was not as triumphant as I'd hoped. About a day later, when only one day's march remained to the city, a detachment of horsemen caught up with me. Headed, unsurprisingly, by Viscount Kurpatsky. But the viscount looked so alarmed that I even tensed when I saw him. Even battle-ready. Who knew what had happened in the two days that I was gone? Had I suddenly been declared a dangerous dark one and sentenced to death? It never ends! However, the situation turned out to be much more complicated:

"Praise the Light, we found you! Max, leave the khorib behind and grab a fresh horse! You are urgently needed in Hearth! We know where Bishop Zwat and Magister Meram have gone! They hid in the rift, and today the beasts started climbing out!"

"Rift creatures hate the sun!" I frowned.

"That's the thing! They're burning, melting, but they're still crawling all over the place! There are thousands of them! The people are fleeing in panic from the city, the duke and the High Priest with their retinues are locked in the palace, Mother Alia with them. May the Light keep their souls. The monsters are dying by the hundreds, but this doesn't stop them—they will destroy the city. I don't even want to think about what will happen to Hearth tonight, when the sun stops dealing them damage! A call has already been sent out to all our neighbors, troops are being deployed, but they'll only show up in a few days, after nothing remains of Hearth! Mother Alia sent me to find you, Max. She said if anyone could help us, it would be you. Hurry, if we're quick, we'll make it to the city just before sunset!"

Monsters pouring out of the rift in droves? A chill went down my spine when I realized what must have happened. Had the dark madmen summoned another Wave?

Chapter 19

"ARE YOU SURE those two hid in the rift?" I shouted, galloping beside the viscount. The horses were galloping furiously. In order to have a normal conversation, we had to yell with all our might.

"Nobody has seen them!" came the shocking reply. "But there is simply no other place they could be! Creatures don't flee from the rifts by themselves!"

"Are you sure they're coming from the rift?" I asked. "Kronas? Or something different?"

"Kronas! While it was still just beginning, several guardsmen infiltrated the town hall and came out alive! A crack in the basement! What are the chances?"

"At this time of day," I muttered, still not believing that the dark creatures of the underworld were so mad that they were ready to crawl out into the sunlight. Even if someone forced them out.

"The city!" shouted Kurpatsky, pointing to the rising clouds of smoke. We still had quite a long way to go, but it was already clear that something unprecedented was happening. The city was on fire, which was strange—the creatures didn't like fire any more than they liked sun. Driving the horses harder, we reached the first houses. We had to move through the fields—the roads were filled with distraught civilians, blinded by fear as they fled from the monsters. The creatures themselves were not far behind. Exuding acrid smoke, they jumped through the streets, destroying the townspeople with frenzied haste. Toothy mouths easily tore through bodies, and the space was filled with a terrible crunch of grinding bones. The monsters ate their meal on the spot, restoring their sunburnt bodies. And, as I could see, very soon there would be nothing there to burn—the bottom tip of the sun was already touching the horizon, giving rise to long shadows.

"Don't stop! We need to get the duke and Alia out!" I shouted and activated *Healing Aura*. It had no enhancements other than cost reduction, but the sixth level stone really proved its worth. A thirty-meter circle of light covered the space, turning dark creatures into corpses in a matter of moments. I didn't even have to linger to hold it on them longer—the kronas crawling out of the rift proved to be incredibly weak.

For me. But not for the rest of the city.

The Duke of Turb, his guards, Alia and even

the High Priest himself had barricaded themselves in the Durnikovs' house, not far from the central square. There were an order of magnitude more creatures here than on the outskirts—their proximity to the town hall had worked against them. We reached the main gate without slowing, and the viscount began to beat at it with a steel glove to attract the attention of those inside. A small viewing window opened, revealing reddened eyes.

"Viscount! You are alive!" came a delighted voice, followed by the sound of furniture being pushed aside. The gate opened, allowing us to look inside—everyone who was in the building was hiding in this room. The rest of the passages were blocked off and something was slamming into them repeatedly. As soon as I came closer, the blows subsided as the creatures that had burst into the house ceased to exist.

I looked around at the crowd. The Duke of Turb looked fantastic, despite numerous cuts. The impact of my aura was already affecting him and cuts began to overgrow before my eyes. Alia gave a wry and pained smile as she put down her heavy crossbow. Even without a single magic stone adorning her soul, she had fought along with everyone else, defending her own right to live. Of the twenty guardsmen chained in armor, five had survived. No—five were left standing. Three more were lying against the wall, breathing heavily. I immediately handed over the three recovery elixirs, hoping that it would help. And finally, there was High Priest Urg, along with Father Dvar, head of security. That was it! The ordinary guardsmen, mercenaries and servants of the Light had laid down their lives to save the top brass.

"We need to get out of the city! Follow me!" I ordered. "Horses?"

Alia shook her head. Not far from the entrance to the house there was a wagon, but only bloody footprints on the stones remained of the animals inside. The kronas had devoured every last scrap.

"Viscount, hitch ours up! Everyone in the carriage! You'll have to remove your armor." I looked at the guardsmen. "There are too many of you for the pair to pull us all."

"We'll cover the retreat," one of them said gloomily, making me nearly smack him in the head with *Dark Spike.*

"I! Said! In the carriage!" I don't think I've ever yelled at another person like that. Even the guardsman, who had seen his fair share of things, stepped back, my aura was so heavy at that moment. I really was ready to kill!

"Follow orders, sergeant," said the duke, and, setting an example, he was the first to take off his breastplate. "Armor won't save us."

"Yes, Your Radiance!" The guard nodded. Kurpatsky obeyed unquestioningly. While I was helping to carry the wounded, he harnessed the horses we had ridden to Hearth on. The poor animals had nearly died while we were rushing here, but the healing aura made them feel much better. The dark creatures seemed to have sensed that their prey was leaving. They fell on us like an avalanche, despite the losses. There was the impression that the dark ones from all over the city rushed to the central square in order to stop our escape.

As soon as they crossed into the range of my healing ability, they immediately fell to the ground. Not even a twitch or a death throe. Instant death. I didn't get on the cart, running briskly beside. When we got out of the city, the kronas disappeared, as if something kept them inside the city limits. I had no time to deal with this—I urgently needed to close the rift from which the dark ones were pouring before they ate everyone. There must be some people still left hiding in the cellars? Surely some made it on time?

"Alright, go on by yourself!" I hit the horse on the rump.

"Max!" the High Priest said, speaking for the first time. "This isn't us! The Fortress is not involved in this breach!"

"There is a girl sitting next to you, prove it to her instead," I replied, barely restraining my anger. Of course the Fortress has nothing to do with it. Everyone there was an innocent lamb, and all that.

"Try not to die," I heard Alia's tearful whisper. Once she realized she wouldn't be devoured, the girl became so emotional that she could not restrain herself. Which was strange—she went to the fire with her head held high, but here, where death was faster, she could not restrain herself. Although, perhaps, she was worried not for herself, but for the thousands and thousands of people who became casualties of the darkness.

"Leonid," I turned to Kurpatsky. "I have a request. Alia must survive. At any cost. Otherwise, it's all meaningless."

The viscount didn't say anything, just nodded as he pushed the wagon forward. The greater the distance between them and the city, the greater their chance of survival. I drank the mana potion and rushed towards the dark avalanche of beasts. I glanced down the side streets as I went. They really were running at me from all sides. I was more than happy with this—the more of them died now, the less would remain for me to kill off later. When I got to the town hall, I literally had to crawl over the bodies. Thousands of kronas covered the pavement, turning it into a terrible mess.

I even had to crawl into the town hall building, throwing back bodies left and right. The indelible flow kept pouring out. I was glad for one thing: I knew exactly where to go. Follow the stream. Going down to the basement, I finally saw a huge metal door that once closed the entrance. Now it was bent and thrown aside, along with the thick steel pins that held it to the wall. I don't even want to think about the strength it would require to do this.

Pushing my way past the kronas, I walked along the first level and stopped abruptly. A rapse fell on me from the ceiling! The creature had sat back and waited for the ambush, and if it weren't for the dome of protection that constantly hung over my head, I would have been devoured on the spot! It was not always possible for me to put up my mirror while holding the healing aura, so I had turned it off, even while I was in the city. The creature was thrown aside, flipped around in the air and, as soon as its paws touched stone, it immediately rushed at me. It didn't reach its target—*Healing Aura* destroyed it in mid-flight. But this moment made me think a lot about what was really happening with this rift. The creatures continued to advance, already managing to block off passages with their sheer mass. But these were the usual weak kronas that arrived with a Wave. But was it really a Wave? Back at the rift under the academy, none of the creatures were calm—they were all rushing frantically to the surface. This rapse had stayed behind, waiting to ambush me, and didn't lay a finger on anyone else until I arrived. The road was clearly worn, which indicated that it was used often. However, the rapse, for some reason, ignored any who had run by, but chose to attack me. Why? This seemed to be an important question, the answer to which would help me greatly in the future.

I swore. In my current state, I was ready to go beyond the Wall and look for a competent dark teacher who could explain to me everything that was happening to me and around me. I, for one, was already tired of poking around like a blind kitten, using the trial and error method. The price of making a mistake was too high.

Putting my mirror back up so that a random creature would not see me as dinner, I went towards the stream of creatures. I hoped the city would cope a little better if I managed to block the arrival of new arrivals and kill, if not all, then at least most of these toothy freaks. I left the first level behind, then the second, then the third. The onslaught continued, but now I also had to fight with the ordinary inhabitants of the rift as well. Even the mirror did not save me from their aggression when they fell into the range of my healing aura. The monsters recognized the source of their pain perfectly well and tried to stop it as quickly as possible. My mirror stayed up—it was much easier to exist in the rift with it in place, but I no longer relied on it as I burned through hundreds of beasts.

The portal arch was on level five. At this point, my mana was starting to run out, so without any hesitation, I extended my hand and activated *Dark Spike.* The sooner I did this, the better. The strategy for destroying this gate was the same—a string of numbers popped up above the portal, indicating its durability, which decreased by almost twenty percent! In terms of structural integrity, this arch was not even close to the one that I had to destroy at the academy. Hit. Hit. One more. On the fifth and final time I activated *Dark Spike,* I sincerely hoped that a horned head would pop out to figure out what in Skron's name was happening, but it didn't. Those beasts had either grown wiser, or they were all dead, or they had nothing to do with this gate. As soon as the structure collapsed, I felt an unprecedented relief. In some mysterious way, I knew that all the kronas that remained alive on the surface were now turned into motionless statues. The city was saved.

"Well, you did it anyway. My congratulations," I heard an old man's voice say somewhere off to one side. I acted instantly—before even turning around, my hand was already pointed in the right direction. Magister Meram, if it really was him, was standing against the far wall. Bishop Zwat was next to him, but just one glance at the churchman was enough to understand that the bishop was no longer a tenant of this body. He, like all converts, had his hands raised to the sky, muttering his mournful melody. Now that the blaze of creatures being burned alive in the healing light had faded away, I finally heard that muttering.

All this happened in tandem with my attack. The dark spike was already flying towards its target. I crouched down, preparing to charge and take them in close combat, but I couldn't do it—I happened to see the result of *Dark Spike*. It flew to the enemy, came into contact with his body and simply evaporated, as if absorbed by an aura or protection. This had never happened before in my experience, so I was confused. Exactly two seconds until the icon became active again. The second spike took off, but this time my target was not the magister, but the bishop. The convert must not be allowed to finish his song. As the churchmen always affirmed.

"No, young man, not so fast," the old man made an imperceptible movement and shifted, standing in the way of my spike. It once again crashed into his body and disappeared without a trace or explosion. Which shocked me for another two seconds. Again, until the ability became active. I sent the third shard of darkness into the stones right under the old man's feet. This time the result was achieved—the spike exploded, enveloping my enemies in darkness and small pebbles. I immediately rushed forward to finish what I started, but the impact of the magical barrier threw me back against the opposite wall. Five meters! My own dome softened the blow, but my mana hovered just above zero. I had to reach my last vial and restore it—the healing aura also absorbed an unacceptable amount of blue liquid.

However, when the darkness cleared, I saw something incredible: the old man continued to stand between me and the bishop, and in front of him was a pile of small pebbles. His shield had saved him. I prepared to shoot again, even as the old man made a pass with his hand and a symbol blazing with fire appeared in the air right in front of him. Assessing his creation, the master breathed on his open palm, sending the symbol in my direction. I moved out of its trajectory, but the symbol somehow managed to change its trajectory, and no matter how I tried to dodge, it slammed into my shoulder. The speed of dark magic was beyond my comprehension.

The only thing I managed to do before being touched by dark magic was use *Analyze*. Now that I had plenty of mana, I needed to find out who I was dealing with.

Gray Magister Meram. Human.

Actually, it was this line of text that distracted me and prevented me from dodging properly. Gray?! How was that possible?!

You are under the influence of the symbol "*???*"
Curse "Wither" has been obtained.
Your mana is zero. Duration: 30 minutes.

"Perhaps this will allow us to have a calm conversation," the old man said as if nothing had happened. Suddenly, the bishop broke off his chant and, taking out a knife from somewhere, slashed his throat, after which he drove the knife into his stomach, revealing his intestines. Strikingly, the body did not fall, but remained standing and, terrifyingly, moving! Taking out the entrails, the bishop threw them into the air in front of him, and goosebumps ran down my spine as they formed another portal passage arch! The blood that was leaking from his throat crawled towards the archway, forming a thin red film in the center. As soon as it was finished, the bishop collapsed as if he had been cut down, and the film bulged as if someone was pushing on it from the other side. In less than a second, the red veil was torn and a pair of two-meter tall creatures ran into the cave, looking like well-trained humans with bull heads. But they weren't quite bulls—fiery steam emanated from their nostrils, their mouths were filled with sharp teeth, and their eyes completely absorbed by darkness as they stared at me, trying to penetrate the depths of my consciousness. Only my mirror and ring prevented this.

"Go back," ordered the old man, brushing off the bull-men as if they meant nothing. "I can handle myself here. I needed a portal to leave."

"Yes, Magister Meram," one of them boomed and I went numb. These creatures could talk? What was going on here, anyway?

"So, young man, let's talk," the old man approached me without fear, stopping a few meters away. I didn't even think about activating the katars and attacking him, despite the fact that *Analyze* did not show any magic stones on the gray one. It was all about this being's stats, despite the fact that Skron or the Light called him a man. No human could have such numbers. The gray Magister Meram had ninety-two open parameters, and none of them had values below a thousand percent. No, I was lying—there were several, but they were shown in a separate line, and all the values in this line had one hundred percent: immunity to the elements, immunity to poisons, immunity to physical damage, immunity to darkness. Protection from all known types of damage at one hundred percent! Killing him was simply impossible!

The old man made another pass with his hand, and the symbol appeared in front of him again. Also unknown to me. The sigil crashed into my chest, and for a while, stars danced before my eyes. When it was over, I sullenly stared at the inscription:

You are under the influence of symbol "???".
Curse "Truth" obtained.
You cannot lie. Duration: 30 minutes.

Master Meram sat down on the corpse of a krona without any particular disgust.

"Your name?"

I was silent. The symbol did not oblige me to respond.

"No, young man, that won't work. I might start getting upset. Might start having bad thoughts, someone might suffer for it. Might suffer badly."

"Like thousands of innocent civilians?" I couldn't help but retort.

"Random sacrifices, all to bring you here for this conversation. I knew that you would come down into the rift and close the gateway. There was no way you wouldn't. Too bad that you were too late, but that's your problem. I summoned the weakest beasts, so it would be easier for you. Who can be blamed for the fact that it took you so long to get here? So the blame for their deaths lies entirely on your head. My name is Magister Meram, I am a runescribe. This, as I can see, you already knew. Maybe you could introduce yourself? It's impolite, you know, to keep your name a secret when your opponent has given his."

"Max," I said, surprised that my tongue, for some reason, did not want to add the sobriquet "Hunter of Darkness." So my name change was not yet Fortress official.

"No, I'm not interested in the nickname that the churchmen gave you. I want your real name."

"Baron Maximilian Valevsky."

"Nice to meet you, Maximilian. That's much better. Although I admit I knew your nickname before this—the bishop told me of your little escapades in extremely unflattering terms. Dark, but recognized by the Fortress, able to close rifts up to level eight on his own. Is it not a miracle that the Light Ones have their own contender for the first time in many hundreds of years?"

"Contender for what?"

"That's not important right now. You are too weak to even consider it. But you're making progress. I even admire your sense of purpose— attacking the residence alone, without knowing what was inside...What is it? Madness? Clear calculation? The order of the Light? But it doesn't matter. The beings that I represent, yes, the beings, I will not call them people, have an extremely negative view of your excessive agility. Rifts exist for a reason, and the fact that there was one trickster who utilized their power to his advantage was just impudence, you know. After you attacked the residence and I realized who I was dealing with, I contacted my patrons. They urged me not to destroy you. It turns out that even among the dark ones, the true dark ones, there are those whose interest you pique. And I cannot say that this is a positive thing."

"Contacted? So there is a symbol that allows you to communicate with another being?"

"Oh! Don't tell me you also know the abecedary? The alphabet?"

"I take it you're not talking about the standard alphabet? The dark one? I have the symbol *Yat.*"

Just because I had to tell only the truth didn't mean I had to tell the whole truth. Some parts should probably stay hidden for later.

"Is that right?" The old man looked at me with interest. "How did you get it?"

"I saw a pictogram that one of the dark ones was preparing."

"Adaptation," Magister Meram nodded knowingly. "Your brain somehow adapted to the pictogram it had seen and presented it as a symbol. Very interesting. Of course, I have heard of such cases, but they are exceptionally rare. A number of different conditions must be met. I take it you're a mirror? Not an ordinary one, but dark?"

"Yes. I can reflect auras," I didn't want to say

this, but the words themselves fell from my lips. Damned symbol!

"That clears up a lot. I guess my patrons were right to watch your development. Maybe it will work out."

"Teach me about remote communication and those symbols that deprived me of my mana and forced me to speak the truth," I blurted out, amazed at my own boldness. So what? Before me was probably the only person in the world who could teach me this. I did not ask what "gray" meant. I had no desire to talk about what kind of magic stones I possessed.

"Teach?" My words had surprised the old man. "You, a person who is light down to the very bone marrow, are asking me, a gray being, to teach you the symbols of the original alphabet?"

"It would be nice to know what this alphabet is and what 'gray' means." If I was going to be bold, I might as well go for broke.

"Okay, let's say I agree to give you one lesson. What do I get in return? You don't even have to offer your rings. The yellow one's off the table, and the red, albeit interesting, is tied to mana. I don't need it. So?"

"A favor?" I said unexpectedly. It would be naive on my part to offer a material object or information. I had nothing to interest a being of such power. But a favor was an abstract concept. A lot of things could be hiding in this word.

"A favor," said Master Meram, tasting the word. "I can't even imagine what favors such a mysterious figure could offer me. You know what, Skron take you. Let it be so. One symbol for one favor. You have two...no, one opportunity to choose a symbol for yourself. I will teach it to you and show you how it can be used without paint. If you can handle it, great. If you can't, no big deal, there's always chabre. Are you ready to choose? Keep in mind, the favor could be anything. Up to and including asking you to say...kill the emperor. Or plant new roses in the garden. Anything, Maximilian Valevsky. Absolutely anything."

"One symbol and an honest answer to two questions," I promptly offered.

"Who taught you to bargain?" snorted the old man. "One character and, well, one question. And even then—only one that you have already asked."

"Two, Magister. Two questions. Because one was about the symbol, and the other wasn't even a question—more of a clarification. It's not every day you meet a gray being."

"So you're interested in what the original alphabet is and why I'm gray? Yes, I'm willing to agree to that. So, choose your symbol."

"Remote communication. I am in dire need of that. But before you give it to me, tell me how it works? Maybe you need to make a hundred human sacrifices for each call?"

"Oof, you're white to the core," he grimaced. "Don't tell me you also stand for world peace and happy people everywhere. No, you don't need souls for remote communication. All you need to do is paint the symbol on yourself and the one you want to communicate with, and for two months, a magical connection will form between you, allowing you to hear each other."

"Does this only work with one person at a time, or can there be several?"

"You can speak with the whole empire, as long as you have enough space on your body. The symbol's size cannot be reduced, and they cannot overlap. To call the other side, you must touch this symbol, so the back doesn't always work. I usually limit myself to three contacts. This is enough to resolve most problems."

"Got it. In this case, in order to make the final choice, I need to familiarize myself with the entire original alphabet."

"What a cocky, arrogant and stupid young man. You got your one question. You'll learn about the original alphabet elsewhere. Are you ready to get to work?"

"Ready," I muttered angrily.

"In that case, memorize the movement. The basis of rune art is that it does not require mana. Only clarity and smooth movements, coupled with knowledge and skills."

The skill "Runescribe" is available to you. If you acquire the skill, the Alchemist branch will be closed to you.

Would you like to acquire this skill?

Naturally, no additional descriptions or explanations were given. Why would they be? This was more fun! But I had to accept—it didn't say anything about this skill being exclusive to dark beings, and most importantly, I had no idea what a skill was at all. This was the first time I had heard this word applied to a person's parameters. So yes, I couldn't refuse.

The status bar blinked actively. The pictogram with symbols disappeared, but a new picture appeared—a golden hand folded into a strange gesture. By mentally focusing on the icon, I opened a new window, which contained all the symbols I knew, as well as a number of unfamiliar ones that I had seen, but failed to learn. I focused on *Yat* and a projection of a hand appeared before my eyes, performing a beautiful movement. My hand automatically went up, repeating the movement. My first attempt was clumsy, but by the sixth, my hand synchronized with the projection, generating the symbol *Yat* directly in front of me. I imagined this symbol coming towards me and touching my shoulder, as a new message appeared:

Received *Yat* buff.
Physical stat growth rate increased by 50%. Duration: 14 days.

"Already?" The old man was genuinely surprised. "In just five minutes? I think I'm beginning to understand why the patrons are interested in you. Your new symbol, Maximilian Valevsky. I have fulfilled my end of the bargain, now you owe me a favor. Not now, of course, but later. When you get stronger. If you survive."

Symbol "Word" learned.
Upgrades available: 4. Upgrades used: 1.

"As for your question, it seems very naive to me. What makes you think that the world is a binary? Light and dark? Good and evil? Isn't that stupid? Locking yourself into the paradigm of your society, not daring to take even a single step in another direction? No, that doesn't work for me. That's why I turned gray. It's for those who only work for themselves. An independent person who can ignore the foundations of the Light or Skron's machinations. There are quite a few like me. There are even some in this empire, but that's another question. I can't tell you about how to became gray—this is not included in our agreements. And I'm not interested in providing that information. Now on to the sad news. Your presence here is no accident. I've been asked to make sure that you don't grow too bold—my patrons don't want the rifts in the Zarak Empire to suddenly run dry. Nobody needs that. Not us, not you. That's why I had to lure you here, away from people, closer to the darkness. Don't think that I'm doing this of my own free will or for some personal reason. I'm just doing my job!"

The old man again made a pass with his hand, and five symbols flashed in front of me at once. I didn't even budge as they hit my chest.

What was the point of running when you were up against an immortal being?

Combined curse: *Campaign Limiter.*
You cannot visit more than 3 Rifts in a calendar year. If you enter a 4th within this time, your system will self-destruct and your body will fall apart. Duration: indefinite.
You have visited 1 of 3 valid rifts.

"As you can see, my patrons don't want you dead. They give you the right to walk the rifts, but only a limited number of them. They decided that three a year would be enough for this cycle. This is the first iteration of the spell, by the way. If you continue to pique their interest, the restrictions can be amended. But we must all survive until then. All the best, Maximilian Valevsky. Tell the High Priest that our annual meetings are over. The Zarak Empire is no longer of interest to me."

With these words, the old man approached the bloody archway and boldly stepped inside. The Bishop's entrails collapsed to the ground, having fulfilled their purpose. The gray magister had left the rift and the empire behind.

Chapter 20

THREE RIFTS A YEAR... I opened my list of curses I was under once again—there was a whole icon on the status bar allocated to this. *Truth* had already expired, but the memory of it remained in the form of a deactivated curse icon, as well as the symbol in the alphabet. There were no descriptions, only an image. I couldn't use this icon, or any of the several previous ones. As I focused on any of the four active symbols, a translucent hand appeared before the eyes, demonstrating the gesture. But things weren't as peachy keen as they seemed at first. I looked into the inkpot where the chabre powder was stored. About a third of the contents of the jar had disappeared, and without any warning. Exactly as much as it took me to apply the symbol to the body. It turns out that the skill only facilitates the process of drawing, but in no way eliminates the requirements imposed on the symbols. Bad news. Symbols that require human lives will remain inaccessible to me.

Rising to my feet, I trudged to the exit, trying not to look around. The rift had turned into one big feeding trough. The creatures that Magister Meram had summoned were dead, but the monsters that lived in the rift hadn't gone anywhere and now they were in a hurry to devour the massive mounds of flesh. And I wasn't going to kill the ones that lived here. Let them eat and give their Riftmaster additional strength—what if it had already reached level eleven? The ugly old man didn't tell me if I could leave and come back to the same rift. Would my counter increase by one if I left, even for a moment? I didn't want to find out.

Reaching the first cave of the first level, I began to clear the rubble from the bodies of the kronas in order to clear the passage. There was no doubt that sooner or later, someone would get curious and check what was going on in the rift. I needed this curious person. If I was going to make it to the Master, I needed food, water, and Alia. I had a new symbol to inscribe on my personal attendant.

Word. *Reinforcing symbol. When applied to the bodies of two people, it binds them with a mental thread, allowing them to communicate at a distance. To communicate, you need to place your hand on the symbol. To end communication, you must remove your hand from the symbol. Each person needs their own symbol. Duration:*

indefinite. Requires chabre powder to use.

I liked the idea of remote communication. As well as the Runescribe skillpath in general. The main problem, as always, was training. Where could I find competent mentors? After all, as practice had shown, you didn't have to cast individual characters, you could make whole words out of them! Surely these words were what had transformed that old man into a true force. Magister Meram could never have drunk so many enhancement elixirs in his life. Even if he absorbed all the enhancements from all the guards in the world, it still wouldn't be enough to get +1000% to ninety-two different stats. It wouldn't be enough. So, it was all to do with the symbols, words, and even sentences that the old man used on himself. Because an omnipotent being, capable of holding the whole world under his right heel, must not be here simply to draw symbols on the ass of Father Pithr. He came to our empire to earn some sort of payment, whatever that may be. Would I have to press the High Priest against the wall and find out how the Fortress paid him?

Having cleared my passage to freedom, I settled in the center of the cave and waited. They obviously wouldn't come by today—people were still too scared. Maybe not even tomorrow. But the day after tomorrow, when the most acute emotions had subsided, the fear would recede and the inhabitants would slowly begin to return to their homes, and there would definitely be some little boy peeking into town hall. He couldn't help himself!

Surprisingly, I only had to wait a day. When the voices were heard, I was sleeping peacefully in the center of the already cleared cave. The creatures of the rift quickly dealt with the flesh of the summoned kronas and even picked at some corpses in the town hall. But without much enthusiasm. Like me, the dark monsters were adamant about not wanting to leave their favorite rift. Opening my eyes, I stared at the four warriors dressed in armor who entered the rift, with shields at the ready and spears outstretched toward me. I got to my feet and, just in case, put my hands up, showing that I was unarmed.

"Max?" came an astonished voice, in which I easily recognized The Countess. "What are you doing here?"

"Sitting here, waiting for you," I replied, unable to suppress a grin.

"Is it safe here?" asked Rabblerouser, lowering his spear, but not lowering his shield.

"In the first cave, yes. I didn't clear the rest. I need your help, guys. Call Mother Alia here, my attendant. It's important."

"You can't leave the rift?" the Countess guessed, also lowering her weapon and raising her visor. Still the same beautiful and world-weary woman.

"I can, but there's a caveat. I destroyed the portal that created the creatures, Magister Meram escaped, Bishop Zwat, who was converted, is dead and has already been devoured by the beasts, and I have not yet cleansed the rift. But that's not even the main part. If it's not too hard, could you bring me something to eat, eh? Three days without food and water does little good for anyone."

"Take it." A small backpack flew toward me with minimal rations, but the doomed soldiers were still in no hurry to embrace me. They were afraid to approach me. For who knows with Dark Max? Skron knows why he couldn't leave the rift. Maybe he himself has already become a convert?

"Gimlet, bring Mother Alia here, chop chop," the Countess ordered, sitting down on the stones. "Max, can you tell me what happened here? Or is it a secret?"

"No secret," I replied. "They really fucked me, from all angles and in every position."

While Gimlet was running to fetch my personal attendant, I gave a colorful account of what I had gone through over the past several days. I had no idea what story the churchmen and the imperials would agree on, so the more people who know about what really happened, the better. I started with the estate, and ended with the rift and Magister Meram, who had put a rein on my rift diving.

"So you're going to hang around here until the very end, until you close it?"

"It's a ten-level," I said, causing the other doomers to whistle in appreciation. "Yes, the bishop has been cultivating it for a long time. You could say he nurtured it. I don't think I'll have any problems up to level eight, but I'll suffer on the ninth and tenth. How much, I have no idea. The eighth took me more than a week, so it'll definitely be longer here. That's why I need food."

"I heard that you have a meeting with the emperor in three weeks," the Countess said thoughtfully. "Also that you freed three doomed soldiers."

"I did," I confirmed. "Don't forget—I closed the eight-level. I received *Amplify*s, which I exchanged for my group."

"And this is a ten," the Countess said, and looked directly at me.

"I understand where you're coming from, Countess, but I don't understand what I gain from it? You yourself know that losing four *Amplify*s for the sake of four people with whom I've only crossed paths a couple of times in my life is not the most reasonable course of action."

"Flask is an alchemist. Not the best one, but not too shabby either. Where else can you find an alchemist dedicated only to you? Rabblerouse is the head of the city guard in a city in the eastern region. I don't need to tell you about his skillset. Gimlet is a mage who served in a secret office in a past life. During their time as doomed soldiers, my people's fighting skills have been honed to perfection."

"That's right, they're your people. If I take them, who will they serve? Me or you?"

"You. As well as me. The Countess is not just a nickname. Before I was in the doomed legion, I was a countess. Governed a city, almost single-handedly conducted all its affairs. In me, you will find a governor unlike any other."

"Are you so easily agreeing to exchange the Fortress for the unknown—me? What you're talking about is the same kind of hard labor you're doing already, only without the "doomed soldier" affix. You're only three or four years away from your release. Don't tell me you don't know about the ten year decree?"

"I do," the Countess nodded. "But my group has been sent to more and more places where return seems nigh impossible. A few days ago we were sent to a three-level in the northern region. Just the four of us, no backup! An hour ago, we made it to Hearth, where the High Priest canceled the previous task and sent us here. We were not even told the depth of the rift—they demanded we clear the first two or three levels. If this is really a tenner, then the creatures on the third level will simply devour us and whole. But who cares about that? What's important is that everything is cleared so that the resource miners can begin their duties. Before that, there was an eighter and entire crowds of doomers who perished in it. Every month the rifts become more difficult, we don't have the strength. I resigned myself to the fact that we simply won't live to see our time, but if you help us get out, you won't find a more loyal bunch. None of us need play the roles that I have described. We even willing to be simple peasants, if it suits you better."

"Is that just your opinion or everyone else's?" I looked at Rabblerouse and Flask.

"I don't want to die," Rabblerouse nodded. "I think I've already made peace with what I've done in the past. The dead cannot be returned, and Skron is with them. If there is a chance to get out—I will use it. The Countess is right—you will not find truer people."

"Don't even look at me," Flask made an expression that only true drunkards have. "I don't really care where I die. What is free, what is broken. The old me died, a new one did not grow in its place. What remains is a limp body that requires nothing. But I will not betray the group. That's for sure. And the work that they give me, I will do in good faith."

"You can think of it as a kind of yes," the Countess explained. "Flask is on his own level. It's because of what he did and how he's resigned himself to it, but this does not affect his abilities in any way. You will get the four of us. Our time, our strength, our loyalty. We don't have anything else to give."

"Okay," I nodded. "If I manage to get four *Amplify*s from this rift, you will gain your freedom. I need people, you're right on that point. And—"

I didn't have time to finish my sentence—the sound of quick footsteps were heard, and Alia literally flew into the cave.

"Where is he?!" she shouted, and as soon as her gaze settled on me, the girl threw herself around my neck, not in the least embarrassed by the doomed soldiers, or her status or the fact that her nose was bleeding and she was smearing it all over my clothes. As far as I knew, this was the first time Alia had entered a rift. Her first time feeling the dark influence.

"You're alive!" Tears streamed down her cheeks. "Why? Why didn't you come out and say so? I... I thought you..."

"I'm pretty much fine." I stroked the girl's hair. I didn't know what else to do. I hadn't yet been in a situation where I had to soothe a fanatic minister of the church. Or even a girl crying into my shoulder. The Countess tactfully took the rest of the group and left the rift, leaving us alone. She made her proposal, I told her my decision, why continue hanging around?

"What does 'pretty much' mean?" Alia wiped her tears away with her sleeve and took a couple of steps back. "Were you hurt?"

"Sit down, I have a lot to tell you. I'll start, perhaps, with the main thing—I cannot leave this rift. Now the details..."

Once again, I had to recall the events of the past few days, but this time in much more detail. Moreover, the girl demanded I started with the estate—what, where, how and with whom? She was interested in everything, but I did not hold back, voracious gobbling down the food that the Countess had thrown me between sentences. Simple bread and cheese now seemed the pinnacle of culinary excellence, and warm water—the finest hundred-year-old wine. If there was such a thing,

"Actually, that's why I sat here and waited for someone to show up. I thought some of the local kids would drop by, but then the Countess's group showed up. I won't leave here until I finish the Master and get ten upgrades. Even if the Fortress strikes a pose and forbids me to move on."

"The symbol you were talking about… How does it work?"

"Like this," I made several passes with my hand, generating the "Word" symbol in front of me. Or rather, two characters at once—for two carriers. Alia's eyes widened in astonishment at something she'd never seen before, and then they almost popped out of their sockets when I pointed one of the symbols in her direction. Without any difficulties, it penetrated through the clothes and seeped into her body. As did mine.

"Max!" the girl exclaimed in shock and jumped to her feet. Instead of answering, I put my hand on the symbol and whispered:

"Can you hear me? To answer, place your hand on your shoulder where the symbol is."

"I hear you," I heard Alia's stunned whisper in my head. She continued backing away from me until her back rested against the opposite wall. The distance between us turned out to be about twenty meters, but this did not affect the connection in any way. The voice seemed to come straight into my head, bypassing my ears. But the connection only applied to speech—when I tried to mentally communicate with Alia, there was no result. Or the girl was simply silent, not wanting to answer.

"Can it be removed?" Alia asked, staying away.

"In theory, yes. In practice, we need to study everything. We need archives on runescribes, we need everything related to the grays. Ideally, two to three hours of training with Magister Meram. But all this later. First, let's take a look at what happened. Alia, forgive me, but I didn't have any other opportunity to somehow establish a connection with you."

"How far is the range?"

"Any distance. Gray contacted a dark being from behind the Wall."

For some time we chatted at a distance, finding out the way it worked, until finally the girl came up to me and hugged me, as if she still did not believe that I managed to escape.

"Yes, it is more convenient. Now I will always know what is happening to you. And just see what happens if you don't answer! I'll eat you alive! Stay here for a while, I need to think it over."

"Bring food. Yes, more..."

I had to wait three days before a delegation descended on me. It's good that I had food and I spent this time at level eight, trying to get used to the influence of the ninth. What immediately surprised me was the power of this influence. The transition seemed significantly smaller than it had been from the seventh to eighth. However, as soon as I took off the red ring, everything immediately fell into place—I almost died. It is good that the ring did not fall out of my weakened hands and that I managed to pull it back on. Finally, one of its properties had been made clear: "reducing dark influence." With this, I can get used to the ninth level in a matter of days. By the end of the third, I was already at the ninth, but only at the very beginning. I had no desire to approach the Warden's Cave. But I knew for sure that judging by the number of exclusive creatures that I had encountered on eight and the ones I could see in the caves on nine I would be guaranteed four *Amplfy*s. There were loads more monsters in this rift than in the eight. It is useless to talk about the rift under the academy, since many creatures were pushed into the sun by the Wave, and I simply did not get to them.

As for the delegation itself, I was in quite magnificent company. The High Priest Urg, together with Father Dvar, the Duke of Turb and Viscount Kurpatsky, Mother Aliya and—my eyebrows shot up in surprise—the chancellor of the magic academy, Kimal Sarento with Magister Zurgan Shor. Seven people representing four branches of power, if we consider Alia a separate structure, and the academy as an independent organization.

The servants of the Light, as the "owners" of the rift, brought chairs, and had even dragged in a table for us to all sit at. Throughout these three days, I was constantly in contact with Alia. There were furious debates on the surface about what happened and how to move forward. Judging by the fact that everyone was gathered here today, they had come to some kind of decision. The High Priest started first, as his status dictated:

"The breach claimed the lives of more than ten thousand inhabitants of Hearth. If you hadn't closed it, twenty thousand more might have died too. As would I. And the duke. And Alia. You and the Viscount were just in time. Max, I will not beat around the bush—we had to work hard to turn down the heat in the empire. What happened is unacceptable. The highest representative of the Fortress turned out to be connected with the dark ones, and at such a level that it is only right to dissolve our entire organization and start building it anew. Actually, that's why it took us so long to come to a unanimous decision on how to present what happened to the public. One thing is clear: we must not disclose the truth."

"The Empire agrees that now is not the time to rock the boat," said the Duke of Turb. "Despite the bishop's betrayal, the Fortress must remain a stronghold of faith and people's hope for salvation from darkness. A guarantee that the dark ones will not be able to capture our world, despite all their superiority."

"The academy is of the same opinion." Kimal Sarento, still looking unimpressed, finished the introductory component, allowing me to piece things together for myself.

"So you want to retell the whole story? Cast Bishop Zwat as a victim?"

"Not a victim," Father Urg corrected me. "A

hero. Bishop Zwat will be the hero who saved Hearth. Who managed to keep the dark ones from seizing the central region and organizing a foothold here. The main culprit of the incident will be recognized as Father Pithr, the manager of the city hall. Everything that happened in Hearth is the result of his betrayal and deeds. Perhaps his body will not be preserved well enough, but it will be burnt in the central square as evidence that Father Pifr gave himself up to darkness.”

My temples pulsated in anger, but I decided to keep my opinions to myself for the time being. They had come to an agreement, they said! Trying not to growl, I said as calmly as possible:

“Before teleporting out of the rift, Gray Magister Meram asked me to tell you, High Priest, that he would no longer visit the Zarak Empire.”

“Yes, this was another reason for our long deliberations. The Fortress admits to working with the gray being. Not dark, please note. But gray. Those who are not under the influence of Skron. Yes, we admit that we did use doomed soldiers who were not suitable for crossing the rifts for our own purposes. But we acted strictly in adherence to our internal principles. It was not my decision— the council of bishops decided so.”

“Roll up your sleeve, Father Urg,” I said.”

“You have the right to demand such a thing, and I am ready to obey this demand. As you can see, I even prepared for this.”

With these words, the High Priest rose from his seat and pulled his robe over his head. He had absolutely nothing on underneath. The naked old man twirled around, not at all embarrassed by the audience, after which he put the robe back in place. His flabby body had age spots and was covered in scars, but there was not a single symbol on it. Not one.

"Neither I nor any of the remaining bishops have symbols. We invited Magister Meram, but not for ourselves. To protect Karina Fardi. The one we thought would be our future star. A Sweeper that would be able to close five-, six-, and even seven-level rifts on her own. We had to do this because of the constant attacks on the princess, whom we could not reason with. Even with the help of Sir Chancellor. But Karina Fardi left the church, and the doomed soldiers will have to go back into the rifts."

"Into the rifts that you yourselves create?" I couldn't resist.

"Neither I nor any of the remaining bishops have symbols. We invited Magister Meram, but not for ourselves. To protect Karina Fardi. The one we thought would be our future star. A Sweeper that would be able to close five-, six-, and even seven-level rifts on her own. We had to do this because of the constant attacks on the princess, whom we could not reason with. Even with the help of Sir Chancellor. But Karina Fardi left the church, and the doomed soldiers will have to go back into the rifts."

"Into the rifts that you yourselves create?" I couldn't help but ask.

"We do create them," the High Priest agreed. "Because the resources we extract keep our world going. Yes, rifts can occur on their own. About one in ten cases, and they are a huge problem. Uncontrolled, spontaneously developing, absorbing the strength of the territory on which they stand. All the others are created by us. Because, I repeat, as long as we extract resources, the world has the ability to resist the darkness."

"Creating darkness for the sake of fighting darkness and ruining hundreds of human lives in the process?" My face contorted in a grin that was more like a grimace.

"Do not idolize doomed soldiers. I won't lie—not all of them deserved to go there, but the vast majority are monsters. Even worse than those who are killed. A trip to the rift is a delayed execution. Sooner or later, it will take place. The only difference is that this is how a doomed soldier benefits our world."

"Actually, that's why we are here, Max," Kimal Sarento smiled. "For the good of our world. As everyone knows, this is a ten-level. Below are ten guards and one rather harmful Rifmaster. We all know how you go through the rift and what's left behind for us when you're done. Or rather, that there's nothing left behind. Given your new and interesting status, we came to you to negotiate."

"Not to dictate terms, but to negotiate?" I grinned.

"Precisely!"

"I am grateful to you for saving Hearth, for

saving me and my people, but I cannot ignore what we may be losing out on if you absorb all the energy from the dark beings. Especially the guards," the duke said glumly. Or at least he feigned it well, averted his eyes, the cynical bastard.

"In the eight-level that you closed, each guard gave eight pieces of yem," the High Priest explained. "One for each level. With one yem, you can create six to ten enhancement elixirs. One elixir costs…you know perfectly well yourself. Thirty percent of this rift will go to the central region. Thirty to the Fortress. Another thirty to the magic academy, as a compensation for the error of destroying the fifteen-level rift. Ten percent in monetary terms will go to you. But at the same time, you must not absorb any guards or exclusive creatures. Nothing. We advise you not even touch the Riftmaster, but the rift won't close unless it dies. These are our requirements. If you do not agree with them, you will leave this rift without closing it. It's easier for us to be content with six or seven levels and the lives of thousands of doomed soldiers than to not get anything at all."

"Alia?" I looked at my personal attendant, who was sitting with her eyes downcast.

"I couldn't help it, Max. Their rationale was solid."

"I need exclusive beasts," I looked into Father Urg's eyes. "I need four *Amplify*s."

"Forty-eight red beasts," the high bishop immediately calculated. "A counter-proposal: don't touch anyone here and you'll get four stones. Even better, you'll get the four doomed soldiers you were about to release. These are for the Countess' group, I assume?"

Everyone stared in surprise at Father Urg, but he didn't flinch.

"Quite a reasonable choice, given this group's composition. For everything they've done for the Fortress, I should have released them long ago. Now their numbers have been pulled. Don't touch anyone but the Riftmaster and I will issue a decree that they have found the four *Amplify*s and are free. Not only that, stones will be provided as evidence. Will this option work for everyone?"

"The Empire has no objections," the duke replied.

"The Academy supports any decision of the Fortress," Kimal Sarento smiled. "That does not conflict with the profits collected from the rift."

"Okay, let's say I agree. Ten percent in the form of gold would be most welcome to me, plus the four doomed soldiers. But what we still haven't determined is what I'll get in exchange for my silence regarding the true cause of the rift in Hearth. Why should I hold my tongue, just because you all came to a consensus?"

"Actually, that's why they invited me." The smile never left Kimal Sarento's beautiful face. "Your silence is highly valued. So much so that the Fortress and the empire united their resources and bought from me one interesting sheet of paper that I received in the distant past. If you accept all our conditions while you're still Max, then along with my official invitation to finish your studies at the academy, and completely free of charge, you will receive this nondescript ticket.

Kimal Sarento put a card on the table and pushed it towards me. I turned my head, reading the lines, and a flock of goosebumps ran down my back. It looked like I was going to get my way after all. I've got you, you bastard!

"This card ensures that the carrier will become my pupil. Gray Magister Meram. Runescribe. Al-Khorezm, Shurgan Empire.

End of Book Three

Want to be the first to know about our latest LitRPG,
sci fi and fantasy titles from your favorite authors?

Subscribe to our **New Releases** newsletter:
http://eepurl.com/b7niIL

Thank you for reading *Condemned!*
If you like what you've read, check out other sci-fi, fantasy and A LitRPG series published by Magic Dome Books:

Reality Benders
a LitRPG series by Michael Atamanov

The Dark Herbalist
a LitRPG series by Michael Atamanov

Perimeter Defense
a LitRPG series by Michael Atamanov

League of Losers
a LitRPG series by Michael Atamanov

Chaos' Game
a LitRPG series by Alexey Svadkovsky

War Eternal
a LitRPG series by Yuri Vinokuroff

The Hunter's Code
a LitRPG series by Yuri Vinokuroff & Oleg Sapphire

An Ideal World for a Sociopath
a LitRPG series by Oleg Sapphire

Kill or Die
a LitRPG series by Alex Toxic

The Way of the Shaman
a LitRPG series by Vasily Mahanenko

The Alchemist
a LitRPG series by Vasily Mahanenko

Dark Paladin
a LitRPG series by Vasily Mahanenko

Galactogon
a LitRPG series by Vasily Mahanenko

Invasion
a LitRPG series by Vasily Mahanenko

World of the Changed
a LitRPG series by Vasily Mahanenko

The Bear Clan
a LitRPG series by Vasily Mahanenko

Starting Point
a LitRPG series by Vasily Mahanenko

The Bard from Barliona
a LitRPG series
by Eugenia Dmitrieva and Vasily Mahanenko

Condemned
(Lord Valevsky: Last of The Line)
a Progression Fantasy series
by Vasily Mahanenko

Loner
a LitRPG series by Alex Kosh

A Buccaneer's Due
a LitRPG series by Igor Knox

A Student Wants to Live
a LitRPG series by Boris Romanovsky

The Goldenblood Heir
a LitRPG series by Boris Romanovsky

Level Up
a LitRPG series by Dan Sugralinov

Level Up: The Knockout
a LitRPG series by Dan Sugralinov and Max Lagno

Adam Online
a LitRPG Series by Max Lagno

World 99
a LitRPG series by Dan Sugralinov

Disgardium
a LitRPG series by Dan Sugralinov

Nullform
a RealRPG Series by Dem Mikhailov

Clan Dominance: The Sleepless Ones
a LitRPG series by Dem Mikhailov

Heroes of the Final Frontier
a LitRPG series by Dem Mikhailov

The Crow Cycle
a LitRPG series by Dem Mikhailov

Interworld Network
a LitRPG series by Dmitry Bilik

Rogue Merchant
a LitRPG series by Roman Prokofiev

Project Stellar
a LitRPG series by Roman Prokofiev

In the System
a LitRPG series by Petr Zhgulyov

The Crow Cycle
a LitRPG series by Dem Mikhailov

Unfrozen
a LitRPG series by Anton Tekshin

The Neuro
a LitRPG series by Andrei Livadny

Phantom Server
a LitRPG series by Andrei Livadny

Respawn Trials
a LitRPG series by Andrei Livadny

The Expansion (The History of the Galaxy)
a Space Exploration Saga by A. Livadny

The Range
a LitRPG series by Yuri Ulengov

Point Apocalypse
a near-future action thriller by Alex Bobl

Moskau
a dystopian thriller by G. Zotov

El Diablo
a supernatural thriller by G.Zotov

Mirror World
a LitRPG series by Alexey Osadchuk

Underdog
a LitRPG series by Alexey Osadchuk

Last Life
a Progression Fantasy series by Alexey Osadchuk

Alpha Rome
a LitRPG series by Ros Per

An NPC's Path
a LitRPG series by Pavel Kornev

Fantasia
a LitRPG series by Simon Vale

The Sublime Electricity
a steampunk series by Pavel Kornev

Small Unit Tactics
a LitRPG series by Alexander Romanov

Black Centurion
a LitRPG standalone by Alexander Romanov

Rorkh
A LitRPG Series by Vova Bo

Thunder Rumbles Twice
A Wuxia Series by V. Kriptonov & M. Bachurova

Citadel World
a sci fi series by Kir Lukovkin

You're in Game!
LitRPG Stories from Our Bestselling Authors

You're in Game-2!
More LitRPG stories set in your favorite worlds

The Fairy Code
a Romantic Fantasy series by Kaitlyn Weiss

The Charmed Fjords
a Romantic Fantasy series by Marina Surzhevskaya

More books and series are coming out soon!

In order to have new books of the series translated faster, we need your help and support! Please consider leaving a review or spread the word by recommending *Condemned* to your friends and posting the link on social media. The more people buy the book, the sooner we'll be able to make new translations available.

Thank you!

Till next time!